Wisteria Drive

Identifiers: LCCN 2024915617 | ISBN 979-8-9890390-2-9 (paperback) |

ISBN 979-8-9890390-3-6 (eBook)

To my amazing family.

Part 1

Chapter 1

Wisteria Drive was the American dream distilled into one strip of road. The houses lining the gated-in cul-de-sac were the kind passing children would imagine playing in. That one lonely, isolated street was idyllic and beautiful, kept immaculate by plenty of fussing and more money than the Montgomery family cared to admit.

First, visitors had to get past the monstrosity of a gate guarding its entrance.

Naturally, this massive expanse of fencing was the first thing Amy Montgomery noticed as she approached her family's new house. It stood with strict duty, surrounding the sprawling properties and appearing assertive despite the luscious homes stretching beyond it. Just behind the gate, Amy caught a glimpse of extravagance, perhaps excessive yet mesmerizing all the same.

The gate was the first thing that Ryder noticed, too. From the backseat of their Range Rover, he chirped, "Mommy, is that to keep the bad guys out?"

"It sure is, buddy," Amy answered.

Her husband, David, finished punching in the passcode and the gate slowly peeled open, swayed by those magic six digits. When the window was rolled back up, he put his free hand on Amy's thigh and gave it a squeeze.

"The code is 08 25 80, the day my parents got married," David told her before directing his next comment to Ryder. "No bad guys can get in here," he said. "Grandpa made sure of it."

Ryder gave a passive, little-boy shrug. "I bet I could fight them if I had to."

Amy stifled a giggle behind her hand. David cracked a smile, sharing Amy's amusement. "I bet you could, buddy," she said.

David eased the car further down the street, and Amy felt her lips part unintentionally. She snapped her mouth shut quickly enough for David to miss it. Or at least she hoped. She didn't want him to see that the Montgomerys' wealth could still shock her.

One would think Amy would be used to the Montgomerys' extreme opulence by now, but her instinctive reaction toward the splendor of Wisteria Drive suggested she was far from it. She should have been desensitized by their all-expenses-paid, lavish Cabo honeymoon and the excessive comfort Amy was given just before Ryder was born. But even now, seven years after their marriage, the Montgomerys' wealth left her speechless. It still sucked the air out of rooms and made conversations fall silent.

Amy's mother, Emily, used to say that the Montgomerys had more money than God. Amy had always agreed passively, not concentrating on the thought for too long. The Montgomerys' status was not exactly hidden from view, but she never imagined she would see their wealth quantified into houses, rooms, and pools in such a way.

Wisteria Drive was filled with houses that people like Amy dreamed of renting for a time in their wildest fantasies but never dared to imagine buying. But, of course, Lily and Richard Montgomery had made sure they owned all of the houses on the street and generously distributed them among their sons. In Amy's opinion, no one should have the type of money it took to buy an entire street of impressive mansions and make it their own.

But the Montgomerys did.

The Montgomerys viewed Wisteria Drive as a strange sort of necessity. The intention of it had always been ease and to keep the close-knit family together.

She and David had been standing in their Charlotte apartment when Amy finally broke down and agreed to the move. The apartment had been David's bachelor pad before Amy won him over. Every crevice of that apartment had held a memory, one that Amy could reach out, touch, and recall in an instant. She already missed the sectional couch she and David had shared their first kiss on, the kitchen they had spent so many lazy Sunday mornings in, and the window in the sitting room that overlooked the city that had raised her. That apartment had grown to become a part of her, always present to assuage her worries, especially after they had raised their son there for the first six years of his life.

The night she agreed to take on Wisteria Drive, Amy had been looking out over the stretch of city, admiring the way the lights of the surrounding buildings dotted the sky and the ground like an aggressive, man-made stamp.

"It'll be a big house," David promised her from behind as she admired the city she had lived in her whole life. "It will be quiet. And safe. Think about Ryder. He needs a backyard to play in. He should be close to his family."

To your family, Amy thought bitterly. Moving to Wisteria Drive meant moving away from her mother, who lived in Charlotte happily and would likely never have the means to uproot her life and follow them down to Florida.

Amy didn't know how to tell her husband that the idea he was proposing was suffocating. She had put up with her in-laws well enough on the few occasions they had interacted. She could even admit that she enjoyed the way they were eager to spoil her, especially in instances regarding Ryder. In fact, they often did not care for her at all unless it was in the context of her son. She never seemed to even cross their minds unless it was as an accessory to what Ryder was accomplishing, which, in a way, suited Amy just fine. She was glad to shrink into the shadows and avoid their scrutiny. But now, she would not be allowed the luxury of being forgotten, and the idea of moving everything she knew to be closer to people she only vaguely understood had always made her uncomfortable.

She knew she couldn't admit this to David, though. Amy had maneuvered around the offer of their designated home at 4 Wisteria Drive since their engagement. The argument had become the center of some of their worst disagreements. Amy felt worn down, whittled away like wood against sandpaper.

"I don't want to pull Ryder away from what he knows," Amy tried. It was an angle she had worked a dozen times before and she knew how he would combat it. "He's so young," she continued. "He needs stability."

"He needs a home, not an apartment," David countered, as expected. "We can't grant him the freedom to run around outside here. He's a kid. We need to let him explore like a kid. Besides... My parents mentioned the possibility of them cutting me off if we don't 'invest in the family more.'"

Amy had whirled around to look at him, exhausted by the argument and quietly frightened by this new revelation of his allowance and trust fund. This was a fresh and seemingly unprompted approach to their exhausted argument.

She had been wary to give herself up to David's family and go from those endurable experiences on passing occasions to being confined into an eternal conversation with them. It was one thing to survive their company at a birthday party or Christmas dinner, but it was an entirely different expectation to tolerate them as her neighbors.

But that night, staring out at the vast city that had loved and raised her since she was a girl, she thought of Ryder. She pictured him in a lush Floridian backyard or on a sandy beach running from the waves creeping up the shore. And she folded.

As they crawled up Wisteria Drive, Amy surprised herself by only feeling wonder. All five houses were French colonial style and imposing with vast green lawns and beautifully kept shrubbery that was somehow thriving in the Floridian heat. There was a glamor to Wisteria Drive that simply couldn't be denied or suppressed.

Ryder stirred in the backseat asking, "Is that our house? Well, is it that one? This one?" at the homes they passed.

David steered the car into the driveway of 4 Wisteria, and Amy's heart pounded against her ribcage with newfound, mounting excitement.

The house could have easily held a family of ten. The hulking structure was made of gray bricks with a large, black front door that four people could have entered side by side. The perimeter of the house was lined with hedges that had been trimmed to a precise length. Flowers bloomed brightly in small explosions of pink, yellow, and white by their front door as if welcoming them home.

"This is insane," Amy found herself saying. David laughed coolly beside her, unfazed.

He put the car in park and turned around to look at Ryder, whose eyes and mouth were wide in awe.

"Welcome home, bud," David said.

"It's a castle," Ryder said. He had only known home to be the size of their comparatively compact three-bedroom apartment.

David smiled. "Let's go inside and explore it. See if there are any dragons inside."

Ryder flinched as if this was a very real possibility. Amy rushed to add, "There won't be, buddy."

David led their little family with a confident, almost eager stride. He didn't use a key to enter. The front door had been left unlocked for their convenience. Amy wondered if they would ever need a key in a neighborhood of family members.

The entryway smelled of lavender, rushing out to greet them in a surge, and Amy noticed that the air was cool, almost cold when juxtaposed with the heavy summer humidity outside. What little furnishing Amy could see from the front hall was warm and cozier than she had anticipated.

Her gaze snagged on the massive, sprawling bouquet of flowers placed on the table at the center of the entryway. Two curved stairways leading to the second floor snaked up the sides of the walls with their ends meeting in the middle and spilling out nearly to the foot of the large bouquet.

As she walked, Amy's heels click-clacked against the spotless marble flooring. The sunlight shining through the many windows was unfiltered and golden.

Despite her awe, she could not dismiss the unsettling feeling that she was an outsider, someone who was touring the house but would never buy it, never live in it.

A noise from deep in the house made Amy turn to her husband. He seemed unworried, though. Instead, he grinned and strode further inward, Ryder trailing excitedly after him.

Behind the massive obstruction of the bouquet, the house gave way to a beautiful kitchen, dressed in marble and white wood cabinets. In the middle of it all, standing at the island, was David's mother, Lily. Her head was bent in concentration as if slicing fruit was very serious business. She looked up with widened eyes like she had been caught off guard.

"Oh my!" she exclaimed. "I didn't expect you all for another hour."

Lily was a pretty older woman, though Amy was certain she would've preferred to be described as elegant. She was never without copious rings on her knuckles, polished nails, and a face of dewy makeup. Lily had a beauty that Amy had always quietly suspected was kept alive by artificial means, especially her vibrant red hair, which was probably the result of frequent touch-ups. It was very unlikely that Lily's hair would remain so bright, shiny, and vividly red in her early sixties. But if she was kept youthful with dyes and injections, it was hard to tell what she had gotten done. Lily seemed to know just the amount to make it still look natural and effortless.

"Hi, Mom," David said. He went to her and kissed both of her cheeks.

"Oh, it's been so long. Too long," Lily said.

Amy hugged her mother-in-law and felt the cool metal of Lily's large, heavy necklace touch her skin in the embrace. She resisted the urge to flinch.

Lily turned her attention to Ryder, who hung back as they reunited. She beamed at her grandson in a warm and genuine expression that seemed to twist her features unnaturally. Amy rarely saw such a bold expression from her mother-in-law, but when she did, it was usually reserved for Ryder.

"My, you've grown so much since I've last seen you, little Ryder," Lily said. She spread her arms for him to rush into, but he merely stared back, clearly confused, with his head cocked to the side in curious observation. Lily waited with her arms open expectantly for an awkward beat. Ryder didn't move. He had grown up rarely seeing the Montgomery side of the family.

"Ryder, go hug your grandma," Amy instructed, and Ryder finally moved to meet Lily, his feet dragging as if they were weighed down by cement shoes.

Lily smiled as she buried Ryder's face into the hug, closing her eyes as she smelled the top of his brunette head. When they broke away, Ryder staggered backward, his eyes still large at the place, the moment, and the woman in front of him.

Lily turned back to what she had been working on. She scooped up the strawberries she had been chopping when they walked in and put them in a large glass bowl already teeming with other fresh fruits.

"I wanted to have a little gift set up for you when you came," Lily explained. "I didn't want to leave you empty-handed, and I know how much a growing boy has to eat." She cast another grin at Ryder. "Besides, I didn't know if I could rely on Amy here to cook as soon as you arrived. The thought of you having to wait to eat..." She shivered before her eyes popped wide as though she had just remembered something.

She lifted a small shaker filled with white powder that had been placed by the bowl and began to shake it on top of the slices of fruit.

"Sugar is the secret ingredient," Lily said. When she was finished, she wiped her hands on a paper towel and disposed of it promptly in the trash can before locking eyes with Amy. "That's where the trash is, in case you were wondering."

Lily paused suddenly, standing back to admire the family for a second, a pleased smile spreading. "I'm so glad you're finally home."

"We're excited to move in," David said.

"Yes, well, all of your furniture and belongings have already been placed throughout the house. I directed them on where to put things. Of course, you can always move everything around. They're just suggestions. If you want to carve out a man cave, feel free."

"Will do," David said, plopping a cut strawberry in his mouth and chewing with relish. He was looking at Ryder, who had started to retreat behind his legs, still regarding Lily with cautious interest.

"Well, I'll leave you all to it," Lily said. "We have a big family dinner at our house on Sundays at six. It's a good way to get together after church and everything while everyone is still all dressed up. We usually gather an hour or so before we eat to hang out and throw everything together. I've told you about it, David, of course. I know you don't go to church yet but that doesn't mean you're not invited. We've been waiting for you to come for so long."

She gave Amy a tight grin. Amy could see a silent look of accusation fleeting across her mother-in-law's features. It was as if that moment was slowed down, lasting minutes between them. But it was there and gone in a blink.

Lily kissed her son on the cheek goodbye and gave Ryder's cheek a pinch that made him cringe and rub the spot she had squeezed.

"Hope to see you all there tomorrow!" she said, her heels clicking crisply against the floor.

"We'll be there, Mom," David called after her.

Lily blew one final kiss in farewell and then left the family to themselves.

Amy suddenly felt every inch of emptiness in the home as it settled into silence. She moved to fill the quiet urgently.

"We'll have to bring something to the dinner tomorrow," she suggested. "Cookies or wine or some kind of snack to contribute."

"Yes," David agreed. "We should."

"I can make some cookies tomorrow so they're fresh. We can get the ingredients when we go to the grocery store later."

"Sounds good," David said. He turned and ruffled Ryder's hair, seeming to snap Ryder out of a trance as he poked at his cheek where Lily had pinched him moments before. "Let's go take a look at the rest of the house."

The self-guided house tour took longer than the average exploration should have but there was a lot of ground to cover. They surveyed the house's nine bedrooms and twelve bathrooms, finding each one more striking than the next. Every room seemed to follow its own color scheme until each shade of the rainbow was given a designated space, though none of the rooms could compete with the vast blue bedroom that Amy and David were eager to claim as their own. Ryder showed particular interest in the smaller red bedroom facing the street and was fascinated by the pool that sat stagnant and waiting, its surface as calm and still as a mirror. Ryder touched everything he could with eager hands, and Amy had to scold him when he got distracted touching the shiny glass bottles at the basement bar.

What was left of the day was spent organizing the meager belongings that hadn't already been moved in, shopping for groceries to pack the various spaces available to them, and eventually settling down for the night over some take-out Chinese food upon Amy's suggestion. David had initially protested but gave in when Amy told him that she was too tired to cook up anything besides a frozen pizza.

Their dinner was pleasant and quiet. There was so much quiet, in fact, that it was as if they were living not only in an excess of space but in an excess of silence as well.

As Amy and David settled into their California king-sized bed that evening, Amy was overcome with the scent of fabric softener and inhaled deeply. Even the sheets smelled like something from a five-star hotel, luxurious and floral, not at all like the Tide detergent she had grown up on.

David turned over promptly after they had consummated the new house with sweaty, almost brutal urgency. Soon, his panting evened out into soft, rhythmic breaths, leaving Amy to lie in the dark room, distinctly hearing the lack of noise yet again. She reflected on how odd it was to go from the frequent noises in the heart of Charlotte to the absolute stillness of the Floridian coast. Amy listened for the waves of the ocean, nearly a mile off, hoping that if she strained enough, she would find a sound to fill the emptiness. But there was nothing. Unlike during dinner, this quiet was eerie and the unfamiliar calmness filled her with a sense of dread without anything to hang on to and distract her. Only the muffled sound of insect chirps substituted the void that was usually occupied by cars and passing late-night chatter. She tossed and turned endlessly for hours without relief.

For most of the night, she listened to the occasional shuffling of their sheets infrequently filling the room. As Amy finally found herself drifting off, though, somewhere around four in the morning, she thought she heard footsteps coming from the floor below them. They were soft, almost timid.

Amy sat upright, struggling to confirm what she believed she had heard, waiting for more footfalls to send her into a panic. She listened intently for several minutes but heard nothing more. Convincing herself that it was simply a hallucination of her wandering, sleepy mind, she allowed herself to turn over and attempt to sleep again.

Amy didn't know it then, but this otherwise gentle patter marked only the beginning of the strange occurrences on Wisteria Drive.

Chapter 2

The next day, Amy woke feeling unbearably tired. It was seven in the morning when she stirred, and the first light of the day was already rudely streaming through the cracks between their curtains. She groaned softly as she came to, stretching to wake her muscles, which were stiff from the cramped car ride the day before.

Beside her, David slept soundly. He was on his back looking delicate and peaceful under the morning glow. Amy smiled to herself and couldn't resist placing a gentle kiss on his forehead. Her husband was a heavy sleeper and did not so much as move despite the disruption.

Amy rose from the bed, slipped on a pair of fuzzy slides she had set by her nightstand, and walked down to the kitchen. Her loud yawn temporarily filled the quiet.

When she walked by the front door though, she paused, remembering the sound of footsteps the night before. It didn't seem as though their house had been ransacked, but even if it had been, how was she to know? There were too many rooms to account for and too many belongings to keep track of.

Amy twisted the doorknob and found that the front door was unlocked. It opened slightly when she pulled, letting a stream of unadulterated morning sunlight flood in. The revelation sent a cold chill down the length of her spine, which she immediately tried to push aside. She was certain that she had locked the door the night before as she followed David up to bed. It seemed she had misremembered, but she could not place why the thought of leaving the door unlocked all night left her so unnerved. They lived in a gated neighborhood and the only people around them were trusted family members. Besides, Amy had been exhausted and half asleep when she had supposedly heard the noises and she had likely been so tired from yesterday's travel that she had forgotten to lock the door.

Amy flipped the lock to silence the vexing voice encouraging her fears. David might trust his parents' security entirely, but it never hurt to have a little extra precaution.

When the coffee was made, Amy sat back into one of the kitchen chairs Lily had undoubtedly picked out and listened to the world begin to wake. The absence of commotion was still palpable, but the twittering of birds and the occasional rustle of branches were rising to fill the stillness.

Amy felt exposed as she sat in the middle of such a large, empty home. Until David, she had spent all of her life in the same cramped, too-small apartment with her mother, listening to the sounds of sirens, car horns, shouting, and conversations through thin walls to lull her to sleep. When she had moved into David's apartment, she had taken it as a significant, unparalleled upgrade. Wisteria Drive was an entirely different type of improvement.

She couldn't imagine how she must seem to the Montgomerys, who were so used to the vastness.

The Montgomery family was powerful and beautiful, their words and intentions always precisely measured. Amy had, over time, begun to regard the Montgomerys as the bootstraps myth manifested. They had pulled themselves up from a middle-class beginning and became so wealthy they were able to afford a neighborhood all while never failing to maintain their appearance and standing in society. They were unrelentingly polite, but Amy couldn't shake the feeling that some of the things they said were like the sugar on a Nerds sour candy; they were the sweet before the sour.

Amy often wondered if it was merely her perception of families that led her to prematurely judge the Montgomerys. They were so unlike Amy's own family—a miserably small and tattered disarray—that it was almost comical. Amy's mother had had to work two jobs after Amy's father had run out on them just to keep the two of them eating. Emily had become disillusioned in the process; to her, the bootstrap myth was just that: a myth. The struggle had made the two of them incredibly close, though.

Amy sat at the kitchen table in reflective thought until Ryder came staggering down the stairs, rubbing sleep from his eyes.

"Hey, bud," Amy said. "It's early for you."

"I had trouble sleeping," he complained before yawning dramatically. "Too quiet."

"Me too," Amy said, rising to start breakfast.

Amy made pancakes and bacon for Ryder and David. Whipping up their favorite foods was her attempt to make the new house feel more homey. She had always cooked for the two of them back in Charlotte, and she hoped that Ryder would taste her familiar cooking and feel more at ease. Amy couldn't tell if it had that effect as Ryder dug into his food happily, but he at least seemed content for the moment, and the process of cooking seemed to quell her, too.

She was snacking on the refrigerated fruit salad Lily had made for them when David finally walked into the kitchen at nine o'clock. His face was still puffy from sleep.

"Morning, honey," he said. He took in a deep, exaggerated sniff. "Bacon. My favorite."

Amy wiped her hands off, clearing them of any fruit juice, and sprung into action. "And pancakes. I'll make those fresh, though."

David smiled drowsily and took a seat, waiting to be served.

Amy had long since learned that David valued home cooking above most other attributes. Perhaps she had Lily to blame for this. Like Amy, Lily had been a stay-at-home mom, toiling around in the kitchen to fill her ample time. After Ryder was born, Amy had slipped into that same role easily, learning recipes and cooking tricks to pass the day away. She suspected that David would have perhaps preferred she had taken on the role all along, though he had never said as much aloud.

Amy served her husband breakfast and got to work on the cookies for the evening's dinner. As they baked, growing more fragrant by the minute, a tight knot formed in her stomach at the idea of spending the evening with the Montgomerys. Their performance—and more specifically hers—would set the tone for how their living situation would proceed. She would need to be perfect, to play the role of the doting, loving wife impeccably.

She watched the cookies rise as Ryder retreated outside to frolic in the large expanse of yard behind their house. The grass he rolled in was thriving and green, well-kept even after all of those years without an owner to oversee its care.

David came up from behind and gave her ass a playful squeeze. Amy jumped out of her thoughts and turned to kiss him.

"Sorry I fell asleep so early last night," he said, his face inches from hers.

"You were driving all day, honey. I didn't blame you at all," Amy said.

David grabbed a lock of Amy's freshly dyed red hair, twisting it between his fingers thoughtlessly. He liked it colored vibrantly red, despite her hair already having a naturally orange hue to it. His appreciative attention and closeness always made her cheeks flush.

"How do you like it here so far?" David asked.

"Everything is so beautiful," Amy said. It wasn't a lie.

David gave a short chuckle. "And huge. My whole family could live in just this one house if they wanted to."

"We certainly have enough storage space," Amy said. "And I guess it's nice that if my mom visits, she'll have seven guest rooms to choose from."

David gave a lingering smile. "Yes," he agreed after a moment. "She will definitely have options."

Amy touched his chest, feeling the warmth of his body through his thin shirt. Her cheeks blushed even brighter like an embarrassed schoolgirl. He noticed and smiled wider, pleased that he still had that effect on her after seven years of marriage.

"I should call her," Amy said, trying to break his concentration from her crimson cheeks.

Amy and her mom called several times a week to talk, whether it be to discuss updates about life or hold meaningless conversations. They were bonded unbreakably, welded together by distrust and trauma like two pieces of metal immortally forged into one. They might not have been picture-perfect like the Montgomerys, but their familial love was just as real.

David let the heavy moment fester for a beat longer, allowing the electricity that sizzled in the limited space between them to consume her. "Alright," he finally said. "I'll be outside with Ryder."

When he walked away, it felt as though he was peeling himself from her like tape off a surface. Amy still found her face hot even after David was outside getting Ryder's attention to go play with the foam swords they had bought while shopping the day before. She had always loved the way David had a demanding presence over her. It had been what had drawn her to him that night they met at the Hangover, a Charlotte bar that she had frequented during her college days with a distinct smell of hops and sweat. She touched her cheek and found that the feeling was still there, alive and fresh after so much time had passed.

Amy checked on the cookies once more, determined they needed much more time in the oven, and then strode to the kitchen table, where she plopped down and called her mom.

Emily picked up in one ring.

"Oh my god, Amy," she said before Amy could even say good morning. "I was waiting by the phone."

"I texted you that we got here safely yesterday," Amy reminded her.

"I know," Emily said. "How is it?"

Amy's eyes swept over the showroom appearance in front of her, taking in the immaculate yet unfamiliar furniture once again.

"It's big," Amy said. "Huge, really."

"In a good or a bad way?" Emily pressed.

Amy tapped her fingers against the table for a moment, thinking. "I'm not sure yet. You really could get lost in it."

"I'm sure it's quite the adjustment. You were in that apartment for so long."

"Yeah," Amy agreed. "But I loved that place. This is a big jump."

She watched Ryder run by the window, chased by David brandishing a foam sword. The two were laughing, taking full advantage of the large space now at their disposal. The scene pulled at something in her chest, deep and stubborn.

"Ryder seems to like it," Amy added. "He thinks it's a castle."

"From what you've told me, it almost is." Amy had also texted her mom the day before about the nine bedrooms, the pool, and the alarmingly large backyard. It was all an image of wealth that neither of them could have ever fathomed. It was also something that Emily seemed to be particularly fixated on because she could have never given her daughter such a life even after her years of endless labor.

"The sleeping is going to be hard to get used to. It's so quiet here that Ryder and I could barely sleep at all last night."

"David was ok, though?" Emily asked.

"Yeah. But he spent all day driving, and he lived in the suburbs growing up, remember? He's used to it. Ryder and I are just going to need a while to adjust."

"You should get one of those noisemakers," Emily suggested. "White noise or whatever. It could help fill up all that empty space."

The call continued for fifteen more minutes going back and forth like that. They caught each other up on everything that the other had missed within the last twenty-four hours, with Amy taking up most of the time describing Wisteria Drive in great detail. She painted a picture of the array of rainbow rooms, the fully stocked downstairs bar, and the bouquet of flowers in the front hall as vividly as she could.

They talked about every detail of Wisteria Drive except for one. Though she told her mother practically everything, for some reason, Amy refrained from bringing up the footsteps she thought she had heard the night before. She could almost hear Emily calling her paranoid now or reassuring her that the noise was just the house settling. Even thinking of it in the light of day made the brief fear she had felt seem like a distant, silly thing.

Before they hung up, Emily said, "You'll call me if you need anything, won't you?"

"I always do, Mom," Amy said.

"I know, I know. This is just the furthest we've ever been apart. I'm so used to you and little Ryder visiting at least once a week. It's very new for me."

"It feels weird for me, too. You can always have the guest bedroom of your choice when you come to visit, though."

"I'll have to soon." It sounded like a promise.

"Just let me know when," Amy said.

"Alright, honey. I should let you go. Let me know how dinner goes tonight!"

As they spoke, Amy was scooping up cookies off the baking sheet and displaying them nicely in a basket. Her stomach twisted once again at the reminder.

"I will, Mom," she said. "You know that."

Almost the instant that they hung up, Ryder and David scooted into the kitchen, breathless from play with large grins spread on their faces.

"That kid really whooped my ass," David said as he sat down at the kitchen table. Amy shot him a look to remind him to watch his words in front of Ryder. David held up his hands defensively, his face full of amusement.

"Daddy said I could be a real sword fighter!" Ryder exclaimed.

"I'm sure you could," Amy agreed.

"The cookies smell amazing," David said.

Ryder, seeing an opening in the conversation, sprinted in the direction of the nearest living room, tearing toward the television at a speed that nearly blurred him. Amy had no idea where he found all of that energy so early and with such little sleep. Amy would need to take a nap soon if she wanted to be even somewhat present and friendly for the first impressions she would be making at dinner that evening.

"I hope your family likes the cookies," Amy said.

"Unless you somehow baked a hair into them, I'm sure they'll love them," he said.

Amy felt the knot in her stomach tighten at the idea that she might have unknowingly done just that.

"I think I need to take a nap," she declared. "I've been feeling a little paranoid because I didn't sleep much last night."

"Was it the bed?" David asked. "I thought it was really comfortable, but if you don't think so, we can always buy another."

"No, no, it wasn't that." Amy remembered the soft silk and the pleasant, floral smell of the sheets. "It was the quiet. I'm used to sleeping through noise."

"Ah," David said. "Yeah, that will take some adjusting." He kissed her on the forehead and gave her a lingering look as he brushed back her hair to better see her full face. "Go get some sleep. We have a big night ahead."

Chapter 3

Amy stood in front of the large front door of 1 Wisteria Drive with one hand holding the basket of cookies and the other fidgeting restlessly with her dress.

David rang the doorbell again and the three of them stood there for a long time waiting for someone to answer.

When David caught Amy adjusting her skirt to ensure that it was perfectly straight and without wrinkles, he grabbed her hand to still it.

"It looks fine," he said, taking in her red Calvin Klein wrap dress. "You look great."

His warm smile made her feel awash in comfort, even if the relief it brought was only momentary.

"Where are they?" Ryder asked, pouting impatiently.

"They're probably busy making dinner, buddy," Amy explained.

David rang the doorbell again as Amy tapped her foot. Finally, Tiffany, one of David's three sisters-in-law, peeled the door open. Upon recognizing the little family, her face broke out into a wide and contagious smile.

"There you are!" she exclaimed. She pulled David into a hug, then Amy. "It's *so* good to see you. It's been too long. And you don't have to ring the doorbell! Just walk on in!"

She waved them inside, and Amy was glad to step out of the oppressive, humid heat that had settled on the evening.

Inside, 1 Wisteria Drive was like something out of a dream. It was at least twice the size of Amy and David's home, and it smelled of citrusy cleaning products. Every surface shined.

Instinctively, Amy began to kick off her shoes, but Tiffany looked almost scandalized by such a silly idea.

"Oh, no, no, no!" Tiffany said. "Keep them on! They're cute shoes. Don't waste them trying to maintain the floors. Sydney–she's been cleaning here for years–will just clean them tomorrow anyways."

"Oh, alright, my bad," Amy said, reaching to readjust the shoe on her foot. Her face felt like it had been lit on fire, and she knew that her cheeks were glowing an embarrassingly bright red.

She was somewhat relieved to be granted the ability to keep her shoes on, though. Amy was wearing the kind of footwear David had always liked. They were strappy with thin heels, colored in an unobtrusive neutral beige. Throughout their marriage, Amy had noticed that most of his compliments were directed at what she was wearing, and the slim heels had never failed to meet his approval. She had even begun wearing them around the house. They often made her feel like a supermodel or well-to-do actress. And it didn't hurt that David liked them as well.

She saw with a glance that Tiffany was wearing a pair of pumps too and wondered if Tiffany's husband, Jason, was also fond of the footwear. Tiffany had paired her heels with a tight, knee-length skirt and a long-sleeved blouse that flowed to her wrists in a shiny silk cascade. Tiffany looked stunning even if the outfit seemed a bit out of season with its excessive coverage. Amy couldn't understand how she could stand being so covered up in the stifling heat.

Tiffany waved them inward again, and they followed her deeper into the house. As they passed numerous rooms, she explained their purposes.

"Ryder, honey, you can play in there," she said when they passed a large room filled with children's toys. Sunlight poured through huge windows onto a shelf filled with every board game Amy had ever heard of, a giant plush elephant, boxes filled with tiny figurines and Barbies, and a Playskool bakery set.

A small girl was bent over one of the boxes filled with Barbie dolls in various stages of undress. Her head was bowed, and her silky chestnut hair shielded her eyes shyly. A little boy with brown curls that were a shade or two darker than Ryder's was stacking Legos. He could not have been more than two years older than Amy's son and was actively ignoring the four of them as they stood in the doorway.

Ryder's eyes were wide, taking in the possibilities of the playroom with astonishment.

"That's Kayleigh and Braxton," David said. "Do you remember them?"

Ryder nodded but showed no signs of recognition. He was too occupied processing all the toys.

"Go on, buddy," Amy said, giving him a gentle, encouraging nudge in their direction.

At first, Ryder was hesitant, drifting toward where Kayleigh was adjusting the tulle dress on a red-headed Barbie doll. Watching his timid approach made Amy's chest ache. Ryder had never had close friends his age to play with in Charlotte.

"Come here," Braxton called out to Ryder. "Let's build something."

Ryder's attention snapped to Braxton across the room, sitting in an ocean of colorful bricks. When he glanced back at Kayleigh, she hadn't so much as raised her head in acknowledgment.

"Boys don't play with Barbies," Braxton said. "We play with Legos."

Amy watched confusion play out on Ryder's face. It seemed like an unwarranted, exclusionary thing for Braxton to say. She felt inclined to correct the statement, but Tiffany was already calling out to them, having taken a few steps deeper into the house while Amy was lingering in the playroom doorway.

"You can throw your purse in the parlor there, Amy," Tiffany suggested as she gestured to a room further down the hall. Amy hurried after her and did as she was told, quickly tossing her bag on top of the little mountain of purses that was forming on a small blue couch.

Finally, they made it to the kitchen, where Lily and all of David's sisters-in-law were fussing about, preparing the meal, and gossiping enthusiastically with each other. Amy could hear their conversation about Sydney's new haircut from down the hall.

When they entered, Lily stopped what she was doing immediately and hustled over.

"Oh, David!" she exclaimed, pulling him into a hug so abruptly that her many golden bracelets jangled loudly. "You're here! Finally!" It was as though she hadn't seen him at all the day before or she had expected him to flee overnight.

Behind the embraced pair, all of the women watched on with pleased smiles. David's sisters-in-law all had a similar appearance. The women were tanned, slim, and on the shorter side with various shades of red hair, both artificially and naturally colored. Amy and Lily both fit the description as well, making it seem to any passersby as if all of the Montgomery women could be sisters or at least somehow related by blood instead of marriage.

Lily moved on to Amy, giving her a quick hug and kiss on the cheek that Amy was sure had left behind a red circle of lipstick. Amy rubbed at her cheek to wipe it off when Lily turned.

"I brought cookies," Amy announced, setting the basket down on the marble island.

Her addition to the feast seemed meager compared to the array of food that the women were already working on. In the oven, a whole turkey was cooking, scenting the kitchen with its delicious, savory smell. Corn and beans were simmering in pots on the stove, and Jenn—who was married to the youngest Montgomery son, Tyler—was cutting up potatoes to season and cook. Various rolls were already prepared and displayed prettily in a wicker basket. The other women were still hurrying to work on other options.

"Yummy," Jenn said, giving Amy a warm grin. She had always been particularly nice to Amy and her comment felt like a lifeline.

"Go ahead and put those off to the side," Lily instructed, gesturing to put the cookies away from the dinner at work. "David, the boys are all out back on the deck. There's plenty of beer out there. Richard made sure to get IPAs, so there should be something for you."

Amy felt a tug at Lily's directions, wanting David to stay with her, to shield her from his family for just a little longer. Their eyes met, and he gave her a small shrug that said *I have to.* She knew that she would have to get used to spending private time with the Montgomerys, but it all seemed so soon, and Amy felt unprepared.

"See you in a bit, hon," David said, and he kissed Amy's cheek lightly as if in reassurance.

"See you at dinner," Amy said before adding quietly, "Have an IPA for me." She knew that the women were not drinking and that getting a beer from the boys' cooler would likely be frowned upon as they worked. For now, she would flounder in the kitchen with the women, uncomfortable and painfully sober.

She watched as David sauntered out, his tall, broad build moving deftly. David walked with the grace of someone who knew what they were doing at all times, who fit into every venue like it was natural to him. He looked good in that house. He looked like he belonged.

When Amy turned back to the women, she felt as though she very much *didn't* belong despite evidently looking the part of a Montgomery wife. All of their eyes were on her expectantly, as if she were a specimen under examination, placed on a slide that had been slid beneath a microscope to be analyzed.

"So," Amy began awkwardly to fill the silence. "How were your weeks?'

"Rather uneventful," Lily answered. "Amy, would you like to hop on over and help Jenn with the potatoes? She'll show you how they're made."

Like David, Amy did as she was ordered to. Jenn handed her a second knife and flashed a smile that seemed to poke humor at Lily cracking the whip. Amy was just relieved to retreat toward someone a little more welcoming.

"My week was alright, in case you were wondering," Jenn said. "Ty and I went to the beach on Wednesday and drank wine with sand up our butts. That's pretty much the highlight."

Amy laughed quietly. "That sounds amazing."

"How was the move-in process?" Jenn asked.

Amy looked around to see the other three women bent to their work, engaged in a conversation about plans to go to Disney World together later that year that they seemed to have already made without her. "Overwhelming," she admitted in a hushed voice.

"Yeah, I bet," Jenn said, equally quiet. "It was for me, too. I can't imagine moving in with a kid."

"I don't think Ryder liked Charlotte much," Amy admitted. "I think he'll fit in here better. He's already in the playroom with Braxton and Kayleigh."

"There's certainly enough to keep him occupied here," Jenn agreed. "You'll have to take him to the beach soon. The Montgomerys own a bit of private land, so you don't have to be near anyone else. It's really nice. Ty and I could go with you to show you where it is if you wanted."

Amy felt her tense muscles relax at the invitation. "That would be great. Maybe sometime this week?"

"I've got nothing but time." Jenn was also unemployed, though she was not taking time off to raise a family the way Amy was. Instead, Jenn was known to complain often and loudly about how there was nowhere around Wisteria Drive hiring someone with a half-complete journalism degree. Over time, though, it seemed that she had settled into the role of a housewife nicely.

On top of the turkey, corn, beans, potatoes, and rolls, Miranda—married to the second-oldest Montgomery brother, Matt—made a green bean casserole, and Tiffany tossed a salad together with home-made dressing. Lily had gotten to work on an apple pie for dessert.

Of all of the tasks the Montgomerys hired others to complete, Amy reflected that it seemed they found a comforting ritual in cooking. It was not chaotic or stressful. The women appeared to be at peace with their work, content to put together food that everyone would gush over. It pleased them to please.

They talked among themselves as they flitted in and out of the kitchen, not seeming particularly cold but seeing no urgency to include the new girl. For now, Amy would chop her potatoes quietly, speak to Jenn in a lowered voice, and listen.

***

Dinner was ready at six o'clock promptly. Jenn told Amy as she slid the potatoes into the oven that dinner was never served earlier than six or later than six-thirty. By five minutes after six, all of the men had been called in to eat and all of the children had been served portioned sizes of the most nutritious food.

The dining room was already set with placemats and gold silverware lining a table that was long enough to fit at least five more people even when including the addition of Amy's family. The feast was set below an array of three grand chandeliers that looked as if they were made from real crystals. Amy wouldn't have been surprised if they were.

The men came back inside talking boisterously, each with a fist securely wrapped around a can or bottle of beer. All of them had similar faces, the familiar, almost repetitive characteristics of brothers. Anyone would have been able to tell they were related at a mere glance. All five of the men had beautiful caramel hair, broad shoulders, and naturally hard faces that relaxed handsomely when they grinned. They looked like men who had grown up in wealth. There was not a crease on any of their faces, save for some light sun damage on Richard. Stress had never touched their complexions.

Amy watched as Richard Montgomery, the patriarch of the family, fell into his seat at the head of the table in booming laughter. Lily took her seat at the opposing end of the table with a tight, practiced smile. She did not appear to enjoy their loud disruption to her quiet, tidy home.

The children sat down in front of their pre-made plates, with Ryder grinning excitedly as he talked to Braxton. Amy watched her son with a fresh sense of reassurance as he took his fork and began to scoop corn into his mouth.

Suddenly, Amy felt the air shift and grow tense. Some of the family members were glaring daggers at her. Glancing back at the children, she knew the reason immediately.

Braxton and Kayleigh sat poised in front of their food, waiting for an unspoken cue to eat with polite patience that seemed strange for children their age.

Lily cleared her throat at the end of the table, to break the men's oblivious conversation about the Red Sox's last game. It seemed that all of the men had been ignorant of Ryder's faux pas. Ryder hadn't noticed either. When he turned to see what Lily was about to say, Amy shot him a stern look to put his fork down. Ryder obediently dropped the silverware onto his plate with a clatter. Amy felt her face grow hot again as some of the men finally picked up on what had occurred.

"Everyone grab each other's hands," Lily instructed. "I'll say grace tonight."

Around the table, everyone folded their hands into their neighbors'. Amy clasped David's on her left and Jenn's on her right, feeling strengthened by their touch. She was glad when everyone closed their eyes and bowed their heads as it gave her face some time to return to its normal color.

"Bless us, O Lord, and these, Thy gifts, which we are about to receive," Lily began. Amy peeked at Ryder and caught his bewildered look. She would have to teach him the prayer soon. "From Thy bounty. Through Christ, our Lord. Amen," Lily finished.

"Amen!" Richard's voice thundered from the other end of the table. He lifted his bottle of beer and took a long sip.

Within moments, the dining room was filled with a chorus of clinking and clanking as forks and knives went to work on the array of food set before them. Bowls were traded around the table so often that Amy barely had time to take a bite between passes.

For the first few minutes, there was little conversation. Then, Richard took aim at David.

"How was your drive yesterday?" he asked, pointing his fork in David's direction.

"Long," David joked. A few of his brothers tittered in respectful laughter.

"I wouldn't have been able to stand it, staring at the road for all that time would drive me nuts," Matt said around a mouthful of food.

David shrugged. "It wasn't so bad."

"I bet you miss all of the commotion of the city," Lily said. "We're quite boring by comparison."

"I think we'll have plenty to do," David said.

"I'll keep you busy at work," Richard promised. "We can always find something for you to do at Treasensure."

Richard's company, Treasensure, supposedly created malware protection and removal software. Though the description of Treasensure had always seemed rather vague and confusing, it was clear that the Montgomerys' wealth had soared decades before Amy met David when they were some of the first to start pushing this technology. When Amy had first looked into David's family's business back in the early days of their relationship, she had found little written about Treasensure no matter how deeply she dug. David had merely laughed about it when she brought it up to him. "That's intentional," he had said. "We don't want to risk the competition finding out about us."

Now, David gave a tense grin in response before he looked down at his plate of food and began to push corn around with his fork. Amy's compromise for the move was relinquishing the city she had grown up in and moving away from her mom. David's was having to work at his father's company instead of pursuing his dreams of working in the business side of the fashion industry. She wasn't sure which of their sacrifices had hurt more.

"You'll be working a man's job, finally," Richard said, mercilessly refusing to let go of the subject. "Make sure you wear your suit and tie."

His monkey suit, Amy thought. She tried to watch her husband from the corner of her eye.

"We have a strict dress code at Treasensure, so don't go making me look foolish by not adhering to it," Richard continued. "You know what I always tell my workers when they ask if they can have a dress-down day?"

He had asked no one in particular but Lily piped up dutifully. "'You do have a casual day. Two, actually. It's called the weekend.'"

Richard gave Lily an approving nod and the Montgomery brothers all produced little, polite chuckles. Jason, the oldest brother, seemed to be especially humored by this, with his laughter canopying over the rest. David stuffed some turkey into his mouth to avoid speaking.

"What do you think of the house, Amy?" Richard asked.

Amy felt all eyes look at her. Even the children stopped spooning messy scoops of their casserole to listen.

"It's very big," Amy said. She could feel all of their stares as if they were physically touching her.

Jenn gave her a small nudge with her heel under the table. *Keep going,* the motion seemed to say.

"And our bedroom is just wonderful," Amy added quickly, almost stumbling over her words. "Ryder already really likes the backyard. Don't you, buddy?"

Ryder gave a quick nod, bashfully quiet in the sudden spotlight.

"Quite the upgrade from Charlotte, I'm sure," Lily said. "Plenty of space compared to that little hole in the wall you were renting, David."

But *he* hadn't been renting it. Lily and Richard had been paying off the rent every month until suddenly the Montgomerys had threatened that the money would stop coming and that the trust fund would go dry. They tactfully left Amy, David, and Ryder with only one place to go, and it was a place that was already paid for and waiting.

"Much bigger," Amy agreed when she saw that David wasn't going to answer. "We're excited to test out the pool."

"I swear by having one," Richard said. "I would never dream of living in a place without one at this point." He waved his hand as if dismissing the idea.

"We love ours," Miranda said abruptly.

"Me and Brax race each other in ours; don't we, Brax?" added Jason. Amy watched him and thought that a stranger to the family would never be able to tell that he was the oldest brother with his shorter stature. He had clearly tried to make up for that by building himself broad with muscles that corded his arms and chest in a way that was intimidating to look at. His hair was also the blondest out of the brothers and was several shades lighter than his son's, making him look the most distinctive out of the Montgomery boys.

"Yes, Dad," Braxton responded. He had already cleared his plate and was sitting patiently, swinging his feet beneath the table to console himself in his boredom.

"Those were good investments if you ask me," Richard said. "I haven't lived in a house without one for over two decades."

Amy couldn't imagine getting much use out of it herself.

For dessert, the Montgomerys ate apple pie from Lily, brownies from Miranda, and cookies from Amy. Jenn had brought a pint of vanilla ice cream as her contribution. Bringing desserts seemed to be a weekly expectation and not, as Amy had assumed, a one-time occurrence.

Amy couldn't imagine eating anything else and declined when dessert was offered. All of the sisters-in-law did the same. Lily, who had mostly eaten turkey and salad, nibbled on half of a cookie. The men, on the other hand, ate as if they hadn't just finished their dinners moments before. Even David topped his plate with two scoops of ice cream, a slice of pie, and a cookie.

Amy allowed Ryder to have a cut of brownie. Across the table, Jason sternly told Braxton how much he was allowed to eat.

"One cookie, do you hear me, Brax?" Jason said. "You want to be in shape for football, right?"

"Yes, Dad," Braxton said. He took a generous amount of time choosing the perfect cookie.

Amy sipped her water quietly, glad to be forgotten. The men talked about sports and their jobs at Treasensure, where they worked together under the watchful eye of Richard. Amy sat wordlessly and let her mind wander back to memories of Charlotte.

Eventually, Amy helped the women clear the table as the men sat capping off their last beers of the night. David stayed with them to talk and drink, and Amy felt a small pang of anger as she watched him sit back with his family while she helped tidy up. She would let it slide this time and excuse it as making up for the lost time while she and the women continued to work.

A little after eight, once dinner had been cleaned up and the chatter had begun to wind down, Ryder grew visibly tired. The conversation between him and Braxton lulled considerably, and he had begun to slump in his chair. Amy rushed to scoop him up into her arms, feeling his delicate body lazily sag against her.

"Sleepy, buddy?" she asked.

"A little bit," he admitted, while his head lolled to the side.

"It was a big day for you, huh?"

"Mhm," Ryder agreed. His lips were spread into a tired, pleased smile. "I had a lot of fun. I like Braxton a lot, Mommy,"

"I'm glad," Amy said.

David had noticed Ryder's drowsiness and seized the opportunity to leave. He downed the rest of his beer in a deep swallow and announced to his family, "We need to get going. It's almost our little buddy's bedtime."

Ryder looked annoyed at the mention of his bedtime but was too tired to argue and too shy to do it in front of such a crowd.

"Aw," Miranda cooed sympathetically. "We should get going in a little bit, too. Kayleigh will be needing some sleep."

Kayleigh, who had been seemingly silent all evening, gave a curt nod once in agreement.

"I just need to get my bag," Amy told David.

Amy hurried into the sitting area, nearly getting lost in the labyrinth of rooms on the way. Her purse was easy to spot, sitting on top of the pile. Even in the darkened room, though, Amy could see that it had fallen over and spilled. The contents of her bag had poured across the blue couch and some of the rounder objects like her lip gloss and mascara tube had rolled onto the floor. Amy cocked her head as she looked down at the mess. She could have sworn she had zipped it closed and yet...

She bent to hurriedly pick up all that had fallen out before making sure that everything was accounted for. Her wallet, makeup, sunglasses, and miniature brush had all been safely returned, but a panicky feeling bloomed in her chest when she couldn't find her pills.

Amy had been carrying her birth control pills in her purse since they had made their move. Ever since Ryder had been born, she had been especially diligent about taking her pill every evening at eight o'clock. She had made sure to pack the pills that evening since she had known that she would likely still be at dinner around that time. And yet when she spread open the little compartments of her bag and searched the floor around the couch, she couldn't find the package anywhere.

Every few months, she got a refill to last her the next three months, so she had a fresh pack at home, but still, the thought that she might have misplaced it or that it could have fallen out somewhere a Montgomery might find it made her skin heat up once more. She tore out the couch cushions and searched the surrounding floor on her hands and knees but to no avail. It was completely missing.

Her face was hot when she returned to the dining room. She was preemptively humiliated, hoping that none of the Montgomerys stumbled across something so embarrassing at 1 Wisteria Drive.

In the dining room, her husband and son did not seem to notice her alarm.

"It was nice having you all over," Lily said. "Maybe next time you can come with us to church earlier in the day. It makes the perfect Sunday, it really does."

"Travel safe," Richard joked, speaking over his wife.

"Of course," David agreed. "Eyes on the road and all that."

"You all can keep the rest of the cookies. I'll just come back for the basket later," Amy told Lily.

"Alright," Lily said. "Now go get that little one to sleep. A growing boy needs his rest. No one knows how important that is more than I do." She gestured toward her three other sons, who stood with visibly strong bodies and worriless features as a testament to her knowledge on the matter.

David kissed his mom on the cheek goodbye and then turned to his dad. "I guess I'll see you tomorrow, then."

"In your nicest suit," Richard said. "Make a good impression on them."

"Of course," David agreed, but he tore his eyes away quickly, evidently not wanting to think about the monkey suit any longer.

The three of them stepped out into the night air, still heavy with humidity. Amy could feel a storm coming. She hoped the additional noise it would bring might be enough to get her to sleep that night.

"Not too bad, huh?" David said.

"No, not too bad," Amy decided. It wasn't comfortable yet, but maybe over time, the dinners would grow more relaxed as she slipped into place as a Montgomery instead of an outsider.

"The first of many," David said as they walked up the driveway to 4 Wisteria Drive.

"Yes," Amy agreed tightly.

She couldn't help but look back over her shoulder at 1 Wisteria Drive as she neared their front door. The lights were still on throughout the first floor. No one else seemed to have left yet. At 1 Wisteria Drive, the gathering continued without them, as it had for years before their arrival.

Chapter 4

The week crawled into Wednesday and Amy stumbled through the passing hours. Those first two weekdays were especially lackluster. The house sat still for the better part of the day, and all of 4 Wisteria Drive seemed to suck in a sharp breath every evening at around five o'clock when David came home.

David was in a perpetually bad mood those days. He would walk through the front door and immediately undo his tie in frustration before lamenting, "What they do there... It's just not for me," as he sat down in a huff to eat the meal Amy had prepared.

Treasensure was not where he had expected to spend the last year of his twenties, and this was evident on his face every night around dinnertime. The disappointment was heavy and written into every feature. He had grown accustomed to living a life of adventure, one without obstacles. Amy found it difficult to watch reality set in as he was suddenly expected to settle down, to fall in line, and to work realistically.

He groaned about how much he didn't want to return to work at least once every hour that he was home and would often text Amy while he was away about how much he hated it there. His complaints were always unspecific, citing the fact that he never thought he would have to be involved in the family business. Amy often felt inclined to point out that she had yet to openly complain about how unhappy *she* was in the house all day or how hard the move was on *her*. But she continued to stay quiet on the subject. She didn't want to start a fight. Arguing with David was unproductive work. It would only result in him getting loud and blotchy with anger and her bending under his rage, compromising or apologizing to appease him. She didn't like to see him in that state, so she avoided it when she could.

Amy let her displeasure fester in silence. Unlike David—who had plenty of work to keep him occupied, even if he had to dress stiffly for it—Amy was left with nothing to do with her time. There was no agenda on Wisteria Drive. She laid out on the back porch and read gossip magazines in the sun on Monday. When the words lost their intrigue, she went inside and surrendered to watching television for hours. On Tuesday, she woke up and retreated to the television all day again, taking breaks only to make food for Ryder, who lost himself for chunks of the day in his video games. Amy was left to call her mom as a last resort when she was in desperate need of adult conversation.

On Wisteria Drive, there was no such thing as walking to your favorite clothing store or venturing out on brisk strolls with Ryder to cafés close by as they had grown accustomed to doing in Charlotte. Now, those luxuries were miles away. Only a shabby hotel sat just off the highway, a twenty-minute walk away, seemingly plopped down in the middle of nowhere years prior with the expectation that the little town nearby would expand over time. Otherwise, places to go were absent, leisurely pastimes were unavailable, and the Montgomerys were utterly isolated, left to their own devices.

Amy knew that she could, of course, invite one of the Montgomerys over. One afternoon later in the week she sat on their large sectional and debated doing just that, contemplating inviting Jenn to the house to break in the pool, which remained untouched.

So, when Jenn showed up at 4 Wisteria Drive in nothing but a bright blue bikini and a tote filled with a towel and suntan lotion the following day, Amy felt as if Jenn had been reading her mind.

"Sorry I didn't call," Jenn said. "I figured you would be home."

"You caught me," Amy said. "Come on in."

Jenn's wedges made pleasant clomping sounds against the marble floor. She looked around her, doing a dramatic turn as she took it all in.

"Your house is bigger than mine," she observed. "But don't tell Ty I told you that."

"You can have it," Amy said. "It's a little much for me. I'm used to small apartments with leaky showers."

Jenn nodded with a serious expression that looked strange on her delicate features. "Yeah, I figured. Just don't go telling anyone else that. It'll be gossip for months if you do."

"I wouldn't," Amy said. "You can trust me." It felt important to establish this. Jenn was quick to warm to Amy where the other Montgomery women remained distant. Jenn was open and bubbly in a way that brightened Amy's otherwise dreary existence on Wisteria Drive so far, and she felt like Amy's most likely friend. Amy was determined to secure the relationship.

Jenn smiled. "I'm glad." She looked up at the ceiling, where a colossal, sparkling chandelier hung. "Funny to think that this house was used for storage up until a month ago. Everyone used to just shove their extra crap in here."

Jenn strode further into the house, and Amy followed her as if she were the visitor instead of the host.

She liked the way Jenn walked with a purpose, demanding attention instead of discretion in her barely-there bikini. The rest of the Montgomerys seemed to hold the secret to confidence, including

Jenn, even if she seemed somewhat eager to separate herself from the others and remain mostly on the fringe of their conversations.

"Where's Ryder?" Jenn asked. "I figured we could all go down to the beach today so I could show you that spot. Unless you're busy, of course."

"I'm definitely not," Amy said as they walked into the kitchen. "Ryder's upstairs in his room playing video games or something. I'll go get him and change. We'll be ready in fifteen."

Jenn sat down on one of the kitchen chairs with a sigh. "Bless you. It would take me at least a half-hour to dress just myself."

As promised, Amy and Ryder were changed and descending the stairs in just a little over fifteen minutes. Ryder came bounding down the steps excitedly holding his T-shirt in one hand after refusing to put it on.

"Someone is ready for some beach time!" Jenn exclaimed when she saw him. "Come give Auntie Jenn a hug."

Ryder, despite his usual shyness, ran into Jenn's arms. Amy smiled, pleased to see that he liked her too.

The three of them loaded into Jenn's spotlessly clean Mercedes-Benz. Jenn drove like her intention was to give her passengers whiplash. She hit bends too hard and sped at least fifteen over the speed limit at all times. Amy was careful to keep from commenting on it and spent a lot of time hoping that Ryder wouldn't give them his two cents from his booster seat.

Amy was relieved when they pulled up to the beach without comment from her son. In fact, Jenn did that for them as she put her car in park.

"Sorry I'm such a bad driver," she said. "Ty usually drives for me. I'm out of practice."

Amy thought that Jenn's driving suggested that she had never been in practice to begin with but held her tongue. Instead, she said, "It's better than what I can do. I don't even have a license."

Jenn's jaw dropped. "No license?"

"In Charlotte, I mostly just walked or biked places," Amy explained. Her mom had also never had the time to teach her between her two jobs, but she excluded that information. Amy had a feeling that it would just confuse Jenn even more.

"I would die if I couldn't go anywhere," Jenn said. "Not that I venture out all that much. But still."

When they got out of the car, the smell of summer air and the tang of saltwater hit Amy as if she had just walked into a wall. It was intense and lovely. Amy breathed in deeply before turning to help Ryder out of the backseat.

Ryder bounded out of the car holding a bucket in a tight, sweaty fist as soon as Amy had unstrapped him him from his seat, tearing toward the beach like an unleashed puppy. Jenn and Amy chuckled as they watched Ryder fall to his knees in the sand, picking up handfuls of the stuff in wonder. He had never been around sand in his life and had only ever seen it on television. His boyish awe made Amy's chest ache.

Ryder was quick to get to work on constructing a sandcastle. As Amy and Jenn set up their lounge chairs, he began to scoop sand into his bucket.

"Make sure you wet the sand, Ryder, so that the castle stays together," Jenn suggested. Ryder said nothing but turned to the ocean and eagerly ran down to collect some water.

"He's a quiet one," Jenn said as she leaned back into her red-striped chair.

"He always has been," Amy said. "He's more of an observer. I'm hoping Braxton and Kayleigh will help take him out of his shell. He didn't really have friends to play with back in Charlotte."

"Tough luck cracking Kayleigh," Jenn said. She relaxed in her chair, her chin and chest proudly pointed toward the sky, drinking in the sun. "She's had a rough time of it around the Montgomerys. Not much for her to relate to with most of them. I'm sure you've noticed it's sort of a boys' club at times. Kaleigh's even quieter than your kiddo. Braxton on the other hand… I think he's a closeted troublemaker."

Amy took her seat beside Jenn and trained her eyes dutifully on Ryder, who was splashing about at the ocean's edge. If he ventured deeper, she would need to intervene. In the meantime, she curled her toes in the sand, appreciating its soft, warm embrace for the first time.

"They both seem like good kids," Amy said.

"Maybe," Jenn allowed.

Amy decided to change the subject. "So, when did you move in?" she asked, talking loudly over the crashing waves. David had told her that Jenn and Tyler were the second-to-last Montgomerys to move onto Wisteria Drive.

"It's been almost a year now," Jenn said. "It was last summer. Sometime in July after the Montgomerys' cookout for the Fourth."

"You'll have to show me all of the tips and tricks to keep from getting bored," Amy prompted.

"Well, this is one of them." Jenn gestured toward the sky. "The Montgomery boys love nothing more than a golden-skinned redhead. Seems like a contradiction for the natural ones, though. Good luck finding a redhead that doesn't burn. Luckily, I have the fake stuff and good Italian genes."

Amy laughed and sat back in her chair to better welcome the sunlight. Her own hair had always been tinged with an orangish hue that had been made more intense over recent years with dye. Fortunately, she was not susceptible to burning either. Her eyes were still focused on Ryder, who was now trying to outrun the waves as they crept up the shore.

"You'll be bored a lot of the time," Jenn admitted. "Especially with your husband at work. At least you have little Ryder. I doubt he's much of a handful."

"I'm just dreading when he goes back to school," Amy admitted. "All that empty space in the house…"

"It's not fun," Jenn confessed. "But the Montgomerys can be nice enough once you get used to them. They sometimes invite you places with them to keep everyone busy. Mostly everyone just cleans and cooks in their free time. Or sunbathes when it's warm. Sometimes they all work out together, too."

"I was thinking about finishing my degree with all of this extra time," Amy admitted. She had put her education on hold during her sophomore year of college when she met David at the Hangover. He had taken up her whole world from that moment on, promising her a life beyond anything she had ever dreamed of. Adventures around the world and a life without responsibilities had all seemed plausible when he pledged them to her over pillows in darkened rooms. And she had believed him so deeply that, by her junior year, Amy was married and in Cabo conceiving their son.

Amy had learned to be disillusioned with men at a young age. In her earliest years, she had determined that men too often used and left women just as her father had done to her mother. By the time she went to college, she had decided that they were rather simple-minded. She could often boil down their interests to sports, sex, or booze.

But then came David.

When Amy met him, he had appeared just as any other man would, though perhaps more handsome and better groomed than the average bargoer. His words were enchanting, telling her everything she wanted to hear with a voice that was almost musical in his deep baritone.

David's money hadn't been a well-kept secret with the designer clothing he wore even on the night that they met, but Amy had always seen wealth as an obstacle more than a luxury. It was something she had to compete with and measure up to. Anything they bought or owned was his. It made her feel indebted, especially at the beginning of their relationship.

At first, she couldn't tell what he had found attractive about her. She was a simple beauty, only slightly above average, and a mere college student to top it all off. Amy had no outstanding accomplishments to speak of, yet David had zeroed in on her, made her feel special, and when she married him, he had also given her a home, promising her safety and security. And she had loved him for it, believed in all of his promises, and trusted in all of his talents.

"Interesting," Jenn said, breaking into Amy's flood of memories. "Going back to school will at least kill some time, that's for sure."

"I went to school for business for a few years. I figure now I can do most of my classwork online and then see if I can maybe start some sort of baking business down the line."

"I don't know," Jenn began. "I might get bored from time to time but I've never wanted to work. I figure our boys are doing enough of that for us."

Amy thought of her mom, who had worked herself until she was too tired to even talk some nights. There had been countless experiences her mom had sacrificed so that Amy could grow up in the city with more opportunities. Her mom would have been appalled by the way the Montgomery women breezed through their day waiting for dinnertime and their husbands' arrivals to liven things up.

"I obviously wouldn't have to for money," Amy said. "It would just be for something to do."

Jenn shrugged. "Suit yourself."

The two reclined side-by-side for a while, listening to the low roaring of waves and the frequent squawks of passing gulls. Amy kept focused on Ryder the entire time and watched as he began to build his castle into a sprawling structure, packing down wet sand into clumsy shapes.

The world was so pleasantly still that when Jenn spoke again it almost made Amy jump.

"I want one so badly," she said. Her voice was soft with longing.

"One of what?" Amy asked.

"A kid." Jenn's eyes were trained on Ryder too, her face despairing behind her overlarge Gucci sunglasses. "All this free time... it would be different if I had a kid."

She tore her attention from Ryder and looked at Amy. When she met her gaze, Amy noticed that Jenn was resting her hands across her lower belly as she spoke. "You know we keep trying? We've done all of the little tricks we can think of. All of them. Some of them are so embarrassing I can't believe we tried them. Tyler said it's probably from his side of the family. Slow swimmers or something. Tiffany and Jason tried for almost a whole year before Braxton caught. She was so desperate to get pregnant." She lowered her voice as if divulging some dark secret. "Kayleigh was IVF."

Amy and David hadn't had any issues conceiving Ryder. In fact, he had been a complete surprise. Amy had never had any intention to get pregnant at twenty, but she also didn't regret it. If David had consumed Amy's world when they had first met, Ryder had consumed the entire galaxy when he was born. Amy made no effort to tell Jenn this, though.

"I think Lily and Richard are wondering what's up, too. Especially for Ty and I," Jenn continued. "We've been married for two years now and there's nothing to show for it. Lily's started to get a little cold recently, especially when babies are brought up. I think she blames me for it."

"That's ridiculous," Amy said quickly. "You can't help it."

"Maybe," Jenn said. "I'm getting frustrated too, though. So is Ty."

Amy remembered the discomfort of her own pregnancy. She had been mostly bedridden in her third trimester due to preeclampsia. At that point, she had been content to resign to it and was simply thrilled to be off her feet.

Shortly afterward, David quit his job as an apparel account manager to be with her. Upon hearing the news of Amy's rough pregnancy, Lily and Richard had traveled to visit them for the first time since their wedding.

Neither Amy nor David had expected their visit, so when they appeared at the door of David's apartment, he had been shocked, and Amy had been embarrassed. She was lying in bed, acutely aware of her unbrushed hair and the musk she was giving off after not showering for several days.

That was perhaps the first time Lily had ever shown Amy true warmth. She had come into the bedroom with a bouquet of roses, a basket of fruit, and the largest smile Amy had ever seen on her. It had been almost disturbing to see her appear so happy.

Lily had rested her hand on Amy's swollen belly at one point, and Ryder had come up to meet her touch with a kick. The movement sent tears to Lily's eyes. This was even more shocking than the smile had been. Amy had never seen Lily show such emotion, not even when her last son was married off to an unemployed college dropout.

"It's a miracle, isn't it?" Lily had asked. "Babies are life's answer. They're our calling."

Amy had thought they were sharing a moment and finally having a breakthrough. For a while afterward, Lily had even been kinder and gentler to her, as if proving Amy's assumption.

"The Montgomerys love three things," Jenn said as she held up three fingers. "Tanned redheaded women." She put down a finger. "Babies." She put down another finger. "And money." Her hand closed into a fist.

Amy swallowed dryly before adding, "You forgot pools."

Jenn threw her head back and laughed at the sun. "That's true. Four things, then."

The three of them stayed on the beach until three-thirty, giving them just enough time to get home, settle in, and get dinner started for their husbands.

As they loaded their belongings back into Jenn's car, Amy said, "I can't wait to hear about how awful David's day was. Again."

Jenn shut the trunk and lifted her sunglasses to give Amy a firm look. "He'll have to learn to keep that quiet. It's best just to fit in here. Trust me, it's easier to roll with the punches and go along with things."

She pointed at Amy sternly with her car keys, jabbing them in her direction with every other word. "And I don't want any of what I said today getting back to any of them. It's our secret. There's none of this talk on Wisteria Drive, okay?"

Amy felt her mouth go dry again. Jenn's sudden attitude change alarmed her. "I would never."

"Good. We just have to play their game."

Chapter 5

When David came home from work that Friday, cheery for the first time all week, and suggested that they take a night swim, Amy hadn't argued even when she considered how inconvenient it would be to have to shower afterward. They tucked Ryder into bed a little after eight and kept the lights low as they swam. Amy played a playlist of relaxing music from her phone as they swam circles together, disturbing the once-still water.

Despite her initial hesitance, Amy found herself indulging in the moment, enjoying the relaxed minutes they were creating together. With her limbs swaying through the cool water, everything felt incredibly *right*.

David seemed to be enjoying the evening as well. Encouraged by the beer he had been sipping at the edge of the pool, he became quite handsy, and Amy was beginning to think their nighttime swim was only the prelude to the rest of the evening.

Amy swam up to the stairs and sat down. David followed her and stood between her legs. She took a sip of her drink. It was a fruity concoction that was more juice than booze, though she looked longingly at the beer David had just set down. He had taken the last of the case, leaving her to resort to mixing various juices to drown out the taste of vodka. She was proud of herself for doing it all without complaint, not wanting to ruin their evening, even when David had said, "I took the last one, but I figured you wouldn't care, since you could make one of your girly drinks instead."

Now, the sugary mixture was coating her mouth. She tried to ignore it as she ran a hand down his bare chest, her fingertips drifting closer and closer to his waistband.

"One week down," she teased.

"Five days I'll never get back," David said. He stroked her arm as he took a deep swallow of his beer.

"I'm proud of you," Amy said. "I know it's not easy."

David chuckled and ran his free hand through his wet hair. "Thanks. It's not so bad, I guess. But you know I don't care for corporate bullshit."

"I know," Amy said. "You can make work clothes fashionable, though."

"Only to an extent," David countered.

"And you can design on the side or something," Amy suggested. "Collect your money at Treasensure and buy all the clothes that you want."

"Not to be rude, but my trust fund could have already bought all of those. And now that it's secured again, it's not a worry."

Amy knew that it was the stifling of his dreams that really bothered him. She suspected that it wasn't the actual work, but the fact that his parents had given him no choice and dangled the luxuries he had become accustomed to over his head.

"Fair enough," Amy said. She downed the rest of her drink and put the empty glass on the side of the pool to focus on touching David, stroking his arm and brushing her hands against his chest and taut stomach.

"He just runs a tight ship," David continued, echoing the thoughts he had expressed all week. "We learned pretty quickly to shut our mouths and take directions from him. It's worked out for the best so far. Overall, at least. All of my brothers are terrified of him, though."

"I think everyone is," Amy said. Maybe it was the drink that had made her say it, but it wasn't untrue.

"What do you mean?" David asked.

"Haven't you ever wondered why your mom keeps the house tidy or why she's always cooking? Maybe she doesn't want to step out of line." She thought of how Jenn had told her that they needed to play the Montgomerys' game earlier that week.

"My mom likes appearances," David said. "You do the same things as her. Are you afraid of me?"

"No." Perhaps she *had* stepped out of line. "I'm not. I'm just saying everyone's laboring under expectations. It might not be a bad thing. It's gotten the Montgomerys this far."

"I'm just sick of it," David said. "It's only been a week and I'm over it. I never wanted to come back here. Could have gone my whole life without seeing that gate again. And my dad makes me feel like I'm a kid."

Amy, eager to switch the topic from her potential faux pas, traced the top of David's shorts with a finger. His eyes snapped down to look at her with fresh interest. He pulled her closer to him and said, "You know what? I'm tired of talking about my family."

David bent forward and kissed her then, too excited to ease into it. His touch was hard and heavy from the moment their lips crashed together. His hands wandered and so did hers. He seemed desperate, driven to eagerness by a week of utter boredom. Amy felt the same.

When his hand slipped beneath her bikini bottom and began to pull it down, she gasped. "Not here," she said.

"Why not?"

Amy pulled away so that she could see David fully as she spoke. His eyes were wild and hungry, and his hands didn't cease exploring.

"Ryder will be swimming here," Amy explained. "And I don't want to do it out here in the open."

David sighed in exasperation. "Fine."

"We have seven other bedrooms we can break in," Amy added, leaning closer.

The smile returned to David's face. He looked giddy, like the younger man she'd fallen in love with instead of the stressed-out businessman he had become in the past week.

"I'll let you choose which one," Amy continued. "As a treat."

When they got out of the pool, they didn't even bother to dry off. They left their glasses poolside, abandoning them in their haste. As they hurried up to the second floor, they dripped water onto the floors and stairs like a trail to follow. Amy didn't mind the tiny chlorinated droplets puddling throughout the house. The new cleaning staff was coming on Monday to rectify any imperfections they might cause.

"Here," David instructed. He was gesturing toward a door just down the hallway, one where Amy knew the room was overlooking their large backyard, hidden from any peeping Montgomerys who might be looking out at Wisteria Drive that evening. "Let's try for another boy, what do you say?"

As David opened the door, a short, lonesome call came from down the hall.

"Mommy?"

Amy froze as though if she moved, she would be seen. But she had already been spotted.

Ryder came walking down the hallway, holding his favorite pale blue blanket and rubbing sleep from his eyes.

"What's up, buddy?" David asked. There was no hint of annoyance in his voice.

"People are talking outside," Ryder said. His voice was high-pitched as he whined and slurred with sleep.

"What do you mean?" Amy asked. She crouched down as he approached to be more on his level.

"Two people. I think. They're loud. I want them to stop."

"Outside your window?" David asked.

Ryder nodded lazily.

"Were they women or men?" Amy asked. She felt her head flood with concern. It occurred to her then how the neighborhood might appear to a stranger, to someone who wasn't a residential Montgomery. Wisteria Drive was lined with large houses ripe for robbing.

"I think they were Kayleigh's mommy and daddy," Ryder said. "I'm not sure. Can you make them be quiet?"

Amy looked at David sharply, hoping he could explain why his brother would be talking loudly with his wife outside at almost eleven at night. David only shrugged.

"What were they talking about, bud?" Amy asked, turning back to focus on her son.

"Something about Kayleigh," Ryder said. "I don't remember what. But they were loud. So loud."

"Alright, buddy," David said, putting his hand on Ryder's tiny shoulder for reassurance. "Let's go check it out."

The three of them walked to Ryder's room in a huddled group. Amy was growing cold in her wet bikini but knew better than to complain and draw Ryder's attention to it.

Ryder's room was already in disarray, with toys scattered carelessly across the floor and some abandoned clothes tossed about. Amy and

David had to tiptoe around the mess, and Amy thought to herself that she would have to talk to Ryder about cleaning it up in the morning.

Ryder stepped back and pointed at the window in the far corner of his room. Amy's heart was in her throat as she approached it. She leaned forward, not truly knowing what to expect.

But there was nothing beneath Ryder's window but trimmed shrubbery.

Amy and David seemed to hold their breath, listening for talking or shouting but heard nothing even after several long minutes.

"I think they're gone, bud," David concluded, finally. He went over and closed the window they usually kept cracked open, though, for good measure.

"Are you sure you didn't dream about it?" Amy asked.

"I know I didn't." Ryder was suddenly pouty, unhappy to be accused of lying or exaggerating. "They woke me up. They were almost shouting."

"About Kayleigh?" Amy asked. "They were yelling about her?" The idea that Miranda and Matt would be out in the street or screaming from their backyard so late, shouting about their daughter for all of the Montgomerys to hear, was more than a strange concept.

"'Kayleigh was a mistake. I can't do anything about it.' That's what I heard. What does that mean?"

Amy's eyebrows knitted together in confusion. She remembered Jenn whispering to her on the beach about how Kayleigh was the product of plenty of time and money for IVF. She was far from a mistake. Kayleigh was thoroughly planned and wanted. So what else would Miranda be referring to?

"Ok, bud," David said. He didn't appear to believe Ryder either. "Can you try to go back to bed for us? You can come and wake us if you hear it again and we'll take care of it."

Ryder nodded. "Ok."

He climbed back into his small bed, draping the blanket over his body to comfort him.

"Get some sleep, pal," David said.

Amy kissed Ryder's forehead and smoothed out his hair. He seemed eager to go back to sleep.

Amy and David were navigating their way out among the sea of toys when Ryder called from behind them.

"Didn't you hear them too? Isn't that why you weren't in your room?"

Amy felt her face get hot and was thankful for the darkened room shadowing her blush from view.

"Mommy and I just wanted to see if the new furniture was moved into the guest room after our swim," David lied easily. "We didn't hear anything. But if they're out there again, come and get us."

Ryder snuggled deeper into his bedsheets, pulling his blue blanket up to his neck. "Ok," he said.

David shut the door behind them as they left Ryder's room.

"We were almost caught in the act," David said. Even in the poorly lit hallway, Amy could see his face was alight with amusement at their near miss.

"That was too close," she agreed.

"Guess there goes our night. We're on duty now in case he hears Miranda and Matt again."

"Do you think he was imagining it?" Amy asked.

David shrugged, seeming thoroughly unconcerned. "I don't know."

"They could have been in their yard and their voices just carried," Amy suggested. Miranda and Matt were their next-door neighbors after all. "But the idea that we didn't hear anything... And calling Kayleigh a mistake doesn't make any sense."

"First of all, we were a little bit busy finding a room, so I'm not surprised if we missed it. Secondly, kids are mistakes all the time. Ryder's technically a mistake."

"Shh," Amy hushed him sharply. She didn't like hearing it said out loud. It felt wrong. "Jenn told me that Kayleigh is an IVF baby. So she had to have been planned."

"Yeah, I guess," David said.

Amy eagerly pulled on a bathrobe when they got back to their bedroom. Her body was covered in gooseflesh by then and her limbs had begun to shiver.

"I think he was just imagining things," David concluded, after several moments of quiet. "He's only six. Kids that age have crazy imaginations."

Amy sat down on the edge of the bed, thinking of the first night they moved into 4 Wisteria Drive less than a week ago when she had thought she heard footsteps downstairs in the early hours of the morning. Could that have been just a wild imagination too?

She pulled the robe tighter against her as if it could shield her from any of the possibilities. Perhaps she and her son did simply have overactive imaginations, but the coincidence still made her feel even colder than she already had been.

"Yeah," Amy found herself saying. "Maybe he dreamt it, too."

It was as if she had said that to assure herself more than David.

David stripped down and tossed his wet trunks lazily into the hamper. "If Ryder wasn't awake down the hall tonight..." He gave Amy a long look, watching her clutch her bathrobe as if to protect her decency instead of trying to hug herself into comfort. Then he shook his head. "No, I'll be a responsible adult. Tonight, at least." His grin was mischievous. "I'm going to take a quick shower."

Normally, Amy would have joined him. She knew that he wanted her to follow but she couldn't find the energy to. Instead, she merely said, "Ok."

She watched him stalk off toward the bathroom and waited until she heard the water start running before she breathed out the breath she had been holding.

Amy felt jittery and restless. She began to pace by the sliding glass door that looked out over a large portion of their backyard. She was tempted to step out onto the balcony for some fresh air but stopped in her tracks.

From where the door was angled, Amy was able to view a sliver of Miranda's yard. Though she had merely been glancing absently outside, a flash of red caught her eye. Miranda was standing in her backyard, her vibrant hair aglow in the porchlight as her shoulders shook with sobs that were rendered silent through the glass. Briefly, Amy was paralyzed, staring. When she found the ability to move again, she reached for the door handle, prepared to wrench it ajar and call out to her. Amy was not sure if she meant to comfort her or ask what was wrong. In the end, it did not matter.

Before Amy could even unlock the door to open it, Miranda was already turning to walk back inside her house, wiping tears from her cheeks so that Matt would not see them when she returned.

Chapter 6

The residents of 4 Wisteria Drive fell into a rhythm within the next few weeks. Monday through Friday, David would begrudgingly wake for work at a little before eight, don his suit and tie, and kiss Amy goodbye. The rest of the day was spent killing time, waiting for him to come home.

She played with Ryder in the yard, watched him swim laps in the pool, and read magazines in the sun. She punctuated every day with a call home to her mom to have someone besides David and Ryder to talk to, and Emily drank in even the most boring day's summary as if it sustained her. In the evenings, Amy listened intently for the sound of footsteps again until she had successfully convinced herself that she had imagined them that first night.

All the while, though, the memory of Miranda crying on her back porch gnawed at her. Amy hadn't told anyone about it, feeling as though she had seen something revealing and intimate that she didn't know how to organically bring up or articulate. But as the days passed and Amy continued to remember Miranda's shaking shoulders every time she passed the glass door in her room, she decided to seek out the opinion of someone sympathetic—and bored—enough to listen to her concerns.

On a particularly lackluster day, Amy trekked across the street to 5 Wisteria Drive with Ryder in tow.

Jenn opened the door dressed in Versace loungewear with a cup of iced coffee clanking about in a glass.

"Oh! Amy!" Her eyes were wide with pleasant surprise. "And little Ryder." She tousled his hair enthusiastically.

"Sorry to barge in," Amy said. "We just wanted a change of scenery. And I haven't seen your house yet."

"Oh, it's no problem. Not a problem at all. Come in! It's already so hot today. Get in the AC."

Amy was surprised to see that Jenn's house was indeed smaller. Not excessively so but it was noticeable from the moment Amy stepped inside. The entryway was tighter and only one stairway twisted up its walls. Her heels clicked across hardwood floors instead of marble as she walked deeper into the house.

"I hope you don't mind," Jenn began. She was a quick walker, and Amy hung back with Ryder, who struggled to keep up on his short legs. "Miranda stopped by to visit, too," Jenn continued. "She and I were just in the kitchen drinking some iced coffee. I can pour you a glass! And Ryder can have some juice. Is he allowed to have juice if it's sort of sugary?"

Amy felt her muscles tense at the mention of Miranda. Beside her, Ryder looked up with worried, knowing eyes.

"It's fine, bud," Amy quietly reassured him. She was grateful Jenn was far ahead with her back to them.

"What's that?" Jenn asked. "Did you say something?"

"I was just talking to Ryder," Amy said. "But yeah, he can have some juice."

"Oh, gotcha," Jenn said. "Don't be nervous, little guy. Kayleigh's here, too. You can play with her. I have no clue where she's sulked off to, though."

At the back of the house, the hallway gave way to a white kitchen that was immaculate and sparklingly clean. The only items out of place were a large pitcher of iced coffee and the glass Miranda was nursing.

Miranda sat as if her back were pressed against an invisible wall. Her posture was severely straight, and her eyes were intensely engaged. She was dressed in a slightly oversized designer tracksuit. It looked rich and as if it hadn't been worn before. David would have been disappointed in Amy for not being able to place who the designer was at first glance.

"Hi, Miranda," Amy said. She felt Ryder bury himself into her left leg, wanting to disappear from sight.

"Hello, Amy." As Miranda greeted her, she pulled a lock of artificially bright red hair and began to twist it.

"Oh, look at him!" Jenn said, looking at Ryder. "See, I told you little Ryder was a shy guy! He'll get along with Kayleigh just fine."

Amy took a quick look around, but Kayleigh's bowed head wasn't in sight. Miranda noticed her curious glance and said, "I think she went up to the west guest room. She likes to keep some toys up there."

Jenn turned to Ryder. "It's up the front hall stairs and then to the left. She should be in the one that's the second on the right."

Ryder thought hard about the directions before he bounded off, eager to leave the three of them behind for someone his age. Amy was certain he would spend most of his time trying to find Kayleigh.

"Coffee?" Jenn asked when Ryder was out of sight.

Amy nodded. "Yes, please. I haven't had iced coffee since we left Charlotte. It's like you can read my mind."

"I would die without a good cup of iced coffee every day," Jenn said. "Really. Like, I have a cup even in the winter. I crave it."

"Charlotte, huh?" Miranda mused. "A city girl." She took a deep sip of her coffee that felt prolonged. "Must be quite the adjustment to move here."

"It's just very quiet," Amy said. *Most of the time,* she wanted to add but refrained.

"I bet," Miranda said. "I grew up in a tiny suburb. Matt and I haven't ever lived in any other houses together, though. We came here right after we were married so we haven't had a problem."

It felt like a jab at Amy's hesitation to move to Wisteria Drive. Amy wasn't sure how to respond and was grateful when Jenn filled the beat of silence.

"I grew up in a little house in Pennsylvania. Ty didn't have to say much to convince me to move with him. I mean, come on." She gestured around her. "I barely had anything growing up," she continued. "My parents certainly weren't generous with their money. They were sort of absent, so my sister did most of the raising, truth be told. And my parents were quick to cut me off and kick me out the second I turned eighteen. Back then, this was the stuff of dreams."

It seemed that none of the sisters-in-law could've suspected that they would end up where they were. All four of them hadn't come from wealth. The Montgomery brothers had all married beneath them, lifting their pretty young wives up. Amy was no exception.

"I met Ty at a Target. Can you believe that?" Jenn said. "I was buying socks and tampons. I know, so embarrassing. And he was like, 'Big night planned?' It wasn't even a good line, but you should've seen him. You could've convinced me he was a movie star."

Miranda seemed entirely disinterested in hearing Jenn's story, and Amy imagined that she had heard it at least once before. But Amy found humor in imagining the Jenn she knew standing in a Target with her Versace lounge pants. The Jenn Tyler had first met, and the Jenn on Wisteria Drive sounded like very different people.

"I can't picture Tyler in a Target," Amy admitted. She could not imagine any of the Montgomery men fending for themselves alone in a grocery store or any other similarly mundane setting.

"I like to think it was fate," Jenn said, smiling when Miranda rolled her eyes. "And who knows? He didn't buy anything, so maybe it really was just where he was meant to be."

"David and I met at a bar," Amy said. "It was this sticky, gross place near where I lived with my mom. I used to go for cheap drinks when I came home for breaks during the semester."

"How romantic," Miranda teased, but Amy wasn't embarrassed.

"He and I talked until the bar closed for the night and then he asked me if I wanted to go back to his place."

Amy remembered the way he had smiled at her, all mischievous and tempting, daring her to take the leap. When she had told him that she didn't have a license and couldn't drive there, he had thrown his head back and laughed, beautiful in his humor and joy. "I'll drive you anywhere," he had said.

"But you didn't go back with him, did you?" Miranda asked. She looked appalled at the idea that Amy would give up the goods just hours after meeting a man in a sketchy college bar.

"Yeah," Amy admitted. "I did. We just went back to his apartment and talked mostly."

They had discussed deep topics that most people didn't even touch on during the third date. They talked about religion and feminism, and Amy had been taken by the way he had come off so educated about the differences among the waves of the women's rights movement. But those conversations had since dried up and had been replaced by grocery lists and complaints about work. She wondered exactly when that had happened.

But they had not spent that first evening just talking. They had slept together, too. It had been wonderful, better than with any man she had ever been with. He was kind and gentle, doting on her and asking about her comfort every few minutes. She had been hooked from then on.

Amy didn't regret that night. She was convinced that sleeping together so early had tied the two of them together, knotting their fates into a bow. She often wondered if they would have been married today if Amy had been too timid that first night. The truth was, she had been saddened that evening by a failed final exam—which at the time had felt as though the world was crashing down around her—and she was eager to bury her sadness in booze. When David presented himself as an option, Amy had been thrilled to bury her sorrow in him, too. It was strange to think about how that initially solemn night had been necessary to get her to where she was then, standing in Jenn's beautiful kitchen.

"I could never," Miranda piped up. "Matt and I waited until we were married."

"She's very religious," Jenn said flippantly. "I believe in God and go to church and all that, but I couldn't wait *that* long."

"I don't think you have to be religious to wait," Miranda countered.

"But you *are* religious," Jenn said. "And that's why you waited."

"Well, yeah. But I'm just saying I don't think you have to be a Christian to value emotional connection first."

"Fair enough," Jenn said before flashing Amy a quick look that seemed to say *really?*

"I'm not a crazy Christian, though," Miranda said. "We go to church every Sunday with the other Montgomerys, of course, but nothing too wild. Matt can sometimes be hard to drag along, though."

"Ty is usually the one rallying me. I like to sleep in, so it can be hard to get me to go," Jenn said. "He's a believer but sometimes I swear his real religion is sports."

"I heard Braxton wants to start playing football," Amy said. "But isn't he a bit young to be preparing for it? Like, should I be getting Ryder ready to play sports, too?"

"Oh, Jason's just really weird about getting Braxton involved. He was the quarterback in high school, and he played in college, too. It's a big deal for him, I guess," Jenn said.

"I think he just wants to give his son the same experiences he had. Matt wants to have a boy so that he can do the same. He doesn't think there is too much wisdom he can impress on Kayleigh," Miranda said with a shrug. "You know how the Montgomerys love their sons."

Amy took a sip of her coffee.

"You should see the way Lily and Richard fall over Braxton when he talks about football. It's like that kid hung the moon," Jenn said.

Miranda shifted in her seat uncomfortably and drained the rest of her coffee in two long, final gulps. A flash of Miranda crying in her yard tore through Amy's mind before Jenn continued.

"I'm sure Braxton would love to show Ryder how to play if he's interested," Jenn continued. "He's probably itching to be with someone his age. Jason always plays with him, and something tells me he doesn't pull his punches."

"I'll ask Ryder if he'd like to," Amy said. "Maybe we could set up a playdate. I haven't really talked to Tiffany much, so that could be nice."

"Cute!" Jenn exclaimed.

The three of them sat in Jenn's kitchen talking and sipping cold coffee in the air conditioning. It was nice to hang around women and gossip even if Amy kept glancing at Miranda, wondering if it was worth bringing up the fight Ryder had overheard. Ultimately, she decided it was not her place. There didn't seem to be a natural way to bring it up either. Amy hadn't had a girl group to talk to since she had met David and tossed aside college for married life. She was hesitant to put this amiability at risk for the sake of quelling her paranoia. Even while Miranda remained rather cold and proper between her frequent check-ins on the children, Amy still felt refreshed and relaxed when four o'clock dawned on them.

"I should get going," Amy said. "I need to start cooking dinner for David. He likes to eat when he gets home."

"Alright," Jenn said. "Stop by any time! I always have tons of iced coffee, so if you're ever craving it, you know where I live."

"I'll probably make the trip often," Amy said. "Thanks for the offer." She turned to Miranda, who was twisting a strand of her hair again. "It was nice talking with you, Miranda."

"Uh-huh," she said. "Nice talking with you, too."

"I'm going to go find Ryder and head out." She put her empty glass down in front of Jenn. "Thanks again."

Amy ascended the stairs, made a left, and began searching the rooms down the hall. She had forgotten Jenn's earlier directions, and the floor upstairs was carpeted, making it harder to walk in her thin heels. Amy hoped that whatever toys Ryder and Kayleigh were playing with weren't something that could be spilled like paint. Otherwise, the cleaning staff would have a hard time scrubbing the mess from such plush carpets.

The two children were so quiet that when Amy finally discovered them after trying four other rooms, she found that they were playing silently with action figures on the floor.

Ryder was holding a tiny figurine of a buff and shirtless Hulk. He was making the little action figure walk among a pile of lifeless toys that lay on their sides as if either defeated or discarded. Kayleigh was lining up a row of superhero action figures. Superman, Batman, Spider-Man, and Ironman stood shoulder to shoulder, seeming to prepare for a confrontation with the Hulk.

"Ryder," Amy said to get his attention. "Hey, bud."

Ryder snapped out of his play world. "Mommy!"

"We need to get going, buddy."

Kayleigh didn't even look up to see Amy. Her eyes were downcast, her head bent in quiet thought.

"Ok. Can I keep this?" Ryder asked Kayleigh. She looked up to see what he meant, and Amy saw for the first time that her eyes were green like Miranda's. Kayleigh nodded and then looked back down at the lineup in front of her.

"Thanks." Ryder stuffed the Hulk in his pocket and walked toward Amy.

"Bye, Kayleigh," Amy said. "It was nice seeing you." She gave Ryder a little nudge.

"See you. I had fun playing," Ryder added.

"Bye." Kayleigh's voice was so soft that Amy could barely hear it. She didn't look up at them again.

When Amy and Ryder were back on Wisteria Drive, out in the sun and the heat, Ryder looked up at her.

"Mommy," he said. "Kayleigh's really bad at playing."

Amy could only imagine that he was right, but it still seemed rude to hear it coming from his six-year-old mouth.

"It's because she's quiet, bud," Amy explained. "She's really shy."

"Braxton says it's because she's a girl," Ryder said. "He said she's not good enough to play with either of us."

Amy stopped walking as if her shoes had gotten stuck in the asphalt. "He said that? When?"

"Last Sunday," Ryder explained. "We were playing with Legos, and Kayleigh didn't want to play with us. So, Braxton said it's because she's bad at it. Because she's a girl."

"That's not true." Amy stooped down to his level so that she could look him in the eyes as she said it. "Girls can play just as well as boys can. You just have to get to know her more."

Ryder only looked confused. "Braxton said the reason all the moms and dads sit in different places is because the girls can't play as well as the boys."

Amy had never thought of how the children might see the natural split that occurred every Sunday. While the women bustled about the kitchen preparing dinner, the men lounged on the porch and threw back beers out of earshot. She hadn't even reflected on how strange this separation was. It had always just seemed so fluid and practiced that she had never thought to question it.

"Braxton doesn't know what he's talking about," Amy said. "You have to listen to me, Ryder. Girls can play just as well as boys can. They're the same. Equal. Understand?"

Ryder nodded his head vigorously. "That's just what Braxton said."

"So, you don't believe it, do you?" Amy asked.

"Not really. But Kayleigh *is* bad at playing."

"Kayleigh is just shy," Amy said again. "There's nothing wrong with being shy and there is certainly nothing wrong with being a girl. You'll meet plenty of girls at school in September who play just as well as the boys. I promise."

"Ok," Ryder said.

Amy stood and held out her hand. Ryder grabbed it, and she walked him back to their house, fretting all the while. Even the thought of cooking David dinner felt like a betrayal now, like she was buying into some preconceived notion Braxton had impressed upon Ryder about a gender split.

But Braxton wasn't entirely wrong, Amy supposed. There *was* one at play, and it was a split Amy helped to amplify. She and Kayleigh were equally guilty of emphasizing the division by playing the parts they were given.

Amy wanted to lecture Ryder more. She wanted to sit her son down to tell him that the world wasn't black and white or male and female but rather shades of gray and variations of both. The words were there but he was only six years old, and as they entered 4 Wisteria Drive, there was a feeling that the moment had passed, so she let it be.

She would regret that later.

Chapter 7

"I just don't see how anyone watches that show," Miranda commented with her nose scrunched. "Too violent."

Sunday had rolled around once again, and Amy was chopping onions, mushrooms, and carrots dutifully at the island while the Montgomery women around her were busy at work, as usual. They were talking about the latest television shows that had caught their interest while hustling around the kitchen.

Jenn was working on tossing a salad next to Amy. She was dressed in a white blouse and a flowy pale pink skirt with large gold hoops dangling from her ears. Even if she didn't think it, she fit in with the Montgomery image well.

Amy, on the other hand, wore a worn green shirt that she had kept from college and black jeans rolled up at the ankles to draw attention down toward her pumps. She had put very little effort into her outfit. After so many Sunday evenings spent together, she didn't see the point in trying to impress the family, especially since she still refused to feign interest and attend church with them in the morning. The other women, however, continued to dress their best as if they had just come from some fashion event, and all but Jenn shot poisonous glances at Amy when she came into the Montgomery house that evening dressed so casually.

Amy continued to work with her head down, listening to the mindless chatter around her and looking up only to take glances at the window overlooking the back porch. Out there, five brunette heads threw themselves back in laughter. The men drank beer heavily, not caring how drunk they got because it didn't matter. No one would pass judgment on them for letting loose.

Amy watched her husband most of all. She saw his relaxed posture, the way he had slipped into his position among the men with such grace and ease. They had welcomed him without question and embraced him as part of the group. He smiled, listening to stories and conversing with a bright grin on his face that was neither fake nor forced. She hadn't seen him like this since those weekends in Charlotte where he had hung out with his friends and let her tag along. Even if she hadn't contributed much to those conversations, it had been enough to lean into the warmth of David in a dimly lit bar, to share his time and his laughter so openly.

Why couldn't she tag along now?

Amy finished her work, setting aside the cut vegetables into neatly placed piles. The women were happily putting together the last of the meal around her. Only the soup was left, which Lily had said that she would like to make herself because she was using her own recipe.

Amy wiped her hands on a dish towel and looked back out the window, watching the men erupt into laughter once more, and she steeled her conviction.

"I think I'm going to go out back and get a beer," Amy declared. "Do you all need any more help?"

"A beer?" Miranda asked.

"Yeah, from the porch," Amy clarified.

"Like, with the men?" Tiffany asked. Her eyes were wide.

Lily tittered. "Are you going out there to talk about sports and boobs?"

The other sisters-in-law laughed nervously.

"Maybe," Amy said. "Unless you all need help here."

Amy watched the women give sweeping glances at their surroundings, searching for a task to give her. They exchanged nervous looks with each other. Amy felt Jenn's eyes trained on her the entire time.

Then Tiffany and Miranda focused on Lily, the final say, and waited for her verdict.

Lily put her hands up. "Fine by me. Enjoy the IPAs and testosterone."

No one relaxed at Lily's approval, least of all Amy. As she walked toward the porch, she felt eight eyes boring into her back.

Amy slid the door open and stepped out onto the porch only for ten more eyes to set their sights on her. The animated conversation stalled and fell silent.

"Honey?" David asked. *Is something wrong? Why are you out here?* his tone suggested.

"Hi, babe," Amy said. She plunged her hand into the icy water of the cooler. In her head, Ryder's voice echoed softly as she pulled out a cold bottle. She would show them that she could play just as well.

"What's up?" he asked.

"Just wanted a beer." Amy held it up to show them. She looked out at the pairs of blue eyes and felt herself tense as she realized that they felt she was intruding. "The ladies are finishing up dinner, so I'm not much help right now. Mind if I join?"

Like their wives, the Montgomery men exchanged looks and then focused on Richard, at the far end of the circle. He shifted uncomfortably in his chair; his face was emotionless. "You're a grown girl. I suppose you don't need to ask for permission."

Amy swallowed. Her mouth had gone dry. Her heels clunked loudly against the pavement as if reminding all of them that she was a visitor, a person who usually didn't venture onto the porch and shouldn't.

She pulled up a seat beside David, the sound of the chair scraping against the ground filling the unbearable quiet. Matt wasn't able to suppress a wince at the noise, making Amy's skin burn. She hoped for a gesture of reassurance from her husband but received none.

"Does anyone have an opener?" Amy asked.

Tyler silently pulled out a bottle opener and handed it to her without a word.

"Thanks," Amy said. Tyler only nodded his acknowledgment.

"So," Richard started, straightening in his seat. "The ladies weren't entertaining enough for you?"

"No," Amy said quickly. "Just wanted a beer and to see what all of the commotion was out here."

"Commotion?" Richard said with a deep chuckle. "I'd say we're pretty civilized, right, boys?"

They nodded in agreement. David sat stiffly.

"I meant all of the laughter. You seemed to be having a good time, and I wanted to join," Amy explained. Her face was unbearably hot, and she felt betrayed by her skin.

"We were just talking about Treasensure. And all the people there. You probably wouldn't know any of them," Jason said. Out of all of the brothers, he seemed the most opposed to Amy being there. His face was visibly pained, and he had crossed his bulky, oversized arms over his chest.

"Probably not," Amy agreed. "But I'd love to learn."

"I'm sure I talk enough about work when I come home," David said.

This was his way of telling her to back off. She was almost tempted to tell the group that he only talked about his work to complain but held her tongue. Besides Jenn, he was her only ally on the street, and she was beginning to realize that she was not making any friends by sitting out on the porch.

"Will dinner be ready soon, then?" Tyler asked. He was throwing her a lifeline, filling the unbearable silence. He was either too nice to join in with his brothers' cold approach or too stupid to notice it.

"I think so," Amy said. She was grateful for the conversation. "It'll probably be ready in twenty minutes." She wasn't sure if she would make it that long sitting under the intense scrutiny.

"Nice," Tyler said, nodding. "What are we having?"

It occurred to her then that the Montgomery men had absolutely no involvement in the ritual of the Sunday dinner. They merely showed up. They were served.

"Some vegetable soup, breaded chicken, cheesy broccoli, mashed potatoes, rolls, and a salad, of course," Amy listed.

Tyler nodded again. "Cool."

The silence settled back in, chilling Amy to the bone. She took a sip of her beer and made an effort to keep from cringing. She hated the bitter taste of the IPA but didn't want to outwardly show that she couldn't hang.

"We broke in the pool," Amy said to Richard. "It's as lovely as you said. Ryder and I have been using it a lot during the day."

It wasn't entirely true. Ryder had used it a handful of times while Amy sat on the edge reading gossip magazines. Aside from the night she had spent with David swimming about, she hadn't stepped foot in it at all.

"That's good," Richard said. "I love that thing. Everyone needs to have one; that's my philosophy."

"Yeah, it's perfect," Amy agreed.

"So, you're liking the move?" Richard asked. His gaze was inherently intimidating, almost searing. It put Amy on edge, making her feel as if every small movement was being analyzed. It almost undoubtedly was.

"Yeah," Amy said. "The space and quiet have been very different but I think we're getting used to it now. Ryder especially seems to really like it here. He's enjoyed playing with Braxton and Kayleigh, too."

She gestured toward Matt and Jason as she spoke. Matt gave her a quick, tight smile and Jason remained unexpressive, not swayed by the mention of his son's name.

"That Braxton is a good kid," Richard said. "He'll be a good influence on your Ryder. He's a tough one. Braxton'll teach him what's what."

At that, Jason gave a vigorous nod.

"I heard he's starting to play football," Amy said. "I could ask Ryder if he's interested in learning. Only, of course, if Braxton would be willing to teach him."

"He might," Jason said curtly.

"It's a good thing you're doing," Richard said. "Boys should start with sports early. It's good for discipline."

"Agreed," Jason said. "I would have started him earlier if Tiffany hadn't pushed back."

"Ah," Richard scoffed. "She doesn't understand then. You ought to explain it to her."

"I did," Jason said. "She wouldn't listen."

"Make her then. You know how."

Amy tensed at Richard's suggestion. The skin of her arms rose with gooseflesh. Something about the way Richard had said those words had twisted her stomach into knots.

"It's your money that will be paying for it, after all," Richard continued. "He's your son, too."

Amy opened her mouth to speak but David put his hand on her knee then, stopping her as she began to form words. He squeezed her leg, and she caught the look in his eyes as he gave a slight, terse shake of his head. He looked terrified. In that moment, he was not the witty, vibrant man she had always known. Under his father's watchful gaze, David was subservient.

His fleeting expression seemed to suggest there was no winning so there was no need to try. Anger boiled inside of Amy, and she leaned forward, ready to speak her mind anyway.

"I just think..." Amy began but the sliding glass door ripped open abruptly, cutting off her words.

"Dinner's ready!" Lily announced.

None of the men looked at Lily, though. David's father and brothers were staring at Amy, eyes acutely trained on her with severe glares. David merely stared at the ground, embarrassed.

"Perfect timing," Richard said. "Seems Amy here needs to eat something."

Richard stood and his sons all followed his lead, David included. Amy looked at him incredulously, but he didn't notice, or at least he made no effort to acknowledge her. He was already walking inside, leaving her in her seat alone.

Amy drained what was left of her beer, hoping that what little alcohol remained might take the edge off the humiliation she felt.

What a mistake.

Amy brought the emptied bottle in with her, unlike the men, who discarded their trash to be picked up later. She didn't want to leave a physical reminder of their encounter.

As she walked back into the house, she caught a glimpse of the clock above the stove on her way to the dining room. Five fifty-three. Seven minutes early. Lily had broken the unspoken rule about dinnertime always occurring at six o'clock to pull Amy out of there.

At the table, the men ignored her. The women chatted among themselves. The children were occupied talking about the meal in front of them and agreeing that broccoli was horrible.

After Richard finished saying grace, David tore his hand from hers as if it might be carrying a highly contagious disease. Jenn, on her right, gave her a sad, lingering look. *You fucked up,* it seemed to say. *Just ride it out.*

Amy looked down the table at where Ryder and Braxton were laughing over their dinner rolls and swinging their feet beneath the table animatedly while Kayleigh was mute beside them, staring dully at her own plate.

Amy was beginning to think that maybe the problem wasn't that girls couldn't play as well as boys, but rather that the boys wouldn't let it happen.

Chapter 8

Amy felt alone. It suddenly seemed like she was trapped on a street full of neighbors who would look down on her until something gave. Every time she thought of this, a cold hand at her throat seemed to squeeze a little tighter.

She knew that David could feel this pressing sensation, too. Perhaps she had betrayed him by rejecting his family's stupid norms, but he had betrayed her worse by leaving her to fend for herself.

That night, there was no one in her corner. Even Jenn had angled herself away from Amy for most of the dinner, only sparing her another apologetic glance over dessert.

No one stood by her except for perhaps Ryder, who hadn't picked up on the tension directed at his mom throughout dinner. He was happily sleepy when they arrived home later that evening.

"Braxton's dad said he's gonna teach me to play football," he told Amy as she tucked him into bed. David had already said goodnight to Ryder and was no doubt waiting in their bedroom to begin their inevitable argument.

Amy bristled at the mention of Jason, reminded of that awkward encounter on the porch while the wound was still fresh. "Do you want to learn?" she asked.

"Yes!" Ryder said. Even in his tired state, he found the idea incredibly exciting. "Please! I really wanna play with Braxton. His dad said it's what all strong boys learn."

"Well, not all of them," Amy said. She didn't want Jason to poison her son's interests with ideas of bravado. "But do you want to play it because you think you'll have fun?"

"Uh-huh," Ryder said. "I have fun with Braxton."

"Ok then," Amy began. "I'll tell Braxton's dad so we can get you over there to start learning. How does that sound?"

"Thank you, Mommy," Ryder said.

Amy smoothed the comforter over his body and kissed him lightly on the forehead. He still seemed so small, so delicate. The thought of him tackling other boys in such a violent sport scared her more than she cared to admit. But she supposed that it was part of his development. He was growing up and needed to test his interests even if it meant doing so with a man whom Amy felt a strange, persistent discomfort toward.

"Love you, kiddo," she said.

"Love you, too," Ryder returned.

Amy relished that sweet moment, savoring the tenderness of putting her son to sleep with a smile on his face, before returning to her bedroom. David was waiting on their bed, still dressed in the clothes he had worn to dinner. Amy stopped several feet from the foot of the bed and looked down at him. Her arms wound themselves together tightly across her chest, and she felt her eyes narrow into a glower.

"To be honest, I really don't even want to talk to you right now," Amy said.

"So, you want to just let this hang over our heads? Or do you want to discuss it like an adult?"

She didn't like his tone. It took everything in her to remain calm. "Adult? You let your dad talk about Tiffany like that and you want to talk to me about being an adult? Only children are that afraid of their fathers."

"Amy," David said with a sigh. The abrupt exhaustion in his voice almost jarred her out of her fury. Almost. "You don't know him like I do. It really is just better to let those things go, as awful as they sound."

"Well, it *sounded* like a threat to me," Amy said. "And the way you treated me when I wanted to hang out with you all... It was like I walked in there naked or something. The look on your face..."

"We just weren't expecting it," David said. "We were all hanging out, shooting the shit. We're used to just having that time as a family."

This was different. David usually fought with a temper. But there was no shouting or angry discoloration on his face. He seemed almost calm. It was like he knew that he was wrong and wouldn't put the energy into fighting it. She watched as he ran a hand through his hair, looking resigned.

"I'm part of this family now, or have you forgotten? No, you're used to having that time as men, you mean," Amy snapped. "If it was about family, Lily would be out there too. But she isn't. I intruded on your bro time, and you want to punish me for it like I'm wrong but this weird separation thing isn't."

"That's just how it is," David said. "You're not going to change it by barging in for no reason, and you're certainly not going to change it by yelling at my dad. I mean, Amy, what were you thinking with that one?"

"You had no idea what I was planning to say to him," Amy said. She could feel the resentment rising in her, bubbling to the surface. Her voice had slowly risen until she was walking the line between talking and shouting. She had never gotten to this point without David's fury pushing her there before.

"You need to understand—and I never explained it to you so maybe that's a bit of my fault—but no one talks back to my dad. He's never wrong even when he is."

"What's the worst that could happen?" Amy asked, exasperated.

David hesitated for a minute as if the words were catching in his throat. "I don't know," David finally admitted. "They're your neighbors. They bought this house for us. You tell me."

Amy sighed loudly. In that regard, he was right. She would always be at a disadvantage surrounded by a family that had months' and years' worth of history together. She was the intruder, coming in to shake the table.

"I'm here because of you," Amy said, exasperated. "I moved here because you convinced me that it was for the best. That we needed the money they gave us and that they had a great job lined up for you. But this was all at a great sacrifice for me. I have no one here for me but you. And you left me." Amy threw up her hands. "I'm just... I'm really disappointed in you."

"I'm sorry you feel that way," David said. "But you wouldn't understand."

It wasn't a true apology. He wouldn't argue his point with rage for once, but it was clear that he didn't feel sorry. She knew then that he would have done it all again if given the chance.

"At least let me try to," Amy said. "Don't just shut me out like you did tonight."

"There are things about my family you won't ever fully get. There's a history there—traditions and things that we've been through together—that you don't understand. You just couldn't. And I'm sorry for that, I am. But all I've asked of you is to make the most of the cards we've been dealt. I've been trying so hard to make things work, to make them right, but then you go and act like… like you're above it all. Like you run the show."

Amy blinked. "Wow," she said. "Ok, I'm going to sleep in one of the guest bedrooms tonight." Immediately, she sprang into action collecting her pajamas as David watched her move swiftly throughout the room.

"Oh, come on…" he began.

"I really need time alone," Amy said.

She looked back at him as she stood in the doorway. He was still sitting exactly how he had been when she had first walked in the room, but his back was bent as if he had been deflated.

Amy remembered a time when he had threatened to throw punches at men at bars who made her feel uncomfortable. She remembered how David used to proclaim that it was just the two of them against the world over tangles of bedsheets. But it was clear now that his family was the exception to that statement.

"Goodnight," she said.

She didn't wait for him to respond.

Amy picked the purple guest bedroom in the furthest corner at the opposing end of the house and settled down for the night. She changed into her pajamas and laid beneath the sheets, snuggled against the silken pillow yet receiving no comfort from its floral, freshly laundered scent.

Within minutes, she felt herself missing David's familiar warmth to the left of her. Part of her wanted him to burst in and beg her to come back. She wanted him to make a scene and apologize to her like the lovers in movies would. But the thought of his dismissal of her and her feelings left her disheartened. They made her feel sick.

David never came.

Amy lay in the stillness of 4 Wisteria Drive for hours waiting with that glimmer of hope shrinking by the minute. She could have sworn that, after hours of seething, she had heard him moving about below her on the first floor, but the sound quickly faded, leaving Amy to chalk it up to wishful thinking. Eventually, she gave up on the fantasy. He hadn't fought for her at dinner, so she supposed she shouldn't be surprised that he wouldn't fight for her then.

Amy tossed and turned that night. She didn't get a moment of sleep. At eight in the morning, she heard David stir down in the kitchen and loudly prepare for work. She didn't bother to get up and make him breakfast or pack his lunch. If he wanted to act as if she wasn't there, two could play at that game.

Chapter 9

Amy waited until she heard the garage door close before she rose and started her day. She moved to the kitchen, where she sat feeling lonely and drinking coffee until she knew her mom was up.

Despite the distance, Amy was certain that Emily was the only person who would listen and even attempt to understand.

"Hello?" her mom said on the other end.

"Hey, Mom." Speaking to her mother was a relaxing ritual, as freeing as yoga or meditation was to some. Amy felt the stress bleeding out of her.

"Hi, honey," Emily said. "How are things in Florida?"

"Not well," Amy admitted quietly.

"What do you mean?" Emily asked. Her voice was grave. She took matters involving her daughter very seriously, almost to a fault. Amy needed that right now.

She explained the previous night's events in as much detail as she could. At times, recounting the story was painfully embarrassing, and Amy blushed behind the phone at the memory. All the while, Emily listened patiently, not interrupting. It almost seemed like she had hung up she was so quiet.

When Amy finished, Emily said, "That's very disappointing. Especially from David."

Amy chewed at her thumbnail nervously. "So, I'm not crazy? It's bad, right?"

"It's 2016. Those thoughts are archaic. And Richard... I don't like what he was insinuating one bit."

"Me neither," Amy said. "It's like a little cult. Like two little cults, really. All of the women follow Lily, and all of the men follow Richard. It's really strange. I feel like if I were one of the brothers, I would have said something. If I was David, I would have spoken up. But they seem scared to and I can't place why."

"Has David ever told you about his childhood? Maybe Richard ran a tight ship."

David rarely talked about Richard in his stories. Those memories usually revolved around his brothers and the trouble they got into, or the times when Lily had been especially tender or generous. Amy simply assumed that Richard was off working or traveling, too busy to be responsible for his rebellious sons.

"I'm not sure. I guess it could be possible, but he's never mentioned it." Amy continued to chew her thumbnail between words, cracking the red coating of polish on top.

"I think it's smart to keep an eye on David's behavior. And maybe talk to Tiffany. Find out how she's doing and see if there's anything going on there," Emily suggested.

A part of Amy found the request to be almost humorous as if she were some investigator trying to crack a case instead of a woman trying to learn how to navigate her in-laws. But she also saw the value in the suggestion.

"Yeah," Amy said. "That sounds good."

"I'll be honest, Amy, I don't like the sound of any of that. I'm very surprised by David. It seems out of character."

"I know," Amy said. "He's clearly weird around his family. They all seem to be."

Just then there was a knock at the front door. Amy felt a bolt of nerves go through her, making the hair on her arms stand up. There was no one she wanted to see or talk to besides her mother miles and miles away. She hoped against the odds that it was just Meredith coming three hours early to clean.

"Mom, someone's at the door," Amy stated.

"Alright, I'll leave you to it," Emily said. "Keep me updated. I want to know everything. I'm proud of you for being willing to stand up for—"

Another knock.

"Thanks, Mom," Amy said, cutting her off. "I have to go."

"Oh, ok. Bye, honey!"

"Bye," Amy said and hung up.

Another set of knocks came as Amy made her way to the door, feeling chilly all over.

When she looked out the peephole, though, she only saw Tiffany standing on her front porch, holding a Tupperware container. Confused, Amy opened the door.

Tiffany's face lit up with a large smile as soon as Amy revealed herself. She was already wearing a full face of makeup, a fashionable outfit, and a pair of smart heels.

"Hi, Amy," she said. "I know it's early, but things were noticeably tense last night, and I feel like you and I haven't had a ton of time to just talk." She held out the container. "I brought cookies."

Amy accepted them, still feeling bewildered. It wasn't even nine in the morning yet.

"Thank you. Well, come in," Amy said. She opened the door wider to let Tiffany slip through.

Tiffany did so gladly and made her way back to the kitchen with no directions. She sat at the island, continuing to smile as if the grin was painted permanently onto her face.

"I remember we used to store our extra furniture in this place up until a few months ago. It's nice to see everything so clear and clean. You've done well decorating it."

"Thanks," Amy said. She walked over to the coffeemaker and set it up to make herself a pot. She would need some more coffee for such an early, unanticipated conversation. "Lily did a lot of the decorating, though."

"Ah," Tiffany said. "Of course. She's got such an eye for stuff like that. Aesthetics."

Amy crossed her arms over her chest as the pleasant aroma of coffee began to waft up around her. "She's not mad at me for last night, is she?"

"Mad? No! Just confused. Hurt, maybe. I think, if anything, she feels like you thought us girls weren't enough, so you wanted to hang with the boys."

"My son implied that us separating every evening was damaging his views on women. He said that he thought girls couldn't play as well as boys and that's why they were being excluded." Amy left out the part about Ryder getting the idea from Braxton.

Tiffany's smile tightened, then dimmed. "How odd."

"I see now that I wasn't wanted on the porch," Amy continued. "I won't be doing that again; I can promise you that." It wasn't worth the fight. At that point, she would only be seeking out another argument.

"The boys are just very tight, you know?" Tiffany said. "They're brothers, after all. It's hard to penetrate that bond."

"Have you tried?" Amy asked.

"Not as boldly as you did," Tiffany said with a short laugh. "But yes. And I learned quite quickly that they're not accepting any more members into their club."

Amy leaned onto the island. The coffee behind her was almost done brewing, but she ignored the machine as it hissed. "Doesn't that bother you, though?"

Tiffany shook her head and pulled the sleeves of her blouse down below her wrists. "No. I think things are easier when you know where you belong. Once you realize your space, you know what's expected. It's simpler when it's laid out like that."

Amy stared at her for a moment, weighing whether to push the topic further. She concluded she was already in the doghouse with the Montgomerys and thought better of it. "I guess I just don't agree with that," she said. "I actually was going to stop by your house later today."

"Oh yeah?"

Amy poured herself a large mug of coffee and then filled a second mug for Tiffany.

"Ryder told me last night he was interested in learning football, and your husband said that he would teach him. I was wondering if Jason and Braxton would mind having Ryder over some afternoon soon to learn the ropes."

"That would be wonderful!" Tiffany exclaimed. "Braxton really likes Ryder. Up until you moved in, he had no one to play with."

"What about Kayleigh?" Amy asked, remembering them in the playroom at 1 Wisteria Drive together that first Sunday.

"Kayleigh doesn't have the same interests as Braxton," Tiffany said flippantly. "I think Braxton has really been loving having another boy around."

"It's been nice for Ryder, too," Amy admitted. "Although I never pictured him as a kid who would play a sport."

Tiffany looked around the kitchen quickly. "I didn't think Braxton would be that kind of kid either," she said. As she spoke, she said the words with strange hesitance like she was divulging a deep secret. "But Jason was insistent. He says it's good for young boys. Important for their discipline."

They were Richard's words through a different mouth.

"I don't know," Amy said. "I think different boys—or kids, for that matter—need different approaches."

Tiffany looked amused by this. "Possibly. But Jason... he's... well, he grew up with all boys. And he is one himself, after all. I trust his judgment."

"But you don't agree."

"I didn't say that."

No, but Jason did, Amy thought. She was pushing buttons now.

"True." Amy took a sip of her coffee. It was hot and bitter. Unsweetened. "But Braxton wants to do it, doesn't he?"

"He didn't at first, but he does now," she said.

"I see," Amy said.

"I sort of let Jason take the ropes with Braxton if I'm being honest," Tiffany admitted. "He's always wanted a son. You know how men are. When they find the one, they want to settle down in the big house with all the kids running around in the yard. I've always thought it was funny that he wanted the white picket fence and everything when he had already lived that life. But regardless, he's always wanted a little boy. Always. A mini-me. He made that very clear from the start. Braxton was a necessity. When he came, he was like Jason's gift from God after all of that... waiting."

Tiffany looked down at her mug, visibly feeling a shame that should've disappeared with Braxton.

As Amy looked at her, she saw Tiffany's true age for the first time. Tiffany liked to dress herself up in makeup and heels and conservative clothing but could easily have been of an age with Amy, maybe even younger. At most, she appeared to be in her mid-twenties. Jason, on the other hand, was well over that. While she didn't know his exact age, Amy assumed he was in his early thirties. Tiffany was far too young to have felt the pressure he had put on her for the son he was desperate for.

"We tried for almost a whole year, you know," Tiffany said. "Braxton wasn't like your Ryder. We knew we wanted a family even before we were married. We even got engaged after a few months of dating because we were so eager to start one. Jason likes to say it was because he needed to lock me down, but I know his sights were really set on that dream of his. It was both of our dreams, really. If we could fill the whole house with a kid in each bedroom, we would. I just don't know if that's in the cards naturally."

Amy remembered the way she and David used to talk about kids. David had been the one who had first brought it up just weeks into seeing each other. Amy hadn't been scared off by his forwardness, though. In fact, she had valued it and had considered it a good sign that he was eager to settle down and plan out their future. So, when he brought up his vision, including little brunette mini versions of himself, Amy didn't flinch. She thought the idea was quite sweet and gentle, and they began to fill in the blanks of each other's futures.

Children had seemed like distant things at the beginning, though, somewhere after a few years of marriage, at least. The dream was far off, long after she had gotten her degree. But then life moved fast and suddenly she was engaged, and before she could even blink, she was on her honeymoon. When she returned, despite thinking she had been protected by the pill, Amy had missed a night and gotten pregnant. Ryder had pressed pause on the rest.

David had cried with joy at the news of her pregnancy. After that, Amy had only seen him cry on one other occasion, and that was when they had found out it would be a boy.

"You never know," Amy offered.

"We're pretty sure," Tiffany said. "We've been trying desperately since Braxton was born."

Tiffany traced the rim of her mug for a moment, then sat up straight as if startled, a smile quickly spreading back onto her face with the efficiency of a rubber band snapping back into place.

"I'm sorry to be such a downer. And so early, too. I didn't intend to come here and unload," she said.

"It's fine," Amy said. "What are sisters-in-law for?" Amy got the sense that this was something Tiffany had wanted to talk about for a while.

Tiffany brightened. "Yes, I guess you're right. Really, my goal in coming here was to extend the olive branch and tell you there aren't any hard feelings between us. I don't think the other girls hold any either. We were just startled, you know? And I think we took more offense to it than we should have. The rest of the girls will realize that over time if they haven't already."

"There are no hard feelings between you and me either," Amy said. She still felt discomforted by the rest of their reactions, including Jenn's. Most of all, there was still some lingering bitterness between her and David that she suspected would remain until one of them gave in and apologized, and Amy had no intention of doing so.

"Good," Tiffany said. "We're not so bad. Some of us may be a bit more traditional or set in our ways but really, I think over time I've come around to it. I see the benefits now. I'm sure you will, too."

If those traditional ways included husbands forcing their wives to fall in line, Amy doubted she would ever come around to it.

"Perhaps," was all she said.

"I can call Jason around his lunch break and let him know that Ryder will be joining him and Braxton for practice tonight. They usually start close to seven, so just send him over sometime around then."

"That sounds great," Amy said. "I'll let him know over breakfast. Speaking of, I should probably get to work on that. Ryder will be coming downstairs any minute."

"Of course." Tiffany got to her feet without any further prompting. "I should get going anyways. I wouldn't want to distract you. Most important meal of the day and all that. I guess I'll be seeing Ryder in a few hours then. In the meantime, tell him I said hello."

"Will do," Amy returned.

Tiffany left with a polite wave.

Amy listened as her shoes clicked down the hallway and out the door. She lingered for a moment in the kitchen, thinking of Tiffany's smile and her conservative clothes, the masks that she donned so easily. She wondered what lay beneath them and what made Tiffany feel she needed to put on facades at all, especially in a quiet kitchen on a calm morning.

When she tore her eyes away from the hall, she realized that Tiffany had left almost a full mug of coffee, now warm instead of hot. She had also left the container of cookies in her wake. Amy took out one and began to nibble on it. Something sweet to wash out the bitter unease she felt for the woman who had just left.

Part 2

Chapter 10

It wasn't until two days later that David finally apologized.

"I'm sorry you felt I was so rude to you," he said. "And that I made you feel unwelcome."

By that point, Amy felt so isolated that she accepted it, even if she wasn't entirely thrilled with the amount of time that had passed or the little effort he had put into the apology.

They made love that night, and the following morning, Amy went back to making his breakfast and packing his lunch as if it had never happened.

As she was going through the motions, though, she realized how similar to Tiffany she must have appeared. She was whipping up food to smooth over situations and to keep the peace, playing the perfect housewife. Again. Yet now Amy could only think of Tiffany and the tight smile she wore as she went about her busy work.

As she put a skillet on the stove, Amy found herself craving more than this repetition of a ceaseless routine. She couldn't walk to places on a whim the way she could in Charlotte. Her mom wasn't just blocks away, hoping for a surprise visit. Some of Amy's only entertainment was catering to the Montgomerys with food or folding her beliefs away into some dark corner to please them and keep the peace.

She told herself that morning as she scrambled eggs that she would indeed go back to school in the fall, even if it was only online. Tiffany,

Miranda, and Jenn might have been comfortable with staying slack in place, but she couldn't simply live and die on Wisteria Drive.

The doorbell rang then, breaking up her thoughts.

Amy sighed. She was growing tired of the guessing game of which Montgomery was waiting on her front porch.

Despite herself, she was relieved to see that it was Jenn standing in a skimpy, vibrant red bikini with large gold hoop earrings and oversized, dark sunglasses. Beside her was Kayleigh, with her head bowed so low that Amy couldn't see her green eyes. Miranda was nowhere to be seen.

Jenn gave a tiny, almost shy smile. "I missed you," she said. "Looking to break up your day?"

Amy invited them in and asked Ryder if he wanted to play down at the beach again. He all but squealed with excitement. Even with the newfound tension between her and Jenn, Amy's boredom won over. She wanted to bury her morning's worries about a discontented life in the Floridian sand.

When they arrived at their large patch of secluded beach, both children dropped to their knees a few yards from where Amy and Jenn set up their chaise lounges to sunbathe. Within moments, Ryder began excitedly constructing towers from wet sand, and Kayleigh was plunging a sifter into the beach, shaking it gently to see what seashells she could uncover.

With the kids just out of earshot, Amy decided to ask what had been bothering her during the brutally fast car ride there. "Where's Miranda?"

"Doctor's appointment," Jenn explained. "She says it's a physical, but I think it's a consultation about another round of IVF. Just me speculating, though."

Jenn rolled slightly to her side so that she was facing Amy more than the kids. "Sorry about Sunday, by the way," she said. "It was brave of you, you know? But I think I've been here for too long. I don't mess with the Montgomerys anymore."

"Anymore?" Amy prompted.

"I mean, when I first moved here, I didn't want to cook. I hate cooking. Before Ty, I lived on microwaved macaroni and cheese, believe it or not. When I moved here, all I wanted to do was sit around in the sun and read articles about true crime and celebrities. But Lily snapped at me to contribute, so I do now. And I once told them I wanted to eventually move out to Los Angeles. Big mistake. You would've thought I called them some kind of slur."

"I don't really consider that messing with them," Amy said.

"Maybe not to you or me but to them, even the smallest form of rebellion is big. It's really simple to live with the Montgomerys. You just have to be grateful and present. And you need to know when to keep quiet. When things get dicey, keep your mouth shut. That's why I didn't say anything on Sunday. It's not really an excuse but I've been on the receiving end of those eyes before. It's not fun."

That was the best apology Amy was likely to get from her.

"Wisteria Drive is too nice to mess up. A few years ago, I would've slapped you if you told me this would be my life. Really, we moved up the social ladder in a hurry. I do miss partying," Jenn said with a small pout, reflecting. "I think Ty does too, but he won't admit it. He just keeps saying 'This is the life, Jenn.' I mean, I guess he's right, but I miss getting blackout drunk on a Friday night." She sighed. "It's the little things."

Amy agreed outwardly but inside she concealed the thoughts she had turned over just an hour or so before. For now, those ideas were best kept to herself.

They sat abreast like that for a few hours, soaking in the sun's rays and watching Ryder and Kayleigh play. Ryder had stacked a tower of sand up to about his height and was decorating it with broken shells and discarded gull's wings. Kayleigh had a growing pile of fully formed seashells that she contributed to sparingly, saving only the prettiest. The two had only taken a break from their work briefly to eat a quick lunch of chips and peanut butter and jelly sandwiches.

The sun was brutal that day, beaming down on the four of them relentlessly. At around three o'clock, Amy turned to Jenn and asked, "It's sort of unbearable out today, huh? I don't know how much more of this I can take."

"Thank God you said something," Jenn said, fanning her sweatless face dramatically with her hand. "Let's get out of here."

Just as Amy and Jenn concluded that they wanted to leave, Kayleigh came racing up the beach, a mousy, childish grin playing on her face. It was the first time Amy had ever seen her smile and the look seemed unnatural on her features.

"What's up, Kayleigh?" Jenn asked.

"I found something," Kayleigh said.

"What is it?" Jenn sat up straighter in her chair, adjusting her sunglasses to better see.

Kayleigh held out her closed fist and opened her hand to reveal a large, shimmering diamond ring lying in the center of her palm.

Jenn gasped. Amy leaned forward as if she wasn't quite seeing it right. Kayleigh grinned proudly at their reactions, unable to contain her joy.

"Oh my god," Jenn said, pressing a hand to her chest.

"Can I see it, Kayleigh?" Amy asked. Kayleigh nodded in response.

Amy took the ring from her delicately, feeling its heaviness from the moment she had plucked it from Kayleigh's palm. It was sturdy and glimmered brilliantly in the sunlight. Amy had no doubts that the array of large diamonds was the real thing. Her heart raced as she held it.

"Wow," Amy said. She handed it to Jenn, who enthusiastically flipped it over, inspecting it at every angle.

"Looks like Daisy is missing her engagement ring," Jenn said. She was looking inside the band and handed it back to Amy to show her. Amy had to squint to see what was written there in the afternoon sun's glare, but eventually, she was able to make out what it said.

In little, italicized script it read: *To Daisy. 6/29/04.*

"It's not from that long ago," Amy said.

"That's so weird," Jenn observed, shaking her head. "I wish we knew who Daisy was. It's emerald cut, too. I'm jealous. She's probably missing that. I mean, look at those rocks!"

"It's got to be someone we would know, right?" Amy asked. "I mean, it was on the Montgomerys' beach, and they've been here since the early 2000s."

"Probably," Jenn said. "I mean, you would think so. Who knows, though? Maybe a gull or something carried it over."

Amy thought that was very unlikely. She wasn't even sure if seagulls carried anything beyond food and wondered if Jenn was just trying to excuse away the mystery of it. She suspected that it had been lost to the sand for however long it had been missing. It could have also been washed up, sinking into the sand over time.

She turned the ring over again and again, watching the diamonds catch the sunlight in different positions. It certainly wasn't the size of the average engagement ring. It was even a bit larger than her own.

"Kayleigh, do you mind if I keep this? I want to ask Grandma and Grandpa if they know who this belongs to," Amy said.

Kayleigh shook her head. "It's fine."

"Thank you, Kayleigh," Amy said. "You did a great job finding it. That's real-life treasure you found!"

Kayleigh's smile broadened before she looked at the sand between her feet shyly. "Thank you."

Amy slipped the ring into the pocket of her bag, and she felt its presence throughout the entire ride home as if the jewelry could have been weighed in tons instead of grams. During lapses of silence, when Jenn would cease talking about the latest sale she had indulged in or Tyler's plans to go sailing soon, Amy's mind would wander to the obnoxiously large engagement ring in her bag. She found herself drawn to it, wanting to touch it or look at it every few minutes to reassure herself that it was still there.

Amy was certain that the Montgomerys would have to know who it belonged to. It seemed very unlikely that a ring from just a handful of years before would wind up on the surface of the Montgomerys' private beach. Sure, a trespasser could've dropped their prized possession, but Amy felt that was doubtful. If Amy had lost that ring on a beach where it didn't belong, she would've searched for days to recover it.

But what did it mean if it was a person that the Montgomerys knew? Amy could imagine Daisy, pretty in a small yellow bikini, soaking up rays just as Jenn and Amy had earlier and taking off her ring to avoid tan lines. Perhaps she was Lily's friend, vacationing in Florida for a few weeks, and hadn't recovered the ring during her time there. Or maybe it had been an old fling of one of the Montgomery brothers, possibly even a visiting friend of theirs who was missing their beloved jewelry.

When they got back to Wisteria Drive and began to part ways, Amy turned to Kayleigh. "Thank you for letting me keep the ring. I'll take good care of your treasure. I promise."

Kayleigh only nodded sharply, but Amy had seen a ghost of a grin on her face.

Inside 4 Wisteria Drive, Amy waited until around four-thirty to put a pot on the stove and boil water for a pasta dinner. Ryder, tired from the adventurous day, was laying on the couch in the living room, intently watching a cartoon flicker in front of his face.

Amy took the time to change into clothes while she waited for the water to boil. She returned her things to where they belonged. The suntan lotion went back into her bathroom closet, the towel and bathing suit went into the hamper, and the magazine she had brought just in case she grew bored went back on her nightstand. Finally, she pulled out the ring, turning it over before she decided to stow it away. She had kept her valuables hidden in her sock drawer since she was a girl in high school, back before she had a safe to hide away her belongings behind a lock. She was not sure when the habit had started or what had inspired it. Perhaps it had been some movie she had seen as a child. Amy placed the ring beneath a mound of her socks next to the necklace her mother had gotten her for her high school graduation, a vintage broach her grandmother had given her, and the first bracelet she had ever saved up and bought for herself.

Amy returned to the kitchen to finish making dinner before waiting for David to come home. The food was prepared twenty minutes before he returned, so she served Ryder while the pasta was still steaming. Ryder ate his food eagerly, hungry from his day out.

When David finally came through the door, ten minutes later than usual, he was mumbling angrily to himself and complaining about traffic.

"There was an accident on the way home," he said as he entered the kitchen and undid his tie. "Someone ran a stoplight. People really need to learn how to drive."

"How was your day otherwise?" Amy asked as she filled a plate for him with pesto penne. David sat down in his seat at the head of the table, and when Amy set the plate in front of him, he clapped his hands together enthusiastically, impatient to begin eating.

"It was fine," David said stiffly. "I really don't want to talk about it."

He spooned pasta into his mouth, clearly ravenous despite the large lunch she had packed for him.

"My day was interesting," Amy said. "Jenn and I took Kayleigh and Ryder to the beach."

"Nice," David said around a mouthful of food.

"You know, at that patch of beach that your parents bought," Amy prompted.

"Uh-huh," David mumbled.

"Well, Kayleigh found a ring there," Amy continued.

David's chewing slowed as he listened. "Interesting."

"It's an engagement ring," Amy said. "The inside said it was for a woman named Daisy. Do you know a Daisy who could be missing it?"

David straightened in his seat, suddenly intrigued. He looked off at some space behind her head, avoiding her eyes, as he chewed thoughtfully for a long moment. In the evening sunlight, he looked particularly pale as he turned the name over in his head. Eventually, he swallowed audibly and shook his head. "I don't think so. I'm not coming up with anything."

"I just figured since it was on Montgomery property that someone may know her. I'd like to return it, if possible."

"I really can't think of anyone with that name."

"Weird," Amy said. "It's huge too. She's probably missing it."

"Probably," David agreed.

"I was thinking about showing it to Lily the next time I see her," Amy said. "Maybe she knows something."

David looked back down at his plate and stabbed at his pasta. "Probably not a good idea. She's not going to care about beach trash. I promise you she won't know anyone by that name."

"Worth a shot, at least," Amy said.

"Trust me, she won't know anything," David said. He shoveled a forkful in his mouth and looked thoughtful as he chewed. "Say, does Ryder have practice with Jason and Braxton tonight?"

"Yeah," Amy said. She dabbed her mouth with a cloth napkin, careful to maintain her lipgloss while still wiping off any lingering pesto. "I was going to take him over at around seven like normal."

"That's a lot of time for us to be alone together in this big house," David said. His eyes were suggestive, and his lips were pulled into a smirk.

Amy returned the knowing grin. "We still haven't broken in six of the bedrooms."

David cleared his throat. "Well, my night is planned then."

As she cleaned up dinner, though, Amy's mind was preoccupied not by the night ahead with her husband but with the past few moments when he could not meet her eyes.

Chapter 11

F or the first time since she had moved from Charlotte, Amy was excited to go to the Sunday dinner at 1 Wisteria Drive.

That day, she made a cake in preparation and perhaps had gotten carried away in the process. As she assessed her creation, she figured that it could have fed a family of thirty. To finish, Amy decorated it with large white flowers and edible pearls. When it was complete and she pulled away to admire her work, it occurred to her that it looked like a plump wedding cake. She figured that the subject was woven unconsciously into her thoughts.

The three of them went over to Lily and Richard's house at five o'clock. Amy wore a floral Kate Spade dress that evening that she knew Jenn would squeal at. She had always liked the dress for its hidden pockets, and that day, the left one held the little beach treasure perfectly.

Inside, the women were already at work in the kitchen, and Amy set the cake down on the counter between Tiffany and Miranda.

"Oh!" Tiffany exclaimed. "That looks so beautiful, Amy!"

"Thanks," Amy said. "I wanted to make something nice for tonight. As an apology. I didn't mean to offend you all by going out on the patio."

Amy didn't truly think an apology was necessary. She had wrestled with the idea all day, flipping back and forth as she tossed around ideas about how to handle her first visit since the disturbance on the back patio. She'd had to handle the decision-making alone, too. If she had asked David for his opinion, he would have told her to say she was sorry regardless. Yet, Amy didn't feel guilty that she had done it or that it had offended them for whatever reason; she only felt regret that it had blown up in her face. She also didn't like the idea that the Montgomery women now believed she wanted little to do with them, as Jenn and Tiffany had suggested. So, Amy decided that it was better to clear the air, take the high road, and swallow a bit of her pride.

Lily smiled a grin that made it to her eyes for once. Amy hadn't seen her look so pleased since she had first arrived on Wisteria Drive.

"Well, thank you, Amy," she said. She walked over and leaned forward to better see it. "It does look lovely."

Amy realized then that there were only three Montgomery women instead of four. Jenn was nowhere to be seen.

"Are we waiting for Jenn and Tyler?" Amy asked. Usually, Amy and her family were the last to arrive.

"No, Tyler's out back," Miranda said.

"Jenn caught a stomach bug, apparently," Tiffany explained. "Tyler said she got sick yesterday."

Amy and Ryder had gone out with her to the beach just a few days before, and Jenn hadn't shown any signs of sickness then. There had been no hint of any impending illness as they sunbathed, and the idea of Jenn's sudden, overwhelming sickness unnerved Amy.

"That's weird," Amy said. "Do you know what she's sick with?"

Miranda shook her head.

"Tyler just came in a few minutes before you did and said she couldn't come. He didn't tell us what it was," Lily said. "You can ask him at dinner if you want."

Amy nodded, intending to do just that.

When dinner was served at six on the dot, Amy sat down between David and Jason. She missed the way Jenn always found her side and sat down beside her, like a dutiful guardian. Amy was one ally down for the night.

Before them was another grandiose dinner, with numerous options for everyone, along with the Montgomery staples of a salad and some dinner rolls. Tonight, Amy was eager to dig into the steak and sweet potato fries before her and was annoyed that saying grace stood in the way of that.

"I heard we have someone who is eager to say grace tonight," Richard said from the head of the table. Beside her, David nodded.

"And who has the honor this evening?" Lily asked.

Richard gestured in the children's direction, and Amy expected to hear Braxton chirp the prayer obediently. Her mouth dropped open when she heard her own son's voice recite those familiar words.

"Bless us, O Lord, and these, Thy... thy gifts, which we are about to receive," Ryder said. Amy was too shocked and amazed to even bow her head. "From Thy bounty... um, through Christ, our Lord. Amen."

Around her, the table erupted with applause. Amy joined in, stunned. Her hands clapped unconsciously as her mind whirled to try to comprehend how her son had learned the prayer.

"Amen!" Lily exclaimed. "Amen! Amen! Amen!"

Amy tilted toward David. "How does he know that?"

David beamed. "I taught him," he said. "I've been quizzing him on it before I tuck him into bed."

Ryder looked down the table at her and David with smiling, expectant eyes. David gave him a proud thumbs-up, and Amy grinned, mouthing, "Amazing." Ryder beamed and turned back to his food, picking at his plate of vegetables and steak with a smile.

The Montgomerys ate mostly in silence for the first few minutes. It seemed that Amy wasn't the only one who had come to dinner hungry. The chatter that followed was as casual and inconsequential as it always seemed to be, as knives and forks tapped pleasantly against dinner plates.

Eventually, Amy dug deep inside herself to find the boldness to speak.

"So, Tyler," she began. "How's Jenn feeling? I heard she was sick."

"She's got a little stomach bug," he said. "Just hit her like a truck last week. She's recovering but she said that she didn't want to expose anyone to it. Especially the kids."

"She was fine when we hung out a few days ago," Amy pointed out.

Tyler shrugged. "You know how stomach bugs are. I'm sure she was on an upswing when she saw you. Probably was trying to put on a brave face."

Amy still wished Jenn had texted her to let her know she would be missing dinner. It seemed strange that Jenn would have failed to inform her or the other women ahead of time, but perhaps the decision had been made reluctantly right before she and Tyler had been about to leave for dinner. There seemed to be nothing else to it, so she moved on, finding the perfect segue.

"Yeah, she seemed healthy when we were at the beach together," Amy continued. "It's such a shame. I miss her tonight."

Tyler chuckled lightly. "Me too."

"Yes," Lily agreed. "We all miss her terribly. I could've used another hand with these steaks."

The table echoed with polite laughter. When it settled, Amy pushed forward.

"Speaking of the beach, we found a little treasure while we were there," she said. "Didn't we, Kayleigh?"

Kayleigh's face lit up at the sound of her name. She nodded vigorously.

Amy pulled the ring from her dress pocket and held it up. It gleamed brilliantly in the light from the chandelier above their heads, sparkling as if it wanted all of the attention in the room. Amy could feel every Montgomery turn their gaze to it. It felt like the Montgomerys had taken in a sharp inhale and the air had gone still around them as they looked at the magnificent ring clasped between Amy's thumb and index finger.

"Kayleigh found this in the sand," she explained. "Isn't it beautiful?"

There was an odd hush that settled and continued as they all stared. Amy took a glance around the table and saw that everyone was looking at it with wide eyes. Tiffany even slapped her mouth with her hand.

Finally, Miranda said, "It's so big!"

Matt's cheeks were nearly as red as his wife's hair as he stared down the gleaming diamond before glancing at Jason. "Interesting."

"So, this is the ring you were talking about?" David said slowly. "I didn't know you had it."

"Yeah, do you want to take a look?" Amy asked. "Here, actually, pass it around." She was as eager to show off Kayleigh's treasure as if she had found it herself.

One by one, the Montgomerys put down their forks and knives to pick up the ring and turn it over, inspecting it like they worked in a pawn shop and were eager to lowball the selling price.

"It's for someone named Daisy," Amy explained. "It says it in the band. Do any of you know who might be missing it?"

Matt cleared his throat as if to say something, but Lily beat him to it.

"Could've been anyone," Lily said. "I don't know anyone by that name, though."

"Young folks come and walk on our beach all the time. Trespassing. Probably some moron lost it. Quite the find, though, Miss Kayleigh," Richard said.

Amy felt herself deflating slightly. It was not the answer she had been hoping for. "Bummer," she said. "I thought we could return it to her if you knew her."

"Unfortunately, we don't," Richard said as he passed the ring along.

Eventually, it made its way around the table until Jason held it, flipping it over and over between his fingers, examining every inch as if he was positively mesmerized by it. He read the etchings in the band, ran his thumb over the writing, turned the ring around, and then read it again.

Amy held out her hand after another moment passed. "Can I have it back?" she asked with mirth. "Or would you prefer to keep it? It doesn't look like your kind of jewelry." Amy thought it was amusing he would find such fascination in a diamond ring when he had spent years around impressive jewelry. Even the band on Tiffany's finger made the large ring look meek.

"*Obviously* I wouldn't want it," Jason snapped. "It's just interesting. Quite the find, like Dad said. What are the odds?"

He directed the question at Richard, who shrugged dismissively. "It's an impressive discovery is all it is."

"Kayleigh, would you rather me sell it and give you the money, or do you want to keep it?" Amy asked.

Amy felt all of the eyes leave her face and shift to Kayleigh, who turned ashen under the new attention.

Kayleigh thought for a long moment. "Sell," she finally said.

"Alright." Amy slipped the ring back into her pocket and out of sight. She supposed the mystery would remain. "I'll get you some nice spending money."

Kayleigh grinned, the color creeping back into her face.

"How fun," Lily said. "I guess you never know what you'll find on those beaches. I'm just pleased we're uncovering diamonds and not more bottle caps and trash. Speaking of trash, we have been accumulating so much recently after these dinners with our three new guests. We're going to need a bigger trash can!"

And just like that, the topic of the ring died. The rest of the dinner involved conversations that Amy found uneventful. They discussed celebrity drama, new music releases, sports, and favorite alcoholic drinks. When dessert came around, the Montgomerys all gushed over the cake Amy had made. No one commented that it looked fit for a wedding, though she suspected this did not go unobserved.

When they were about to leave, Amy was surprised to see Ryder put up a small, exhausted fight to stay.

"I want to play with Braxton more," he whined.

"You can some other time," Amy said. "You need some sleep, buddy."

"I do not," he protested between yawns.

Amy rolled her eyes playfully. "Come on, bud. Let's go."

They returned home to their quiet, empty house, and Amy put Ryder to bed in his spacious bedroom feeling that things were right with the world. Something felt as though it had shifted on Wisteria Drive, and it left Amy feeling a sudden and rare wave of content. She suspected that it was because she seemed to be back in the Montgomerys' good graces.

As she undressed for the evening, she was careful to put the ring back in her sock drawer, where it would sit patiently until she and

David could find the time to venture out to a pawn shop. She found herself thinking about how difficult it would be to part with it. There was a strange connection that she felt toward the object as though it held some deeper value to her than anything monetary. Daisy was a stranger to her, but for some reason, it felt wrong to sell the ring of this faceless woman.

Amy fell into bed that night tired physically but mentally, she was abuzz. Her mind raced as she turned over the evening, the cake, the ring, and Ryder saying grace. Even after David's breathing had fallen into a steady, sleepy rhythm an hour after they had gone to bed, Amy was still completely awake with sleep nowhere in sight. She found that those noiseless evenings gave her ample time to reflect, for better or worse. The passing hours of fruitless effort were both unhurried and fast, slowing down and speeding up inconsistently with each weary glance at the clock.

Somewhere around midnight, she heard it.

It was distant at first but soon the soft clacking grew louder with proximity. Eventually, the clicking sounded as if it was moving up the stairs.

Amy could've sworn that it was the sound of high heels against the marble flooring. It was a noise she had become accustomed to, one that she heard every day on Wisteria Drive. She sat upright in bed, listening, trying to hear the sound again, when the clicking stopped for a beat. It resumed after several moments that felt like hours. Amy jumped, clapping her hand to her mouth as if to stifle her breath. Eventually, she could hear the sound traveling away.

"David," she whispered urgently. "David! Wake up!"

"Wha..." David mumbled as he rolled over. His eyes were squinted and puffy with sleep.

"There's someone in the house!" Her whisper was sharp with panic. "Listen!"

They sat without moving, straining to hear. Amy did not dare to move out of fear that the footsteps would get lost in the sound of rustling sheets.

Two minutes passed and there wasn't a single noise besides their breathing and the muffled insects outside.

"I swear," she insisted. "There were heels. Clicking. I wouldn't lie, David."

He rubbed his eyes and sighed. "I know you wouldn't." He groaned as he rose. "I'll go check."

"Get a poker by the fireplace," she said.

"Yeah, yeah," he responded as he shuffled out of the room.

Fifteen minutes passed as Amy sat in silence, breathing sharply in measured breaths as she tried to hear any commotion that might arise. The air felt sharp in her lungs, and her limbs were numb. Amy's head felt as if it were buzzing with static, devoid of all thoughts besides irrational conclusions and utter fear. What if their vast house had enticed an intruder? She had also heard Jenn talking about something called phrogging once where people could live in your house for months or years without you even knowing. Amy shuddered. Each minute was painful and unbearably long.

Finally, David came back into the bedroom, leaned the fire poker he had been holding against the wall, and gave an exasperated sigh. Amy allowed herself to exhale after seeing that he was unharmed.

"There's no one here, Amy," he said. "The doors are all locked."

"And the windows?" Amy asked.

"I checked them too. Everything is locked up." David sat down on the bed. "I don't like to say this, but I think you imagined it."

"I didn't, David. I swear on my life that's what I heard. I swear on Ryder's life."

"I'm sure it's what you *think* you heard but maybe you just were half asleep and imagined it. It's happened to me a few times."

"I've heard it before," Amy said. She was incredulous at her husband's dismissal. "The night we moved in I heard footsteps."

David tilted forward and kissed her on her forehead. "Well, there's no one here right now. I checked in all the closets and under all the beds. Nothing. And everything is locked up tight. Plus, we have the gate."

"David..." Amy started.

"I don't doubt that you think you heard something, but there is no one here but the three of us. Go back to sleep, honey."

"But I wasn't asleep, to begin with. That's how I heard it. I swear—"

"Go and check it yourself if you don't believe me."

"I..." she began, then cut herself off. The idea was paralyzing. It made her body feel as if it had been drained of all of its heat, leaving her frozen in place.

"I believe you," she said finally, though as she tossed the sheets back over herself, she wasn't sure that she did.

Chapter 12

The following Saturday, Amy was surprised to get a call from Jenn at lunchtime.

"The girls are all going out to get some food for the Fourth," Jenn told her. "Hot dogs and all that stuff. Then, Lily said she wants to treat us all to dinner. Just us ladies."

"That sounds nice," Amy said. In her head, the clicking of heels below where she slept echoed as it had all week. The sound played in the back of her mind constantly as if it were on a loop. "When are we leaving?" she asked, trying to dismiss the clacking sound.

"Well, are you ready right now? Lily wanted to go as soon as possible."

Amy looked at Ryder and David, who were playing out in the yard again. This time, they were passing a football between them, with Ryder looking particularly pleased every time he caught it.

"Sure," Amy told Jenn. "I'll just tell David."

"Awesome!" Jenn said. "Be over in a second!"

Amy peeked her head out the back door. Ryder and David stopped catching the ball and turned to look at her expectantly.

"The ladies are all going out shopping and then we're going to get some dinner together," Amy told them. "Do you mind being on your own tonight?"

"No, we're fine," David said. "I'll just order something. I'm glad you're going. That could be really nice. You know, to bond with them."

"Yeah, I agree."

"We might go hang with Jason and Braxton later anyways," David said. "Ryder told me he's got a new friend."

Amy smiled at Ryder, who was grinning at the ground bashfully. "Aw, that's great!"

"So, we might be out of the house, too," David explained. "I guess we'll see you later tonight then."

"Sounds good," Amy said. "Well, Jenn's supposed to be here any second."

"Go on," David said encouragingly. "Have fun!"

"Thanks." Amy grinned at him. "You too."

Jenn pulled up moments later, her Mercedes-Benz gleaming in the bright afternoon sun, reflecting light off of its flawless surface. Jenn rolled down her window and beamed.

"Long time no see!" she exclaimed.

"She lives!" Amy said with a laugh.

"Barely," Jenn groaned. "I felt like total S-H-I-T."

"Well, I'm glad you're feeling better," Amy said as she pulled the passenger door open.

"Somewhat. Well, anyways, get in!"

The drive there was rather uneventful and filled with Jenn talking inconsequentially about the latest true crime podcast that had captured her attention. It freaked her out so much that she invested in an indoor camera system that Tyler had been teasing her relentlessly for.

"He can make fun of me all he wants," Jenn said with a shrug. "I'd rather be paranoid than dead. I mean, that poor girl was killed in her own kitchen! I think he likes it too; he just won't admit it. Loves playing on that app. He said he checks in when he's away sometimes. It's good motivation to not look like a slob when he's gone."

Amy endured her graphic recounting of the poor girl's murder until they pulled into a parking lot corralled by a long stretch of stores. They met the rest of the Montgomery women standing outside of their cars despite the heat, all of whom had driven separately for no good reason. Amy was the only one who had been carted along.

They popped into various stores along a strip mall of small businesses whose names Amy could hardly pronounce. Between the deli, the bakery, and a quick stop at a convenience store, they picked out the American staples: hot dogs, hot dog buns, coleslaw, burgers, burger buns, cheese, potato chips, pasta salad, potatoes, and various flavored drinks. Their arms were filled with bags by the time they had finished, and all the while, Lily directed them like a composer, keeping the women running around in an orderly, efficient fashion.

Amy spent most of the time pushing around a cart filled with meat and buns while observing the way the women danced around the stores like practiced artists, heels clicking with determination. She couldn't help but focus particularly on the way their shoes sounded, trying to match their footfalls to the ones that had been imprinted in her memory. They all sounded the same, though, each one rhythmic and insignificant.

Afterward, they loaded all of the food into Jenn's car, stuffing the trunk to the max with their purchases.

"I'm just going to hold onto all of the food for now," Jenn explained. "I have the most refrigerator space because, well, you know."

Amy thought of Jenn's smaller, emptier house and couldn't help but wonder if the task had been passed onto her without any thought of how it cruelly underscored that vacancy.

"I could take some," Amy insisted.

"I don't mind. I have to drop off the extra stuff I bought for myself anyways," Jenn said. "Why don't you go off with one of the other girls and I'll meet you at the restaurant."

"Are you sure?" Amy asked.

"Yeah! Go on! I'll be there in a few minutes. Order me a sweet tea. That's all I ask."

"I can take you there," Miranda said from behind them. Amy hadn't even been aware that she was standing there. She almost jumped at the sound of Miranda's voice.

"Oh," Amy said. "That would be awesome. Thank you."

Miranda whipped out her keys and twirled them around her finger. The various keychains attached to them jangled prettily. "No problem."

Miranda's car was significantly larger than Jenn's. It had an extra row of seats as if Miranda planned to drag large groups of people back and forth. Amy couldn't help but wonder if she had purchased the car as an optimistic splurge or if she had done it before they discovered how difficult it was for them to have Kayleigh.

"So, you don't drive, huh?" Miranda asked.

"Nope," Amy answered simply. The Montgomerys seemed to find this outrageous, but it had never posed an inconvenience until Wisteria Drive. Her mom, despite having a license and a car, had hardly driven anywhere in years and walked most places. She drove to journey long distances but rarely to navigate the city.

"So strange," Miranda said. "That would drive me insane, no pun intended. How do you and Ryder get anywhere?"

"Well, Ryder entertains himself throughout the day around the house," Amy said. "Then, if he wants to go anywhere later in the day, David can take him."

"Matt would be pissed at me if I asked him to do that," Miranda said. "He always comes home from work and just wants to sit around and watch TV."

"I don't think David minds." But did he? He had never complained about it openly to her at least. "He usually just comes home, eats, and plays with Ryder if Ryder isn't with Braxton."

"Your husband sounds like he comes home with lots of energy," Miranda observed. "I'm lucky to get Matt off the couch for dinner sometimes."

Amy imagined the interactions in their house. She thought of Kayleigh, with her head bent and her lonely way of playing, and felt a pang of sadness imagining that Matt was too busy watching a screen to try to pull her out of her shell.

"Thank you for taking Kayleigh to the beach a week or so ago, by the way," Miranda continued. "She said she had fun, and you know she never says anything like that."

"Oh, it wasn't a problem," Amy said. "It was certainly eventful. I still can't believe she found that ring out there."

Miranda's face pinched. "Yes," she said. "She certainly got lucky. She's been talking about their little playdate nonstop. Matt can't stand to hear any more of it. I can't remember the last time she's talked so much."

"I'm just glad Ryder has little friends to hang out with," Amy said. "How did the doctor's appointment go by the way?"

Miranda's cheeks turned pink as they pulled up to a red light. She turned to Amy and gave an embarrassed smile. "Oh, very well," she said. "I heard Jenn was telling people it was for a physical or checkup or something. It wasn't, really."

"Oh yeah?" Despite herself, Amy straightened in her seat.

"Yeah, it was... um... I'm looking at getting some... well, some fat removed."

Amy couldn't help but crease her forehead in confusion. It sounded so out of character for Miranda. "Liposuction?"

"Oh, I hate that term," Miranda said. Her face was growing even redder. "But yes."

The light turned green, and Miranda made a left turn. The little Italian restaurant Jenn had described earlier came into view, sitting atop a slight hill, marking the end of their journey.

"I never thought you... you know... needed that," Amy said. "You look fine. Great, really."

"Well, thank you," Miranda said. "I appreciate that. I just have always wanted it, though. More recently I've been sort of obsessed with the idea."

Miranda pulled into a parking space directly in front of the restaurant. She unbuckled and turned to Amy with her eyes downcast and cheeks still flushed. For a moment, Amy saw a glimpse of Kayleigh in her.

"If I'm being honest, it's hard being around you guys all of the time," she said.

"Us?" Amy asked disbelievingly. She had not thought about Miranda as looking any different than the rest of them.

"Yeah, and I just figure, you know, it would keep things looking fit... for Matt."

"You're getting it for him?" Amy's stomach curled at the thought.

"No! I mean, well, not entirely. Like I said, I've been wanting to get it done. It's just... I know I can't be the only one who's noticed I'm falling a bit behind the rest in that regard. I never really snapped back after Kayleigh. Sometimes I think it all went to waste, you know."

"Miranda," Amy started. "I literally have never thought that. And I don't like the idea of you getting it because of what others think. You're being really hard on yourself."

"I guess," Miranda said. "I just figured since we have the money and everything, why not get rid of an insecurity?"

"Just don't get it to keep anyone else but you happy," Amy said. *A new body isn't going to fix a splintered marriage,* Amy wanted to add.

"I'm not. Not entirely, at least. There are other reasons," Miranda insisted.

Amy opened her mouth to speak but was cut off by a knock on the passenger-side window. She jumped and turned around abruptly to see Tiffany staring in at them. As usual, her smile was wide and unsuspecting. Amy rolled down the window.

"You ladies coming in or what?" she asked. "And if it's some hot gossip you're spilling, I want you to fill me in."

"It's not. We were just talking about school for Kayleigh and Ryder next year," Amy said, covering for Miranda.

"And my surgery," Miranda added anyway. Amy turned back to Miranda, surprised she had said it so openly when just moments before she had been blushing profusely and avoiding eye contact when talking about it.

"Oh! Yes!" Tiffany exclaimed. "Isn't it so exciting?"

Amy was even more surprised by Tiffany's positive reaction. She forced a smile. "Yeah," she agreed.

"Well, come on! I'm starving!" Tiffany said. "We can talk about Miranda's new bod inside."

Beside her, Amy saw Miranda flinch.

At the table, Amy dutifully ordered a sweet tea for Jenn and asked for a glass of white wine for herself. She thought it would help ease the tension she always felt around Lily.

Lily breezed in not too long after the three of them had taken their seats. She placed her Chanel sunglasses on her head, where they sat for the rest of their dinner.

"I cannot believe we decided to eat here of all places," she said as she flipped open the menu and frowned immediately at its contents. "Everything here has double the carbs it should. We're being very naughty today, ladies."

Tiffany giggled as if she agreed they were doing something exceptionally dirty by eating breadsticks and pasta. Miranda looked down at the table mutely. Amy knew that if the Montgomery men had been there as well, they would have had no reaction or concern over the calories listed by the food.

"I heard your Ryder is playing with Braxton," Lily said, directing the comment at Amy. She didn't look up from her menu as she spoke.

"He is," Amy confirmed. "I think the two of them are getting pretty close."

"How lovely. I'm so happy about that. And that Braxton is great with football. He has real potential. And he'll be a good influence on your Ryder," Lily said.

"We've loved having him around," Tiffany chimed in. "Ryder's a good kid."

"Thank you," Amy said. "He's a bit shy, so I'm glad he's starting to socialize more."

"Jason's loved teaching them, too," Tiffany added. "Football is one of his passions, so he especially loves teaching the kids."

"That boy has few passions but the ones he does have he loves intensely," Lily said. "He is quick to love and when he does it's all-consuming."

Tiffany smiled widely to the point where the expression looked rather painful. "Agreed."

"Jenn better hurry up or we'll be ordering without her," Miranda said.

"Poor girl has so much refrigerator space," Lily said. "I usually store all of the drinks and sides for events, but my own fridge is just too full this time. She tells me she only uses half of the space with just the two of them. Poor thing."

Amy remembered Jenn on the beach, longing for her own children as she looked out at Ryder while her fingers grazed the skin of her lower belly.

"Her time will come," Tiffany commented. "Remember how long it took Jason and me?"

"How could I forget?" Lily said. "And little Kayleigh took a lot of time, too. And all that wasted money." Lily folded up her menu and put it aside as Miranda visibly swallowed the comment. "Only Amy here didn't have any problems."

"For better or worse," Miranda mumbled.

"Children are for the better," Lily corrected her. "No matter what or when."

"Ryder was a surprise, that's for sure," Amy offered.

She could still remember the unbearable worry she had felt when she had found out. They had taken precautions, and besides that one skipped night on the pill, she thought they had been playing it safe. Even though she had not wanted to get pregnant, it seemed the world had had other plans for her.

When she had told her mom, Emily made it clear that the decision was entirely Amy's. If she wanted to keep the baby, fine, and if she wanted to abort it, Emily would drive her straight to the clinic. Amy always suspected that Emily had hoped her daughter would rid herself of the baby when she had proposed her options. Amy had been very young, after all, and settling down into David's life so dramatically felt hasty. She and David were already tied by marriage, but children made the bond eternal. Amy, however, had loved her little bump even when it confined her to bed in the later days of her pregnancy. Ryder had indeed been for the better.

"A gift," Lily said. "My boys were the best things to happen to me. Truly. I'd give up all of the money and the houses and the properties for them. All of it. And raising boys keeps things… simple. You just got to set them up right and then they go off and *fly*. God knows I would've done a horrible job with girls. Boys are the ultimate way to pass down your legacy. They make sure your name keeps having meaning after you're gone."

"Jason and I are trying again," Tiffany said. "We're hoping for another boy, of course."

"And we're hoping to try for a boy too in the next few years," Miranda agreed. "We'll probably need IVF again but we're hoping that they put a Y chromosome in there."

"That's smart. Fill up those houses, ladies," Lily instructed. "That's what they're there for."

Amy was grateful when the server came back with her wine. She eyed Lily suspiciously over her glass before taking a sip, thinking of the pack of birth control pills she had never found. She knew that even if Lily hadn't outright taken it from her purse, if it had been left at 1 Wisteria Drive, then it would've been tossed in the trash without question. Anything for the sake of more grandchildren.

She washed away the thought with another large gulp of wine. Maybe she was just being cruel, though.

"We want to raise our children on strict Christian values," Miranda announced, breaking into Amy's thoughts. "When they're older, they can decide for themselves, but so long as I'm their mother they'll be raised on the Lord's word."

"That's what I did," Lily said with an endorsing nod. "I'm disappointed to see how little those teachings stuck. I would've expected all of my grandchildren in church."

Amy blinked, taken aback by the targeted response.

"If Ryder shows interest, we'll take him. That's what David and I decided on," Amy said.

"I suppose that's fair," Lily said though she didn't appear to agree with her in the slightest.

"We just can't imagine raising kids without those ideas being taught," Miranda continued. "Honestly, this country as a whole could use a little more education when it comes to God."

"Amen," Lily said as she held up her glass as if to toast. "I see what's happening to our country and it makes me sick. It really does. Truly, I would rather take a handful of pills and be done with it than see how all of this pans out."

Amy stood abruptly. She couldn't hear any more of it. "I have to use the restroom," she announced.

Lily didn't seem to notice Amy's sharp response or regard it as anything irregular. She was far too engaged with Miranda in a discussion about how these new conservatives represented ideal Christian values. Amy didn't have the energy to start that argument, not when simply sitting on the back patio had given her such grief. She couldn't imagine how debating politics would turn out.

Amy retreated to the restroom and, not having to go, stood in front of the mirror. There was no one else there, and she leaned against the counter, looking at her reflection.

How did she end up hiding in the bathroom of an upscale restaurant in Florida? Just years ago, she had set out to receive a business degree, and somehow, she had sold her voice to a rich familyin exchange for a stable place to live and the hope of a better future for her son.

Within just a few months, she had been taken from her comfortable hometown, had settled among strangers, had been stripped of all titles beyond housewife, and had become isolated from everyone she had ever known. The person she had been in Charlotte felt as distant now as the city itself, hundreds of miles away. She looked her reflection in the eye and admitted how she felt to herself for the first time.

She was painfully unhappy.

Amy sighed. She took three deep breaths to calm herself and quell the tears that threatened to become visible. Amy inspected her reflection closely once more, carefully noting the lack of redness in her eyes. She gave the mirror a grin to see how it settled onto her face despite the disturbance she felt. Finally, when she determined that she was ready, she left the restroom, returning to her place at the table.

Amy was overcome with relief when she saw that Jenn had arrived in her absence and was sipping her tea thoughtfully.

As she sat down, Amy gave Jenn a look, and Jenn squeezed her knee under the table reassuringly.

"Are we ready to order then?" Lily asked. They all nodded like school children being called on to answer a question. "Excellent," she said, and she raised her hand to call over their server.

Amy treated herself to three glasses of wine throughout the dinner. When the third one arrived, she received a critical look from Lily that she ignored. She kept her mouth shut even when the conversation was light and frothy like their discussion on their favorite type of pasta sauce or their opinions on white pants.

When Lily finished her meal, she put her napkin on top of her nearly full plate and said, "Honestly, girls, we need to go somewhere classier next time. Miranda, this was a passable choice, but at the next dinner we eat out together I'll show you what the standard is. This was a treat. My treat. I'll pay the check."

The check came moments after her pronouncement, cutting off Miranda and Tiffany's pleadings to pay for their part. Lily read the charges thoroughly as if, despite her unbelievable wealth, every cent mattered. Eventually, she looked up, her eyes falling on Amy.

"My, you ladies did enjoy your wine today," she said. Miranda and Tiffany had also ordered two glasses each, with their second servings still sitting before them half-drunk. Amy had drained all three of hers eagerly. "For once you didn't indulge, Jenn."

Jenn smiled proudly, her face lighting up at the observation. "Yes," she said. "That's because I have an announcement to make."

Amy froze in anticipation, assuming what Jenn meant before she even said it.

"I'm pregnant," Jenn stated, beaming. Her face glowed as if it were made of starlight. "That's why I couldn't make it last Sunday. The nausea is awful when it hits."

"Oh, my goodness!" Lily exclaimed.

Tiffany and Miranda chattered their congratulations as Lily leaped up to hug Jenn. The commotion was drawing attention from nearby tables, which was something that only Amy seemed to notice.

"Oh, thank goodness!" Lily said, pulling Jenn into what appeared like an unwelcome hug. "What a blessing!"

When Lily finally let go of her, Amy scooped Jenn into another hug. This time, Jenn folded into her happily, embracing her back. "I told you it was a matter of time," Amy said quietly. "You won't have that refrigerator space for long."

Jenn laughed into her neck.

When Amy let go, the other women took turns folding Jenn into their arms. Jenn seemed to soak in their excessive excitement, determined to enjoy every moment of the celebration. It was overdue.

"We were just talking about how babies are a gift before you got here," Tiffany said. "We had no idea you were carrying one. That's wonderful, Jenn, really. I'm so happy for you."

"Nothing like a little miracle," Lily said. "I can't wait to learn the gender."

"Me neither," Jenn agreed. "I'm hoping for a girl."

Amy could've sworn she saw Lily's smile twitch. "Well," she said after a cold, dead moment. "We'll just have to see."

Jenn had never looked so pretty or happy. "I guess I should expect to get very fat very soon," she added. The other women all tittered.

The rest of their short time in the restaurant was spent planning around Jenn's pregnancy. When was she expected to be due? Should they have a baby shower? What sex did she *think* the baby was? All the while, Jenn answered their questions excitedly, the brilliant smile on her face never lessening. Despite not having a visible bump yet, she placed her hands on her stomach, resting them there as if she might be able to already feel the baby's kick meet her touch.

Amy watched Jenn's excitement, remembering her own reaction when she discovered she was carrying Ryder. She was pleased to see that Jenn lacked any of the hesitance Amy had felt initially. Instead, she was all delight, seeming to teem with it.

The bustling joy hung around them even as they left the restaurant and stood on the sidewalk.

"I really liked peanut butter toast when I was pregnant," Tiffany was saying. "Like, I craved it all the time. Get ready for stuff like that. The cravings can get weird."

"Alright, ladies, let's let the poor woman go home," Lily said. "We're so thrilled for you, Jennifer."

"Amy, are you coming home with me?" Jenn asked.

Amy had fully intended to sit in the car with Miranda, allowing Jenn to unwind from their explosive dinner alone. She was very grateful when this alternative was extended.

"Yes," Amy said. "If you're willing."

"Hell yeah," Jenn said. "Well, Amy and I are going to head back then."

Lily hugged Jenn one last time, closing her eyes in the embrace as if she wanted to mold into it. "Drive safely," she instructed. "You have precious cargo."

"Of course," Jenn agreed.

They all waved goodbye, more congratulations were extended, and then Amy and Jenn peeled off. Amy could feel the sensation of relaxation settling in with each step of distance they put between themselves and the rest of the Montgomery women.

In the car, Jenn turned the key and buckled up before turning to Amy. "They really don't want me to have a girl, huh?" Jenn said.

"I don't know if you've noticed but they don't like girls very much. At all." Amy likely would not have been so candid if she were sober, but she didn't think that what she had said was inaccurate either.

"I can't go through what Miranda went through," Jenn said as she pulled out of the parking spot.

"What do you mean?" Amy asked.

"The humiliation of having a girl in the Montgomery family. I can't deal with the comments. I think..." Jenn bit her lip.

"Go on," Amy encouraged. "I won't say anything."

"I think I would rather move away than stay on Wisteria Drive if I had a girl," Jenn said.

"Is it that bad?" Amy asked.

"Why do you think Kayleigh is so quiet?" Jenn asked. "No one is subtle about how much they hate that she was born without a penis."

Amy took a sharp inhale. Hearing the words sent a bolt of energy through her, making her feel awake and oddly nervous at once. She could not help but recall how Miranda referred to Kayleigh as a mistake.

Jenn zoomed through a yellow light and gave a laugh. "Welcome to the Montgomery family!"

Chapter 13

The afternoon of the Fourth of July started as a lovely affair. After the light showers of rain that fell around noon had subsided, the sun broke through and shined in a brilliant golden hue onto the Montgomerys' cookout.

The air smelled of grilled meat and summer, and Amy watched as her son ran across the grass passing a football back and forth between himself and Braxton with a skill she hadn't expected. He was growing before her eyes, old enough to play and appreciate the sport that so many American men revered. It made her both proud and sad to see how quickly he was aging.

The Fourth of July was less formal for the Montgomerys. Without their Sunday best on, they were still dressed nicely, but the clothing was looser and not as dressy. Miranda even wore jeans for the first time since Amy had moved in.

The men and women mixed and mingled over drinks and burgers in the waning afternoon heat. Amy sat on David's lap with a glass of wine as the world dimmed into evening.

Despite the feeling of unease she felt around the Montgomerys, Amy couldn't help but admit that the day, at least, was nice. She was comforted by being so close to David in the summer air, and she felt more connected to him than she had in weeks. He was wearing an oversized button-down that was relaxed and hung loosely on his frame. It reminded her of the way he used to dress when they first met, before Ryder and Wisteria Drive, when his priorities had been dressing nicely and hanging off her every word.

When the sky was finally black, Matt and Jason brought armfuls of fireworks into the middle of the cul-de-sac in view of all of their houses.

"Mom wanted us to do this on the beach," Matt explained to David as he put down his second armful onto the asphalt. "I said, 'That's a perfectly good waste of the space we already have for it.'"

Amy did not note out loud that Lily was exceptionally good at overlooking the things that were already at her disposal.

By nine-thirty—past Ryder's bedtime—they were ready to set off the fireworks. When Amy looked around her, none of the children were standing in the cul-de-sac.

Amy tugged on David's shirt, her chest suddenly aflutter with nervousness. "Where's Ryder?"

"They should still be in Mom and Dad's backyard," David said. "I think all three of the kids are. It's fine, though. They'll still be able to see the fireworks from back there."

Amy's eyes trained on 1 Wisteria Drive, weighing up whether or not she should run back and get Ryder before the first of the fireworks went off.

David noticed this and hugged her to him so that she fell into his hard body and could smell the comforting and familiar scent of his cologne. "He'll be fine. There's nowhere to run to. It's all fenced in. He'll be ok for a few minutes."

"But what if he gets scared of the noise?" Amy asked.

"Honey, you worry too much." David kissed her nose. It made her feel like a sophomore in college falling head over heels for the well-dressed guy across the room.

So, she let his words soothe her as much as they could.

Jason lit the first firework and the Montgomerys watched as it whizzed into the air and exploded loudly into a constellation of red sparks. Matt lit the second and sent a blue burst into the sky. The two brothers took turns putting on a show for their family by alternating between types of fireworks. Some burst into spherical sparkles, others zipped upward with a noise that sounded like a scream before it broke into a flash of golden light. The Montgomerys oohed and ahhed at every new firework that was introduced. Even Amy had to admit that the show was rather spectacular for it just being put on in a cul-de-sac by two brothers.

They shot off their last firework ten minutes after they had lit their first. Everyone standing in the street clapped approvingly, including Amy, who gave Jason and Matt an appreciative smile. The night was abuzz with refreshed electric energy that made Amy feel young and giddy.

"Now where are our kiddos?" Tiffany asked Amy. Tiffany seemed to find humor in not knowing where her child was, so Amy mirrored her relaxed approach.

"No idea," she said.

"Let's go hunt them down," Tiffany suggested. "Miranda! Help us find the kiddos, won't you?"

Miranda joined the two of them as they hiked back to 1 Wisteria Drive through the grass, taking a shortcut into the backyard. Amy regretted following them immediately as she felt her heels sink into the mud the earlier rain had created out of the grass.

When the kids became visible once again, Amy gasped.

Kayleigh lay in the grass, her hands curled into fists, crying wildly with blood on her face. Beside her, Braxton was playing with action figures absentmindedly, as if he didn't notice or care to acknowledge

Kayleigh's hysterics. Ryder was sitting between the two other children holding an Iron Man figurine and watching Kayleigh with a worried expression.

Miranda ran past them, nearly slipping in the mud as she rushed to her daughter's side before pulling Kayleigh into her arms.

"What happened?" Miranda asked. "Kayleigh, what happened?"

Beside Amy, Tiffany had frozen where she stood, petrified with shock as she took in the scene.

Miranda wiped blood from Kayleigh's lip.

"What happened, Kayleigh?" Miranda asked again.

Kayleigh only cried harder, unable to form the words to explain in her state of hysterics.

"Ryder!" Amy called to her son. "Ryder, come here!"

Ryder came forward with his eyes downcast. He dropped Iron Man in the grass on his way over and moved in a shuffle as if he was hesitant to approach. Amy's chest tightened and she swept aside the possibilities that sprung into her head.

When he was in front of her, still focused on the ground, Amy asked, "Ryder, what happened to Kayleigh?"

He gave a small shrug, still refusing to tear his gaze from the ground.

"Look at me," she instructed. "Do you know what happened to Kayleigh?"

Ryder finally met her eyes. His own were shiny with tears. He only shook his head in response.

Tiffany was still frozen to their left. Amy felt an angry flare at her inaction.

"Do you think Braxton would know?" Amy asked her.

It was as if Tiffany had been snapped out of a trance. She blinked hard and rapidly like she was trying to bat sleep from her eyes. Tiffany adjusted the sleeves of her blouse as she called, "Brax! Come here."

Braxton's head snapped up so suddenly that his dark curls bounced. He seemed to be noticing the commotion for the first time.

"Yes, Mom?" Braxton asked as he made his way toward them. His own stride was confident in a way that looked strange for someone so young.

"Is Kayleigh ok?" Tiffany asked. "Do you know what happened to her?"

"I don't know," Braxton said. He looked confused.

Kayleigh's crying subsided as she was soothed by her mother.

"H-Hit, m-m-me," Kayleigh stuttered between sniffles.

Miranda's eyes were wide with surprise. "What? Who?"

But being asked only started up her crying again. She let loose a horrible scream like the sharp shrieks from some of the fireworks moments before. Blood was smeared down her chin and clung to parts of her lips like grotesque lipstick. Her face was a pained pink as she wailed, her ruddy cheeks slick with tears and snot.

"Ryder, what does she mean she was hit?" Amy asked. It all felt so wrong and strange when juxtaposed with the moment of bliss she had experienced just minutes ago.

"I don't know," he mumbled. Amy had no doubts that he did, in fact, know exactly what had happened. And he was lying to her.

"Miranda, do you need any help?" Amy asked.

"No, I think I've got this," she said. Her features were a mixture of anger, terror, and shame.

"I'm going to take my son home and have a talk with him," Amy said as she grabbed Ryder's arm. His eyes fell back to the grass as if there was something of sudden interest at his feet.

"Me too," Tiffany echoed. She also grabbed Braxton's arm. He looked up at her as if he was still perplexed by it all.

Amy led Ryder out of the backyard, listening as Kayleigh's crying softened with distance. She found David still standing in the cul-de-sac talking to Tyler and Jenn. When he turned to her and saw her expression, his face clouded with worry.

"What's wrong?" he asked. Tyler and Jenn turned to look at her too and had similar reactions.

"Someone hit Kayleigh," Amy said. She felt her face fill with embarrassment. They would all consider her son the culprit. And why wouldn't they? As far as she knew, nothing like this had happened on Wisteria Drive before. It only occurred after they moved into the neighborhood.

"Oh my," Jenn said, covering her mouth with her hand in shock.

"We better go then," David said to the couple.

"David, please go get my purse from inside," Amy instructed.

David nodded dutifully. "I'll meet you at the house," he said. She was glad to see him taking it seriously at least. He jogged toward 1 Wisteria Drive with clear urgency.

"See you later," Tyler said.

"Good luck," Jenn added. Her expression was warped with the same deep concern Amy felt.

"We need to leave," Amy announced as they passed the rest of the Montgomerys. She slowed down as they approached the group but didn't stop. "Lovely fireworks tonight. Thank you for the invite."

"Of course," Lily said, looking bewildered. Beside her, Richard frowned.

Jason's face bloomed with some sort of comprehension. "Where's Tiffany?"

"And Miranda?" Matt added.

"In the backyard still," Amy said. "Good night. Thanks again."

She and Ryder hurried home, rushing to get inside and away from the curious Montgomery eyes boring into their backs.

Amy's chest was getting heavy. They had barely made it inside and closed the door before she turned to Ryder and knelt to be at a similar height to him.

"You have to tell me," Amy said, her voice growing desperate. She gave herself a second to calm the flood of feelings, took a deep breath, and then as evenly as possible added, "I need you to tell me about what happened if you know. Please."

Ryder's eyes were still trained on the floor, staring at some point between his shoes.

David came in behind her, putting her purse on the entryway table beside the obnoxious bouquet.

"Has he said what happened?" David asked.

"He won't tell me," Amy said. She felt so weak and pathetic like a helpless stray kitten. Like she had failed as a parent. All of that time spent at home attending to his every need, trying to teach him as best she could suddenly felt like an utter waste.

"Ryder," David said from over Amy's shoulder. "This isn't a game. We need to know."

For a moment there was nothing but silence as Ryder refused to speak. Amy wanted to shake the answers from him but balled her fists up at her sides to keep from doing so. Her heart was beating against her rib cage in suspense.

Finally, Ryder mumbled something inaudible.

"What, Ryd?" David asked.

"Ryder, what was that?" Amy said.

"Braxton." The name dropped from his mouth like it was a heavy, tangible thing.

Amy felt her body relax.

"How did it happen, bud?" Her voice was calmer now.

"She wouldn't answer him," Ryder explained, his voice wavering with sadness. Amy knew that he was close to tears. "He wanted the Superman she had and he... he..."

Ryder began to cry then. It was an ugly child's cry, the kind that racks the body and chops up words like a cleaver. Amy had to keep him on track. She needed to know for sure that his hands were clean.

"He did what?" Amy pressed.

"Hit," Ryder managed to say between sobs. "On the... face... then... pushed... her." Each word was broken up by a sharp intake of breath and said with a shaky voice.

"And you didn't touch her?" Amy asked to clarify.

Ryder shook his head.

"But you didn't help her." It wasn't a question. Amy knew already that her son had been a bystander to the scene.

Ryder shook his head again to confirm what she had already concluded. "He told me... not to... say." He was choking on his words as he spoke.

"Alright, bud," David said. "Let's calm down. You'll make yourself sick."

Amy stood. A chill crept over her like her veins were pumping cold blood.

"I'll get him something to drink," she said.

She left David to console Ryder. As she entered the kitchen, her feet guided her without thought.

The entire situation felt sticky and dark. It reminded Amy of Emily telling her about how her grandparents used to fight and sometimes it would turn into a physical altercation. Her grandpa had always won those arguments.

Yet Braxton's abuse wasn't entirely like the horrors her mom had told her that her grandmother had endured. Those were adults with grown-up anger. This was a child, taking out aggression on a little girl who was often too scared to speak. Amy wondered what shows had taught Braxton such anger, whether his football practices had encouraged or nurtured such violence.

Amy did not need to wonder, however, where her own son had learned to stand by and watch.

Chapter 14

Perhaps it was out of cowardice, but Amy called Tiffany instead of going to her house and divulging the information in person.

"I think... well... Ryder told me that it was Braxton," Amy said into the phone. She received only silence in response for a moment. Amy bit down on her thumbnail nervously before she continued. "Did... did Braxton tell you anything?"

"No." The word hung between the two of them for a moment. Amy wasn't sure if it was in response to her question or in denial of what she was hearing.

"I'm sorry, Tiffany," Amy said. "They're still young. Just don't say that Ryder said anything. I think it would kill him if Braxton turned against him."

"I just... it just... it all doesn't make sense... he hasn't..." Tiffany stumbled over her words.

"I know," Amy said. "I'm sorry. I don't think Ryder would lie, though. He was pretty distraught about telling me."

There was another well of silence that seemed to stretch the seconds into minutes. Finally, Tiffany said, "I believe him. I believe you. I have to... I have to go."

Her voice was laden with urgency. Amy didn't even get to say goodbye before Tiffany hung up.

Ryder was upstairs in his room presumably reading or playing with whatever toys he could salvage. Amy had taken away his video games and his iPad, the things he held most dear, as a makeshift punishment. When she had told him that it was because of his initial avoidance of telling the truth and the way he hadn't intervened, Ryder hadn't argued or seemed particularly angry. He had merely accepted the consequences timidly.

Amy turned her cell phone over in her hands, thinking. The distraught sound in Tiffany's voice echoed in her head like a shout down a vacant hall. It was so unlike the Tiffany that Amy knew, with her constant, white-toothed smile and unwaveringly pleasant demeanor, that it made her uncomfortable.

She could feel the emptiness of the house once again and hear its hush. Throughout the house, there was only space and furniture and her son, who was too embarrassed by his scolding to approach her. She wondered if this was how Tiffany felt too, knowing that she would have to handle matters without her husband, alone in her immense home.

Amy's fingers began searching for the contact instinctively, knowing the best way to fill the quiet and loneliness.

"Hello?" Emily said when she picked up.

"Hey, Mom." Amy leaned against the marble counter, combing through her hair with her fingers. It was a knotty tangle, and she was in desperate need of a root touch-up.

"This is late for you, honey," Emily said. "You're lucky I didn't have a shift just now. I would've missed you."

"I just needed someone to talk to," Amy admitted.

"Is everything alright?" Emily asked.

"I think so," Amy said. "This house is just so... still again."

"You knew it would be like that moving in, though," Emily said. "Can't imagine a private neighborhood and a nine-bedroom house is very busy."

"I just feel it. All of the time. It gets suffocating," Amy explained.

"You probably just have to adjust," Emily said.

But she had tried adjusting for weeks with no success. Amy explained to Emily that perhaps it wasn't just the openness of Wisteria Drive, but rather the people within it that were making her feel so uncomfortable. She told her about Braxton's aggression and Kayleigh's feminine shame. Amy told her about Miranda's liposuction and Jenn's pregnancy. She couldn't keep those tidbits in anymore. They had all begun to weigh on her, each anecdote making things progressively more difficult.

Emily had always been a good listener. Her end was so quiet the entire time that she might have put herself on mute. Finally, she said, "Amy, something about all of that isn't normal."

"I know." Amy could feel the sadness rising in her voice, tightening her throat. It was one thing to find these occurrences strange on their own, but it was another thing entirely to lay them all out at once and have someone else confirm that something wasn't right.

"I don't want to overstep with what I'm saying. This is just my opinion," Emily began.

"Go on," Amy encouraged. She could feel her throat constricting even further.

"They seem to be hung up on women," Emily said.

"Yeah." Amy chewed her nail. "Jenn said that."

"I think it's more than just with the children. Even how Jason reacted when you asked him if he wanted to keep that ring. It seemed oddly defensive. If it's like you described, it goes deeper, like they don't associate with anything feminine unless they can use it."

"Yeah," Amy agreed again.

"Is there any way you could make some friends outside of Wisteria Drive down there? You know, like to connect with someone, oh, I don't know, on social media?"

"Mom, even if I could, I can't drive," Amy said.

"We live in the age of Uber, honey."

Amy sighed and thought of the rest of the Montgomery wives. She had never once heard any of them mention friends beyond their little cul-de-sac. At least not in the present tense.

"I guess you're right," Amy said. "It's just kind of hard when I'm not really going anywhere by myself. I was hoping to start classes again in the fall or winter. Finish my degree. I originally wanted to do it online but... but now I think it's best if I go in person. Meet some people, you know?"

"I think that's probably for the best, too," Emily said.

The idea of putting herself out there was vaguely terrifying. She hadn't done so in years, not since she had taken the jump with David. She would be out of practice.

"Tell you what," Emily continued. "How about I come down for a visit soon? I'll have to give work a heads up of at least a few days, but I wanted to see this Wisteria Drive sooner or later anyways."

Amy tried to picture Emily walking among the sea of red and brunette heads, maneuvering around the stagnant smiles and passive comments. It was asking a lot of her to have her come down and endure that. But selfishly, Amy felt she needed it. The thought of her mom coming down for a visit came with a flood of relief, like the promise of a security blanket being returned.

"That would be great, Mom," Amy said.

"I'll do it then," Emily concluded. "I'll plan for the end of July. And I'll keep you updated on it. When I know, you'll know."

"Really, Mom, that would be great," Amy repeated. "Just remember that they're a little different and they definitely have some odd views on things."

"Oh, you didn't have to tell me that," Emily said with a pleasant laugh. "I remember them from your wedding. They sounded like textbook hypocritical conservatives."

Amy gave a small giggle, too. She was happy someone found the humor in it all at least. Emily's black-and-white view of the world was almost funny in the face of a situation with so much gray.

"Lily is, at least," Amy said.

"Again, I assumed. I promise I won't try to force my views on them if they don't."

Amy could see the Montgomerys doing just that. Since she moved in, that's all they seemed to do.

"It'll be interesting, to say the least," Amy mumbled.

"Well, I have a shift coming up and I was planning to shower before," Emily said. "I'll call you tomorrow, though. But keep me updated if anything strange happens again. I want to be kept in the loop."

"Alright, Mom," Amy said. She couldn't shake the feeling that divulging those incidents to her mom felt like exposing a part of her that she would have rather kept hidden. Each conveyance of Montgomery gossip felt like an admittance of a mistake she had made.

"Bye, honey," Emily said.

"Bye." Amy hung up and the kitchen returned to silence, settling down like a thick, stifling fog.

But when she turned around, she wasn't alone.

Somehow, Ryder had been able to sneak downstairs undetected. He stood in the entryway, looking at her with big eyes filled with tears.

"What's up, buddy?" Amy asked. She went over to him and crouched down.

"I'm sorry, Mommy," he said as he began to cry.

"I know you are." Amy pulled him into a hug as his little body shook with sobs.

When they pulled away, Ryder wiped at his eyes with fists. "Mommy," Ryder said. "Braxton scared me last night."

"Did he hit you too?" Amy's stomach sunk at the thought, but Ryder shook his head vigorously.

"He was so angry," he said. "And Kayleigh was so scared."

"I bet," Amy said. She wasn't sure what the right words were to comfort him. Amy racked her brain as he continued.

"He looked so mean. That's why I didn't... why I couldn't..."

His voice trailed off, but Amy could fill in the rest. Braxton's sudden outbreak had startled Ryder so much it had scared him stiff.

"You'll tell me right away if he does it again, though, won't you?" Amy asked. "This is serious stuff, buddy."

Ryder nodded but she could see on his face it was hard for him to commit to her request.

Amy hugged him again, feeling the seed of worry that had been planted the night before beginning to take root.

Her son was not clean in the situation, but Amy's concern had almost totally shifted to Braxton. Something seemed off about the way he had reacted to Tiffany calling him over and questioning him. The ease of his lying was unnerving.

Something was very wrong with Braxton.

Chapter 15

David came home on Thursday and played football outside with Ryder immediately after dinner. The two of them passed the ball and tackled through fits of laughter as Amy watched them from a chaise lounge on the porch, smiling to herself whenever she looked up from the magazine in her hands.

Since the incident on the Fourth of July, Ryder had been hesitant to go back over to Jason and Tiffany's to practice football with Braxton. When David had asked about it the day before, Ryder's eyes had widened with concern. Amy wondered if he was worried that he would be the next person on the receiving end of Braxton's fists.

This left Amy to be the middle person communicating and softening Ryder's fears to Tiffany.

"I think Ryder wants to stay home today," Amy had said. "He told me he wanted to hang out with David tonight if that's alright. He said he doesn't really see his dad much anymore because of work."

"That's fine," Tiffany had said. "Just let us know when he wants to come over and play with Braxton again."

Tiffany had hung up without any parting words. She was smart enough to pick up on the true reason Ryder didn't want to come over, yet Amy didn't know how else she could have broken the news to Tiffany. "Your son scared mine so badly he doesn't want to be around him right now" didn't sound quite as polite.

David had been more than happy to fill the role of playmate. He was never one to value sports; David was a man who appreciated art above almost any other pursuit in life. His interests were in fashion and music instead of the rough aggression of athletics, but it seemed that David was able to put those preferences aside and was happy to simply spend time with his son. Amy was more than glad to sit and watch them.

Amy had gotten lucky too when Richard and Lily had announced that they would be vacationing in New York for the weekend to go to a designer pop-up shop that Lily was incredibly thrilled about attending. There would be no family dinner that Sunday and Amy was pleased to note that she did not have to see another Montgomery that weekend. She was grateful to have some time away with her family to sort through her thoughts.

This is how it should be, she thought as she continued to watch her husband and son. It was just the three of them in the dying sunlight. There wasn't anyone else around to pass judgment through stares or to comment negatively. Instead, before her was the dream that was promised to her upon moving to Wisteria Drive.

But she couldn't shake the nagging feeling that the moment was a mere blip in the timeline, a pocket of happiness in what had been weeks of worry. Amy missed the intimacy of their Charlotte apartment. David and Ryder could never have played football in that condensed space the way they were in front of her, but she longed for those days when the smaller home seemed to naturally bring them together.

She remembered a time in their apartment when David had shown Ryder how to finger paint. They had made a mess of the kitchen table, covering it with newspaper and splattering coarse paintings with primary and secondary colors. Ryder had painted pages of white paper with yellow and green in thick strokes from tiny fingers.

"Mommy, come paint with us," Ryder had said, holding up his small, stained hands. His face had been lit with joy, and Amy had giggled when she saw the way David was looking at her.

"Don't be scared, Mommy," David had encouraged. "It'll wash off... I hope."

She found herself with her fingers in a puddle of yellow paint moments afterward.

Together, they had painted a scene not unlike the one before her, with the three of them in a vibrant green yard beneath a bright yellow sun.

It was a simple memory, but it was also one of her favorites. Strangely, it stuck out to her as a summary of their time in Charlotte. Happy, creative, and together.

But Amy was now resigned to her seat, not particularly interested in the things that were now beginning to interest her son. Ryder was no longer preoccupied with the simple task of putting careless paint strokes onto plain paper. His hobbies were developing and becoming more complex just as he was. He was growing and this place was expediting it.

Ryder wrapped his arms around David's calves, making him trip and fall to the ground. David chuckled loudly, still holding the football to his chest.

"Nice one, bud," David said.

They lay there on the lawn, breathless and laughing for a moment.

"We have a real prodigy here, Mom!" David called over to Amy.

"What's a prodigy?" Ryder asked.

"It's a very talented person," Amy explained.

Ryder grinned, pleased with himself.

Amy closed the magazine and put it beside her. "I think I'm going to run inside for some water. Do you two need anything?"

"Ryder, do you want anything, bud?" David asked, but Ryder shook his head. "Well, I'll have a water, if you don't mind. And a stick of gum. I feel like my breath reeks from the onions tonight."

"You'll choke on it if you chew it while you play," Amy noted.

"I think we're almost done for the night," David said. "It's going to start getting dark soon."

"Ok." Amy stood, slipping her pumps back on. "Be back in a second."

She poured two glasses of water and left them on the counter to go seek out her purse. She found it still discarded in the front hall closet, where Meredith, the cleaning lady, had placed it after it had been abandoned by their bouquet on the Fourth of July. Amy hadn't left the house to go anywhere since that strange night, and the bag had gone untouched for days.

When she opened it, prepared to dig through the mess, a high-lighter-pink note lying on top caught her eye.

Amy knew that her family's stationery was typically in neutrals, with their sticky notes colored in a softened yellow. She certainly hadn't ever used one that was so vibrant.

The note was not hers.

On it were just seven words, written in a cursive script so beautiful and flaring that it was almost hard to read.

Have you been to your attic recently?

Amy read the question three more times. Had it been meant for her? Of course it was. It was in her bag, after all.

The question was so strange and unprompted. Why were they asking about a room she had never even stepped foot in?

As Amy reread the swirling script, she concluded that someone had left the note for her most likely on the Fourth of July. Someone with beautiful handwriting and bright sticky notes had thought she should go investigate her attic.

Amy could feel every inch of her recoil at the idea. She put the note in her pocket along with a stick of gum, grabbed the glasses off the counter, and returned outside, where Ryder and David were still catching their breath in chairs on the porch.

She handed David his glass of water, then grabbed both of the objects in her pocket and gave them to him.

"What's this?" he asked, looking at the note. He unfolded and read it.

"I found it in my purse," Amy said. "Do you know anyone who has that handwriting?"

David read and reread it just as Amy had, his forehead creased with thought. "No, I don't think so." He handed it back to Amy. "Weird."

"What could they mean?" Amy asked. She didn't appreciate the way he was acting so nonchalantly. In her head, the sound of high heels clicking against the floor below her bed echoed.

"I'm not sure," David said. "I can check out the attic, though, if you want."

Amy nodded. "I think that's a good idea. Thank you."

David sighed softly as if he had hoped she wouldn't ask that of him after all. He threw his head back and downed the glass of water before standing. "Alright," he said. "Give me a few minutes."

"Bring the—"

"Fire poker. I know," he said, finishing her sentence.

When he had disappeared into the house, Ryder turned to look up at Amy. "What's wrong, Mommy?" he asked.

"Daddy just needs to check the attic for something." But what he needed to check for, Amy was unsure. There was no need to trouble

Ryder with the scary truth of the situation, though. Amy tried her best to mask her nerves and pretend that nothing peculiar was going on.

She waited on the porch for David to return in quiet concern. As the minutes ticked by, she bit her thumbnail nervously and trained her eyes on the porch door.

It took David roughly ten minutes to return with the fire poker in his fist. Amy sprung to her feet.

"Well?" she asked.

He sat down and put the fire poker across his lap. "Nothing out of the ordinary up there," he said.

Amy studied his face, looking for deeper answers but found nothing. She only noticed that something in his eyes seemed tired.

"I didn't make it up," Amy said, suddenly defensive.

"I know," David said. "That would be a weird thing to make up but... I think it could've been a prank or something. There's nothing up there worth your time. We can ask the family next Sunday."

"A prank?" Amy was astounded by the idea.

"I mean, what else could it have been?" David asked.

"I don't know but... it's so weird, David, and the..." She looked at Ryder and lowered her voice. "The footsteps."

"I think you're being a bit paranoid," he said. "There isn't anything wrong with that, really. It might be better to be paranoid than relaxed in some ways, but we have the gate, Amy. It's very unlikely."

"Unless it's your family," Amy said.

David looked up at her with a mixture of surprise and anger playing out on his features. "What do you mean by that?"

"I only mean that if it can't be someone from the outside because of the amazing security, it's got to be someone on the inside."

David stood. "You really are paranoid. I'm tired of this witch hunt. Ryder doesn't need to hear this." He turned to Ryder, who appeared confused and rather frightened by his parents' blooming argument. "Bud, let's go inside."

Amy's jaw dropped. "We need to talk about this."

"Maybe tomorrow," David said. "I have work to get ready for, and I'm not interested in going at it right now. I can sleep in one of the guest rooms tonight. It'll probably be for the best."

Ryder's eyes were big with worry. Amy wanted to comfort her son and hug the distraught look from his face, but David grabbed Ryder's hand before she could.

"David…" Amy began, walking behind the two of them. She felt so humiliated, following them like a dog while her son witnessed her appearing so pathetic, almost neglected.

"I need space for the night," David said. "That stuff… You know better. It hurt me."

Amy couldn't help but scoff as they walked back into the house, though she wasn't sure David heard. The line he had used sounded practiced, pulled straight from a self-help book. She stood on the porch for a second longer and squeezed her hands into fists, holding all of her anger and disappointment in with careful concentration. She was becoming quite good at doing this at her expense to keep the peace.

David might not believe her, but she didn't believe him either. As she stood there, feeling pitiful, small, and gaslit, she resolved to investigate matters for herself the next day.

Chapter 16

Amy waited until David had left the following day before she embarked on her journey up to the attic. She ventured there during that sweet spot between eight-thirty and nine o'clock where she was the only person awake in the entire house.

She pulled down the makeshift wooden ladder that led to the attic. The entrance stared down at her like a wide, open mouth. From the moment she put her foot onto the ladder, she felt the heat of the attic billowing down toward her along with the faint musty smell of a room that hadn't been used in a long time. Poking her head out into the middle of the space, her body almost instantly accumulated a thin layer of sweat from the intense humidity. Even in the dim light of the morning on that sunless day, Amy could see that the attic was almost entirely filled.

She squinted in confusion at the stacks and stacks of boxes. David had neglected to mention the mysterious array of items that didn't belong to them when he returned from his search the day before. Amy stepped onto the floor with caution as if someone might be hiding behind the dozens of stacks.

A voice echoed in her mind then, far off and muffled from time. *Funny to think that this house was used for storage up until a month ago.* Jenn had said when Amy first visited 4 Wisteria Drive. Amy supposed the stored items had been simply moved up into their attic.

The fact that no one had told them about all of the things that had been stowed away above their heads was strange. Amy felt as if she was intruding on something private, even if it was in her own house.

She put the bright pink note down on a short stack of boxes. Amy wasn't sure why she had carried it up with her. It was as if she feared that if she let it go it would disappear, fading away like it was just a figment of her imagination.

Amy took small steps to walk around the towers of boxes, her fingers brushing the dusty cardboard and skipping over the worn leather of old trunks. The stacks rose around her, like great cardboard skyscrapers. It would have taken her days to sit down and fish through all of the boxes before her.

As she rounded the corner of a stack of several overstuffed suitcases, her eyes fell upon a worn red trunk that had been pushed into the furthest corner of the attic. It was shrouded in darkness, hidden beneath shadows as if it had been discarded with the intent of being forgotten. Amy thought that its placement had quite the opposite effect. The way that it was separated from the rest of the stored belongings was so starkly abnormal, like a break in a pattern, that Amy felt herself being drawn toward it. As she grew closer, she also noticed that it was lacking the fine coating of dust that all of the other storage containers had.

Her fingers traced the gold embellishments on the corners and clasps. It felt like forbidden fruit. She knew that it wasn't hers to look at. The stacks of belongings at her back weren't filled with her things. But they were in her house, weren't they? Didn't that make them fair game?

Amy thought of all of the secrets surrounding the Montgomerys, recalling the way they liked to strategically hold their tongues on certain subjects and speak openly and brashly about others. It was incredibly odd that they hadn't mentioned all of the items that had been stowed away without Amy's knowledge. They had just assumed the space was available for their abandoned junk.

Her fingers switched the clasps with a *click*, and she threw open the top of the trunk, revealing the contents within.

Well, there's no going back, she told herself.

Her eyes took in the piles of folders before her. They were in various sizes and colors, all appearing as if they had been well used, with their edges frayed and the corners worn down almost to nubs.

Amy wasn't sure what she had expected, but the pile of folders in front of her wasn't it. She flipped through them carelessly, finding old bills and invoices. At first glance, it seemed to be all paperwork.

Frustrated by the anticlimactic discovery, she pulled out the folders one by one and flipped through them rapidly before setting them aside, hoping to find something of interest stuffed away somewhere.

Then, she opened the last folder, a red one from the bottom of the trunk.

There was no writing on the front indicating what it might hold. The contents were scarce, and the folder was thin. There were a few documents within it, one of which was a deed confirming Jason's ownership of 2 Wisteria Drive.

That's odd, Amy thought. She was almost positive that David had no ownership of the house they lived in. Their house was a privilege that could be taken away from them at any moment. They had no right to it and no official claim to their home. But for some reason, it seemed that Jason did. She found this inconsistency among the brothers strange though perhaps not unwarranted. Jason had been on Wisteria Drive for far longer than the rest of them. Perhaps ownership was a reward given over time when it was clear that their residency was permanent.

She brushed back more papers, flipping through until she felt the firm, authoritative stiffness of the final page in the folder. She pulled it out, holding it up so that the light caught on it, and she could better read its content.

It was a marriage certificate.

Amy leaned forward to see if she was reading the names right.

It was indeed a confirmation of marriage, and it was for Jason.

But the woman who had signed off on it wasn't Tiffany. It was someone named Daisy.

Amy dropped the certificate as if it were white-hot.

Part 3

Chapter 17

The Montgomerys had lied to her.

The idea that this woman and her connection to the Montgomerys had been hidden from her and stowed away in a trunk in a dusty attic made it all feel as though this discovery was wrapped in something dark. For the rest of the day, Amy resisted the urge to scream.

Worst of all, someone had wanted her to find it. Someone who didn't want their identity revealed needed her to know about Daisy. Whoever had done it had been too scared to suggest it to Amy in person, implying that there were consequences for leading her to this information.

Amy had the sudden and intense urge to gather Ryder up and take him out of Wisteria Drive and run to... where? She couldn't drive, and she didn't have any friends in the state. Jenn could have been pretending not to know of Daisy as well when she first saw the ring on the beach. Even David was suspect after he had been quick to side with his family the night before, deepening the wedge that Wisteria Drive had placed between them. Was he lying to her too? Did he know about the certificate?

The fight between her and David still lingered, untouched by his request. How could she prove that she wasn't some paranoid housewife with too much time on her hands? He would tell her that she was only being distrustful again.

The folder with the marriage certificate. The forgotten ring. Lily's statement that Jason was quick to love. All of these small revelations were stacking themselves on top of each other.

There was evidence now. Proof. She could link Daisy to Jason with the certificate and discount the Montgomerys' claim that they had no idea who Daisy was.

Perhaps the other brothers hadn't been on Wisteria Drive when Daisy was there. Wisteria Drive had been new then, constructed just two years before the marriage certificate was signed in 2004. At the very least Lily and Richard had known about their eldest son's first wife. She had been here, on the Montgomerys' little plot of beach. Daisy had been on Wisteria Drive long enough to leave her large diamond ring in the sand before she left with such haste that she hadn't bothered to look for it.

Or maybe she hadn't left it.

Amy shook her head, alone in the kitchen as she prepared Ryder's lunch. No. She wouldn't let her mind wander there. That was getting into the territory of pure paranoia just as David had suggested the night before. She couldn't feed into his theory.

Amy navigated the day like a sleepwalker. Her thoughts never wandered from the piece of paper now placed in her sock drawer and the bright, shiny ring set on top of it. She didn't bother to put on makeup or brush out her hair. Even Ryder noticed the change in Amy's appearance.

"Mommy, are you ok?" he had asked her finally in the early afternoon. He had been regarding her all morning with curious, cautious eyes.

"Mommy is fine," Amy said flippantly.

"You're not wearing your loud shoes," Ryder observed, pointing at her feet, which were bare against the cold floor.

"Yes," Amy said. She wiggled her toes and looked down at her feet as if just noticing this for the first time.

"I heard you this morning," Ryder said. "Did you find something?"

"What do you mean?" Amy asked.

"The attic," Ryder answered. "You opened it. It makes a squeak. Like a mouse."

Of course he had heard it. It was just down the hall from his room, and he would have been stirring by then, waking to the soft squeal of the ladder being pulled down.

"I went up this morning," she said. "I'm sorry if I woke you."

"You didn't," he said. "What were you there for? Did you find something?"

Amy swallowed but her mouth was dry. "Nothing that needs to worry you."

"It worries you?" he asked.

"Like I said, it isn't something that you need to be concerned about. Just something that I need to discuss with Daddy."

"Was it something bad?" he pushed.

"It was something that shouldn't have been there," Amy said simply. She wanted nothing more than for the interrogation to end.

"Like finding treasure?" Ryder asked.

That was the last word Amy would've used to describe it. Even finding the ring in an expanse of sand and shells had soured in her mind from a treasure into an omen.

"Not quite," Amy said.

Ryder pouted, disappointed.

"Why don't you go play outside? It's a nice day," Amy suggested. It was still cloudy, and Amy assumed that it would be a rare cool day because of it.

"Daddy said it was supposed to be hot today," Ryder said.

Amy looked out the window above the kitchen sink at the gray layer of clouds in the sky.

"Maybe you can swim," Amy suggested. "Would you like that? I could sit by the pool."

Ryder scrunched his nose. "Braxton said that people pee in pools."

"It's our pool," Amy said. "Unless you or Dad peed in it, it shouldn't have any." She found the idea so childish in light of her heavy worries that it almost made her laugh. "Braxton says a lot of weird things, huh?"

Ryder shrugged. "He says they're what his dad told him."

Amy felt the knot in her stomach tighten at the mention of Jason. "He seems to think he knows a lot," Amy mumbled.

She ended up convincing him to swim until it was time for her to make dinner. While Ryder swam the doggy paddle in his floaties throughout the pool, Amy continued to fret, even if it was only in a different location.

Later that evening, as Amy made a dinner of burgers and fries—David's favorite—the sky opened up and rain began to pour down in sheets. The world roared in deep bellows of thunder and the torrent of rain was violent, obscuring everything beyond their yard. She felt that the sudden turn in the weather matched her mood as she waited for her husband to come home.

Amy became more jittery with each passing minute. Her belly felt like it was contorted into painful shapes, making her almost want to hunch over with discomfort.

Ryder watched her as she worked, noting her silence and flustered movements. He didn't say anything, but his own concern was visible.

Five o'clock rolled around and Amy was shaky with anticipation as she put the array of toppings and condiments on display. She hoped that cooking his favorite meal would soften any blows she sent David's way. It seemed unlikely, but it was worth a shot.

Finally, she heard the large front door open followed by David's heavy footfalls. Each step he took sent a jolt through her, making her heart stutter.

When he rounded the corner, he looked almost as disheveled as she felt. His hair was unkempt and wet from the rain. Deep purple circles ringed his eyes like bruises. He looked as if he was merely going through the motions. Strangely, this relaxed her.

"I like that smell," he said.

His eyes fell on Amy, seeing her bare face and troubled features. He paused as if he wanted to ask her something but then thought better of it.

"I suppose we should talk after we eat," he suggested as he slid into his seat.

"I agree," Amy said.

The tension between them was palpable as they ate, and the discomfort Amy felt kept her from eating more than a few fries throughout the meal. It was a silent dinner, and the quiet around them was smothering.

When the meal had finally finished after what had seemed like hours of stinging wordlessness, Ryder bounded away at the first opportunity, eager to leave them to it if it meant that he could escape.

David sat at the table as Amy cleared the dishes and cleaned up. Both of them waited for the other to begin speaking. Finally, David broke the silence.

"I took it very seriously when you came for my family last night," he said. "And I'm sorry about that. You know we're close, and your accusation... I mean, even you have to admit it's a little wild."

Amy had been scrubbing a pan when he spoke, but she let it fall into the sink with a clatter when he had finished. "I don't feel comfortable here."

She had weighed up what to say all day but, in that moment, those five words escaped her without any thought.

"Ok," David said. He ran his fingers through his still-wet hair, exasperated. "If it's these noises, I really think..."

Amy cut him off. "It's not just the noises. And you know that."

"Look, the note could've been a prank. I asked the other guys at work about it, and they think it could've been one, too. Or a reminder of some kind."

"You asked them?" Amy felt her stomach drop. Now all of the brothers knew she had been tipped off.

Jason knew she had been tipped off.

"Yeah, why wouldn't I?" David asked.

"I feel like you're not taking this seriously," Amy said. "You haven't taken any of it seriously. You don't believe me even when you claim to, and you're so quick to back into your family's corner."

"In my defense, they're my family, Amy," he said. His frustration was growing. She could hear it in his voice and see the first glimmers of it on his face. "You would fight for your mom too no matter what. Don't deny it."

"I've lived with her my whole life," Amy snapped. "Up until you swept me away, I was living with her. You moved out when you were eighteen and didn't come back to base until just a few weeks ago. I know my mom like I know myself. How well can you say you know your family?"

"Very well actually." David's face was beginning to glow red with anger. Usually, Amy would've cowered under his rising emotions but not that day. She was equally angry this time.

"Then who's Daisy?" Amy asked. "And don't lie to me. Who is she?"

It was almost as if David had been slapped. He fell back into his chair, collapsing at the question. "What are you... What are you talking about?"

"Daisy," she said again as if repeating her name would help him make sense of it. "Jason's first wife."

David stared at her, utterly stunned for several long moments. Then, his eyebrows knitted together in thought, and he chuckled. "Amy, what are you even *saying*?"

"I found the marriage certificate in the attic," Amy said. "Jason and Daisy. 2004. And the ring on the beach. It all adds up. Don't lie to me. I have proof now. It's all up in my sock drawer."

David didn't say anything for a long moment. He sat there in thought as Amy crossed her arms over her chest, waiting for him to respond.

"I want to see it," he said finally. She was surprised to hear that his voice was strained yet soft, unlike the rising anger that it had been loaded with before. "The certificate. Please."

Amy fetched the certificate and ring from upstairs. When she returned to the kitchen, David was sitting with his elbows on the table and his head between his hands. For a moment, Amy almost pitied him.

She slid the items to him, and he looked at them, picking them up delicately. He turned over the ring and read the certificate over and over for almost two minutes before he put it back down on the table.

He didn't look up at her; his eyes were still focused on the piece of paper between them.

"Jason and Tiffany got married in 2006," Amy said. "Who's Daisy?"

David shook his head, taking a moment to collect his thoughts. "I don't know. I was in LA with Tyler that year. We lived there until a year before I met you. Jason never..." But the words trailed off and David appeared dazed.

She let him think about it for a minute, allowed him to turn it over in his head and swim in the possibilities just as she had been doing all day.

"So, see," she said, finally. "I'm not just paranoid. I have a good reason. They're hiding things from us. And they're stashing them above our heads."

David put his head back into his hands. "How..." he mumbled, his question trailing off.

"Someone wanted me to find this," Amy said. "They left me a note so that I would go looking for it. I'm sure of that."

David finally looked up at her. His eyes were even more tired than before, and his face was ashen. "Why do you think that someone would want you to find it?"

"Because of the ring," Amy said. "Because I was the only one who was curious about it. And because the proof was in our attic and not anyone else's. At least that's what I'm assuming."

Amy was not entirely sure why it had been just her, though. Those were merely the reasons she had come up with herself. She didn't know why she had been chosen as a gatekeeper for this secret or why the evidence had been stowed away in her attic and not more safely secured in Lily's. Perhaps they had just assumed that it wouldn't have been found and that neither David nor Amy would have ever gone to investigate. Without that note, it would have been unlikely that they had, in truth.

"I just don't understand... Has anyone said anything about this? Or asked you about Daisy? Have you talked to anyone about the note?" The panic in David's words was startling. She had never seen him so jarred.

"No, I was waiting for you. I have no idea who knows about her," Amy admitted. "But I've been thinking about it since I found the certificate. They lied to us and told us they didn't know a Daisy. Jason at least did for sure. But why?"

David ran his fingers through his hair again, combing it back as if restyling it might improve his situation. Then he sighed loudly in frustration. "This is insane. I can't... This is all insane."

"I know," Amy agreed. "As for the footsteps, I could be imagining them. I know I could. But I don't think I am, David. Especially now. I think now more than ever it's very likely that someone has been in here. Does anyone else have a key to the house?"

"They have a spare," David mumbled to himself.

"Who does?"

"Everyone," David said. "We have everyone's spare keys too. They're in the dresser in the front hall. For safekeeping."

This didn't surprise Amy in the slightest. Of course she should have known they would have all had the spare keys to the other homes. In retrospect, it seemed obvious, but while she didn't even emote at the news, she felt her heartbeat stutter in her chest at the revelation.

Amy watched David wrestle with things for another moment, then asked, "So, what are we going to do?"

He stared at her with confusion, anger, and most of all, alarm. His face was one of unfettered feelings, displaying a deep torment. All of the emotions Amy had felt throughout the day were displayed on David's features, raw and unhidden.

"I don't know," he admitted.

Chapter 18

Four Wisteria Drive lost any sense of security. There was no warmth to its walls, no feeling of comfort in its décor. Every polished floorboard, antique table, and frivolous paperweight was starkly alarming.

Amy had held on to the idea that she would warm to this strange home and foreign feeling. She had gambled her happiness on the assumption that it was just something she needed to get used to. And she had lost.

David promised her that he would get answers. He intended to interrogate Jason at the first chance he could, bright and early when they went in for work the next day. But Amy was itching all over to know the truth. She couldn't imagine how Jason would react when he was confronted and cornered even in a professional setting. Then again, his reaction would depend completely on what had happened to Daisy.

The possibilities made Amy chew at her thumbnail, which, in light of recent events, had been gnawed down nearly into nonexistence. She couldn't sleep. How could she when the ghost of Daisy was just feet from the end of their bed, stuffed away beneath a pile of socks?

Beside her, she had listened for David's breathing throughout the night, waiting for it to even out as he slipped into sleep. But it remained uneven, and he turned often, equally restless.

When she suspected that they were both awake at one in the morning, she kissed his bare shoulder gently. He turned over, rustling the sheets noisily as he moved to face her. Their lips met and she felt a tenderness in the kiss that she hadn't received from him in a long time. Too long. He appeared distraught and tired in the moonlight pouring in from the windows, but his touches were gentle and almost hesitant.

Amy climbed on top of him, straddling his hips, and let the next several minutes unfold naturally. When they were finished, she lay beside him and listened as his heavy, ragged breathing slowly leveled out until it was rhythmic and deep with sleep.

Amy had no such refuge. It took her several hours more before she finally slept, but even then, it felt like no time at all before David rising for work woke her once more.

She watched him don his clothes in the dim light of their bathroom. He dressed in a pale blue button-up, gray pants, and a silver tie. From where she lay in bed, she could see him styling his hair and watched his face closely. He was preparing for a confrontation, yet he showed no visible signs of his nervousness. Perhaps that was good.

Amy rose to make his breakfast after a few more minutes of watching him get ready. He looked so handsome that morning, and Amy felt suddenly guilty for not having admired him more in the difficult weeks behind them.

The breakfast was his favorite: crispy bacon, scrambled eggs with hot sauce, cinnamon toast, and orange juice with a cup of coffee on the side. The All-American Meal he liked to call it on days when he was in brighter spirits. But that morning he had only eaten in silence, chewing but seeming not to taste. He left his plate half-eaten when he rose to leave.

Amy kissed him on the mouth instead of the cheek that morning, hoping the gesture would give him some sort of resolve. His lips tasted like bitter coffee.

"Good luck today," she said. "Text me if you need anything. Or if you learn about anything that I should know of."

"Alright," he said. There was something empty in his eyes.

He grabbed his lunch off the marble island and left.

Amy's insides felt like they were being gnawed away by anxiety. It flooded her body like she had drunk a pot of coffee on an empty stomach, leaving her jittery and restless.

She waited with her phone in her hand, clutching it in her palm with a painfully tight grip. Amy was sick of waiting for things to play out, yet she had no other choice.

Above her head, she could hear Ryder stirring. She listened to his little feet tapping the ground. He was starting his day a little earlier than usual. A part of her worried that he might see her reaction if David reported back that the confrontation was negative. She wanted to shield her son from the Mongomerys' mess for as long as she could.

As she heard Ryder slowly descending the steps, a text came in from David.

He's not here today.

There was a ringing in her ears then, pure and crisp, and it was all she could concentrate on. She felt a sudden hollowness as if all of her thoughts and emotions had been temporarily scooped out of her.

Jason knew about the note and that they were looking in the attic. He didn't know that she had found the document, though. And why wouldn't he have just stood his ground or even lied to them instead of fleeing?

She texted back: *That's really convenient.*

His response was immediate. *Yeah.*

Ryder came into the kitchen then, rubbing his fists into his eyes and yawning.

"Good morning, bud," Amy said but it didn't sound like her voice. It was strained and high-pitched. Wary.

"Morning. You ok?" His big, sleepy eyes were focused on her, undoubtedly seeing the panic on her face. She wished she were better at hiding her feelings.

"Everything is fine," she lied. Amy dropped the phone on the counter and rushed to work on preparing his breakfast. "You're up early."

"Couldn't sleep," Ryder said. "Too much going on."

Amy felt her stomach dip thinking he was implying that her and David's stress had rubbed off on him.

"What do you mean by that?"

"The noise," Ryder said. "Outside."

"What noise?"

"Car doors. People talking. Or yelling." He yawned. "Braxton's mom and dad, I think. Uncle Jason and Auntie Tiffany."

Amy stopped moving. Stopped breathing too. "What exactly did you hear, Ryder?"

"I heard them, but I was so sleepy. They live sorta far so I couldn't hear. I don't know what they said. The doors were being slammed over and over."

"Were they shouting then?"

Ryder nodded.

Amy's blood had gone cold. "What time was this?"

Ryder shrugged and rubbed at his eyes again, clearly not seeing the importance of this observation. "Late."

Amy nodded, unable to find the right words. She returned to her work, putting together Ryder's breakfast in shaky silence. Her hands were trembling violently as she prepared the food.

She placed the plate in front of him and then grabbed her phone with an iron grip.

"Mommy has to make a phone call, ok?" she said.

Ryder didn't even look up from his meal. "To Grandma?"

"Sure," Amy answered, eager to slip away.

She hurried into the front hall and took a seat on the first three stairs of the left staircase. Amy sent a quick text to her husband, one that she knew he would be uncertain about. For once she didn't care about what his reaction might be. She was tired of waiting and it felt as though something in the air had shifted drastically.

Amy sent David a text that said: *Ryder heard Tiffany and Jason fighting last night. They might have been packing the car. I'm calling Tiffany.*

She dialed up her sister-in-law seconds after she hit send, not waiting for David's response.

Amy listened to the phone ring and ring and ring with her thumbnail between her teeth. Her leg bounced impatiently as she waited.

Tiffany's voicemail cut one of the bland rings short. The sound of her cheery voice made the breath catch in Amy's throat. Tiffany would likely have been up tending to Braxton by now. She would have been awake with a full face of makeup on already and in a pair of heels. But instead, she was unavailable.

"Hi, this is Tiffany! I'm currently away right now but feel free to leave me a message. I'll try to get back to ya!"

When it was her time to speak, Amy sat in an insufferable quiet, unable to come up with the right words as her heart hammered in her chest.

Finally, she said, "Hi, um, Tiffany. I just was calling to check in. Please don't take this the wrong way. I just wanted to check in because, well, my son, uh, Ryder, he said he might have heard you and Jason arguing last night. And David told me Jason isn't at work today. So, I guess I just wanted to see if everything's alright. Uh, let me know if you need anything. Ok... bye."

She hung up, feeling like she should have said more, but it was too risky.

Within a moment of ending the voicemail, Amy felt her phone vibrate. It was a response from David: *Keep me updated. I'll ask around here to see if anyone knows anything.*

She was pleased that he at least didn't argue with her.

Amy responded: *Straight to voicemail. Getting very concerned.*

Part of her wanted to call Tiffany again, but she knew that it would be fruitless. Yet she was jumpy, and her mind was racing. Four Wisteria Drive felt like a cage, trapping her inside and holding her within its unyielding grip. She couldn't bear to sit complacently any longer.

Amy returned to the kitchen and found Ryder still at the table, his plate nearly cleared.

"Hey, bud," she said. She found that her voice sounded especially tight as she approached him. "Do you mind running over to Aunt Jenn's with me when you're done eating?"

"I like her," Ryder said in answer.

Amy walked over to Jenn's home just before nine-thirty in the morning, her heels moving noisily across the pavement as she strode with purpose. Ryder was in tow, walking just a few steps behind, unable to keep up.

Amy couldn't shake the idea that there might be prying eyes peeking out from between the blinds and curtains of the surrounding houses, watching her walk down the street. She imagined Lily glaring out from behind her window with her arms crossed over her chest but didn't dare to cast a glance in 1 Wisteria Drive's direction.

At Jenn's door, she sucked in a deep breath, bracing herself to knock and calculating how to approach this conversation with everything that she now knew. It was a long shot to confront Jenn. After all, Jenn could have easily been lying to and manipulating her, too. But Jenn, aside from David, was the only friend Amy had.

Ryder stood at her side and reached up to grab her hand. His little fingers grasped hers delicately. Amy knew that he wasn't doing it for himself.

She looked down at him, and he tilted his head up at her. Ryder gave her a small smile and there was a responsive, sharp tug in her chest. Overwhelming guilt flooded her as she stared down into his trusting eyes. She had unknowingly taken him to a place of lies, and she was still unsure as to whether they would be able to squirm free from the mess they were in. She had agreed to the move in the first place because she had seen it as a better place for her son to grow. Now she was doubting that this was the case.

Amy knocked on the door and waited. After nearly a minute passed, she knocked again. Eventually, she heard Jenn's shoes making their way to the door and let herself exhale.

Jenn ripped the door open and peeked out curiously. She was already dressed immaculately, with her face flawlessly painted in a light coating of makeup.

"Oh! I didn't expect to see you here so early," she said. Her bright red lips were pulled into a genuine smile as she pushed the door open further.

"Hi, I'm sorry to bother you," Amy said. She could feel her hand getting sweaty in Ryder's as she imagined the eyes of Wisteria Drive boring into her back.

"No problem at all," Jenn said with a dismissive wave of her hand. "What brings you by?"

"I was just wondering if you knew anything about Tiffany."

Jenn's face contorted into one of bewilderment. "Tiffany?"

"Yeah, um, Ryder here said he heard her and Jason arguing last night. He also said he heard car doors slam quite a bit. And Jason's not at work today. I was just wondering if maybe they went somewhere—you know, like a vacation for the weekend or something—that I just wasn't aware of."

Jenn straightened in the doorway, and she appeared suddenly serious. "You heard all of that, little guy?" she asked Ryder.

Ryder nodded enthusiastically.

"And Tiffany isn't answering her phone," Amy added. "I called her once and she didn't pick up. I just wanted to see if you knew anything about it."

Amy had never seen Jenn look so severe. She seemed to darken at the news like some ominous cloud had swept over her, dimming her typically sunny demeanor.

Jenn pulled the door open wider and stepped to the side.

"Come in," she said. "We need to talk."

Chapter 19

The sun was streaming through Jenn's kitchen windows, brilliant and unadulterated by blinds or curtains. The bright scene was in stark juxtaposition with how Amy felt.

Jenn's invitation had caused a sinking feeling in Amy's belly. It only worsened when they stood at the kitchen island, and Jenn handed Ryder an opened bag of Goldfish, saying, "Why don't you go to the living room and watch some TV? I'm pretty sure SpongeBob is on. It's just down that hallway and to the left. Channel two-ninety-nine."

Ryder looked at Amy curiously, but she only nodded in approval. Ryder let go of her hand and teetered away, walking slowly with clear reluctance.

When he was out of sight, Jenn strode over to the counter where her little indoor camera was mounted. She ripped out the plug and snapped her attention back to Amy.

"What do you know?" she asked.

"What do you mean?" Amy was taken aback. Her entire body felt as if it were buzzing like the static on a television screen.

"Come on," Jenn said with an eye roll. "The Montgomerys think they're so smart. But they're mostly a bunch of privileged boys. They're sloppy and overconfident. Let's compare notes. What did you stumble on?"

Amy swallowed. At that moment she could see how deep her paranoia ran. She wasn't sure she could trust Jenn. How far did this all go? Was Jenn a Montgomery first or a friend?

"Did you leave me that note?" Amy finally asked.

"What note?" Jenn looked sincerely confused. She laid her hand on her lower belly as if it were swelling with her child already, though Amy had yet to see any change.

"Someone left me a note to find," Amy explained. She spoke slowly, watching Jenn's reaction to her every word, looking for a reason to stop speaking. "It said to go into the attic."

Jenn only blinked. "Why?"

"I'm not sure what their intention was," Amy admitted. "But it did lead me to some strange... realizations. I investigated it myself. The place was absolutely filled with boxes, and they weren't our things."

"Lily and Richard must have moved everything up there before you came." Jenn tapped her lips with her pointer finger in thought. "Strange, though. They told us they were moving it all out. Must have gotten lazy. Sloppy, again. Did you find anything important?"

Amy slid into a seat beside Jenn, suddenly feeling like it was difficult to stand. She had the unbearable urge to chew on her nail but resisted. "A marriage certificate."

Jenn smirked. "I knew it."

"For Daisy and Jason."

"Son of a bitch," Jenn whispered. She looked away in astonishment. Her features were a mixture of disbelief and validation.

"Do you know who she is?" Amy asked. She caught herself angling forward and didn't bother to adjust her posture.

"Well, I'm guessing Jason's ex-wife," Jenn said with a scoff. "But Tyler hasn't ever told me about a previous marriage. Only that Jason gets in deep when he likes something and that… he doesn't know how to express it."

Jenn looked down at the hand resting on her belly, avoiding eye contact. "He told me that when I asked why Tiffany wears long sleeves even in the summertime."

Feeling drained from Amy's limbs. "They're always down to her wrists, no matter how hot it is."

Jenn nodded. "I don't think Braxton learned about what he did to Kayleigh from cartoons."

Amy leaned back into her chair, her hand covering her mouth in shock.

"I'm only speculating," Jenn said. Her voice had dropped low as if someone could be listening to them besides Ryder. "But I think it's odd that Daisy has never been mentioned. They won't acknowledge her. I'd never heard or seen her name until the ring." She paused, turning a thought over. "Do you remember her maiden name on the certificate? We could look her up on social media or something. See if she's still… well, see where she is now, I guess."

Amy couldn't remember it off the top of her head. For all the stress it had caused her over the past forty-eight hours, she was frustrated that she had not made the effort to memorize it.

"It starts with an 's,'" Amy said. "I don't remember. Steward or Stone or something. I have the certificate in my sock drawer. I'll check when I get back and text you."

"It's better not to," Jenn said. "I know this might sound a little crazy, but I would rather keep these conversations between us. In-person or over the phone. Just in case. Anyone can read a phone's texts."

Amy felt slightly nauseous. She couldn't believe what they were discussing.

"And maybe don't tell David," Jenn added. "I know, I know. I sound crazy. But I promise you. It's better to play it safe than to be sorry."

"Why can I trust you and not him?" Amy asked.

"I'm an outsider. The wife," Jenn explained. "If what we're talking about has any foul play involved, I'm disposable. They can plow on without me and act like I never happened, just like Daisy. David is not. I have everything to lose. He doesn't."

Jenn rubbed her belly thoughtfully when she spoke the last sentence.

"You don't think... that Tiffany..." Amy couldn't say the words.

"I have no idea," Jenn admitted.

"We could leave," Amy suggested suddenly. Her skin prickled at the idea of staying on that street any longer.

"And go where?" Jenn looked amused by the notion. "We have no money of our own, you and I. Nowhere to run to. You can't even drive. Everything is tied up in the Montgomerys. Besides, we're probably getting ahead of ourselves. Everything could be fine. We're talking about wild speculation right now. Hypotheticals."

"Until it isn't," Amy said.

"At least we won't be blindsided if it isn't. But we also don't want to overreact if it's truly nothing."

"I hear people walking in our house sometimes," Amy said abruptly like the words were forced out of her. "At night. No one else does. David even looked the one night and found nothing."

"Now that's news," Jenn said. "Could be anyone really, couldn't it?"

"I heard heels," Amy added. "The second time."

"Hm." Jenn thought about it for a moment. "I've never heard that here or seen anything weird on our cameras. That's very... well, in light of the conversation, Amy, I'd say that's downright scary."

Amy surrendered and let her thumbnail meet her teeth. She couldn't avoid it any longer. "I know."

"Next time record it. I want to hear it myself. And it's good to have proof. Do you sleep with your phone on your nightstand?"

"Well, I hope there isn't a next time." Amy couldn't bear the thought of those footfalls being real, especially not within the context of their current discussion. "But yeah. I sleep with it right by me."

"Good," Jenn said. "Reach over and hit record *if* it happens again. And obviously, call me if you need to. We're in this together. Whatever it is. Consider us allies."

An ally. That was what Amy had wanted since she moved to Wisteria Drive just a few weeks ago feeling like a schoolgirl walking into a crowded cafeteria and trying to figure out where to sit. She had needed a friend, one that she could be assured would remain loyal to her.

"You're lucky I listen to so many true crime podcasts when I sunbathe," Jenn said with a playful smile meant to comfort her.

"I feel awful about not being able to tell my husband," Amy said.

"David?" Jenn clarified. "Amy, we're allowed to keep secrets too."

Jenn took her hand from her belly and put it on top of Amy's. She could feel its warmth and with it came a shred of security.

Jenn was right.

Amy left Jenn's house not long after, gathering up Ryder and carting him back to 4 Wisteria Drive. Amy trembled the entire walk to the house, shivering despite the Floridian heat as the remnants of their conversation echoed in her head.

Back inside, Amy sent Ryder off to finish the episode of SpongeBob she had pulled him from. He was immediately hypnotized by the brilliant colors, and Amy was happy to see that, even if it was only for a moment, he seemed to forget his mother's worries.

He shouldn't have to be so perceptive, Amy thought. He was too observant for his own good. As Amy watched the back of Ryder's little brunette head, she knew she had done him a great disservice.

When she was satisfied that he was completely zoned out, she left him for a moment to take a second glance at the certificate and try to recall Daisy's last name. She tore open the sock drawer, sending several balls of bunched-up socks rolling about.

Amy plunged her hand into the sea of fabric, letting her fingers graze the bottom where they felt the wood of her drawer. The sensation sent a bolt through her as if she had been electrified. Dread overtook her, and she dug wildly, madly tossing balls of socks behind her.

But there was no sign of the certificate or the ring. At the bottom, there was only wood.

Chapter 20

"Just breathe," Jenn said on the other line. "What's going on?"

"It's gone," Amy said. Her voice was shaky. She felt as though she couldn't take in enough air. "The certifi- the paper. In my drawer. It's missing. It's not here."

"Oh wow," Jenn said. "Do you know if it was there this morning?"

"I... I don't know." The idea that someone might have stolen it in the early morning, during those few short hours of sleep she had been able to get, made her unbearably scared. "I didn't sleep well last night. I only slept for like three hours. I don't think it would've been taken in the night." She couldn't think that.

"And you know for sure it was there last night?" Jenn asked.

"Yes, I showed it to David," Amy said.

"So, someone probably took it while you were at my house then."

Amy slid down to the floor until she was sitting on the hardwood. Her legs were too shaky to stand.

"Someone who was home when we were," Amy stated. *One of the women* was the subtext of that. One of the wives had betrayed them. "Lily or Miranda."

"Or Tiffany and Jason," Jenn suggested.

The thought of Jason wandering throughout her home made her shudder.

Amy gasped as a thought occurred to her. "What if they're still here?"

She sprung back to her feet, nearly tripping back onto the floor as she did so, and began to hurry back down the steps, rushing toward Ryder.

"You didn't check?" Jenn asked.

"No," Amy said. "I didn't even think of it. Ryder..."

She turned the corner and Ryder was still sitting in the middle of the couch, staring intensely at the cartoon in front of him. Amy put her hand on her chest and forced herself to breathe in shaky, uncomfortable breaths.

Ryder turned to look at her with a small smile that faded when their eyes met. "Mommy?"

"Jenn, can we come back over?" she asked into the phone as she kept her eyes trained on her son.

"Yeah. Definitely. I think until we figure out what happened, being together is for the best."

"I'll be right over."

Amy hung up and gave Ryder a strained grin in a pathetic attempt to appear sane.

"We have to go back over to Auntie Jenn's, ok, buddy?" Amy said.

Ryder nodded but he was visibly disturbed and perhaps even a bit annoyed by the instruction.

Amy was careful to lock the door behind her when they left again, though she was not sure what good that would do if a Montgomery wanted to get in. As she crossed the street again, she was convinced that there truly were curious eyes staring out of the surrounding homes. She wondered what they thought of her leaving again and retreating to Jenn's. It wasn't subtle. It would cause a stir and further raise suspicion to anyone who knew what was happening.

Jenn invited them in once more, offering Amy an iced coffee that Amy refused.

"I already have enough anxiety," she said before sending Ryder back into the living room.

"You're right," Jenn agreed. "This calls for the stronger stuff."

Jenn poured a tall glass of red wine for Amy and gave herself a cup of water. Jenn stared at Amy longingly as she drank. "I miss alcohol so much already. Could really use some right about now. This will be a *long* pregnancy."

Amy finally came up for a breath with the glass half drained and the bitter taste resonating on her tongue. "I don't envy you. Can we please talk about something other than what just happened? I don't think I can take more speculation. I'm already sort of lightheaded."

"Sure, I'll talk your ear off. It's a talent, especially when I'm nervous."

Amy soon learned that this was not an exaggeration. Jenn was able to talk about her baby—which was supposedly now about the size of a kidney bean—for hours. Amy was happy to not have to contribute to the conversation, and Jenn seemed content to speak uninterrupted. Amy sipped at her wine all the while, letting the alcohol slowly dull her feelings.

But as much as she drank, the nervous cramping in her stomach never fully disappeared. It gnawed at her behind every unrelated thought, reminding her that she was trapped in a web of drama and lies. There was a sickening sense of nausea that came and went, flooding her and threatening to result in a fit of vomiting that, with some effort, Amy was just barely able to suppress.

Amy almost lost track of time, and when four-thirty rolled around, she glanced at the oven clock lazily only to jump at the numbers.

"Oh my god," Amy said, cutting Jenn off in the middle of her explaining exactly how she wanted the nursery to be laid out. "They'll be home soon."

She had drunk too much and had lost track of time, forgetting to feed Ryder in the process. The realization made her blush. Strike number two against her.

"Jenn, I have to go, I think," Amy said. "Dinner... and David..."

Jenn gave her a look. "Are you ok to do it? I could help you make dinner."

"No. Too suspicious. I..." Her voice trailed off, thinking. "I have to go."

"Ok," Jenn said. "Call me tomorrow. A lot. Or you can come over again if you want but you'll have to make a good enough excuse. Remember, anyone can read your phone."

"What's tomorrow?" Amy asked. Everything seemed hazy and distant. She dug in her mind for the answer but came up empty.

"Saturday."

"Oh god," Amy said. "This will be awkward. And Sunday. The dinner. What are we going to do?"

"I don't know," Jenn admitted. "But we'll figure it out. Together. Now go get Ryder. It'll look better if you're back before David is. And make sure you drink some water while you're at it."

"Ok, ok." Amy felt pathetic like she was a child being chastised, as she went to go get her son.

Ryder looked at her excitedly when she came in. He seemed relieved that she finally came for him, and despite her drunken state, she felt a tug of guilt.

"Are you hungry, buddy?" Amy asked.

Ryder nodded. He didn't seem to be too distraught about his hunger, though. He seemed more thrilled to see his mom than anything.

"I'm sorry, buddy," she said. "Auntie Jenn and I had important stuff to talk about. I feel really bad."

"It's ok," Ryder said. "Are we having macaroni?"

She could see him leveraging her lapse of memory to his advantage and gave a long laugh, perhaps too long for the circumstances, but Ryder didn't seem to notice.

"If you want, bud," Amy said. "I can make some macaroni."

"Yes, please."

So, Amy did just that, even if it was an admittedly clumsy affair. She made enough for the three of them when she realized in the middle of making it that she would like some as well.

She was in the final steps of stirring it all together when David came through the front door, emitting his usual frustrated sigh. Despite the wine in her system, Amy felt her belly jump at the sound of his footsteps.

He was undoing his silver tie when he walked into the kitchen, stripping off his suit aggressively as if he couldn't remove the clothes fast enough. Amy remembered the serene and longing feeling of watching him get dressed just that morning. It felt like it had happened two weeks ago.

"Hi, honey." David's gaze fell on the pot of macaroni, and he raised an eyebrow. "What's for dinner?"

"Macaroni and cheese, as requested by Ryder," Amy answered. She was making a great attempt to appear calm and normal, but even through the fog the wine had created, she knew that it was a long shot for her to be perceived as anything besides unnerved.

"Oh, he's dictating dinners now, huh?" David asked.

Amy couldn't tell him that she had neglected to feed Ryder a proper lunch. "He requested it, and I realized I wanted some too, so here we are."

David took a step forward, appearing darkly curious as he did so. Amy instinctively leaned back as he regarded her with a strangely cold and assessing gaze.

"Amy, are you drunk?" David asked in a lowered voice so that Ryder couldn't hear from his seat at the kitchen table.

Amy felt her face flood with heat. "I'm not drunk," she said defensively.

David gave an understanding nod and took a slow step back. "Just tipsy, then."

"So, what if I drank?" Amy hissed. "This has been a hard few days for me."

"For you?" David looked appalled. "Amy, think about it from my position. And unlike you, I don't have the time to bury my feelings in drinks. You're supposed to be looking after Ryder when I'm gone."

That felt like a slap in the face, especially given the circumstances.

"Don't talk to me like that," Amy said. "Not here. Not in front of him."

"Alright, Amy. Pull that card again," David said. He gave her a tired look that was woven with anger. But he didn't say anything else.

The tension was present throughout dinner. It hung around the family like a physical thing, as though Amy could reach up and touch it.

Amy tried desperately to fill the awkward silence by recounting Jenn's baby plans to David, who only stared down at his bowl of macaroni dimly as she spoke. When Amy felt she had exhausted the topic, David finally asked, "Did you call her today and find all of this out?"

Again, Amy felt her face get warm. "We went over to visit."

"Ah," David said. "Interesting."

"What's interesting about that?"

"Just that you decided to go over there and drink all day," David said.

"You know why I did," Amy snapped.

"I know," he said. "But you're supposed to prioritize our son. Not yourself."

Amy clenched all over with fury.

"I like Auntie Jenn," Ryder piped up.

"There is just one thing I ask you to do all day," David added, ignoring Ryder's comment.

"I'm allowed to blow off steam every once and a while just like you do when you shoot the shit with your brothers."

David opened his mouth to call her out on her use of a swear in front of Ryder, but Amy continued, hurtling forward. "Especially when the certificate is gone. Missing. Stolen."

That froze David in place. She watched his reaction, paying close attention to every muscle of his face. "It's gone?"

Amy gave a hysterical laugh, one that would have made even her cringe if she had been on the receiving end of it. "Stolen, more like. The ring too. Taken."

"Mommy, what do you mean?" Ryder asked.

"One of your aunties or uncles came in and took something that was mine. Ours."

"Don't say that!" David exclaimed as he jumped to his feet.

His sudden outburst made her suck in a sharp breath. Whatever dulling effect that had been carried over from the wine an hour before fled from her, leaving her feeling painfully sober.

"You don't know my family like I do, Amy. You won't ever. They're kind and giving. I mean look at where we are! But you can't admit that because they've always had more than you, so they have to be evil right? That's what this is, huh? Are you taking down The Man, Amy?"

Ryder, with bulging eyes, had begun to sniffle, on the verge of tears.

"Look at yourself," Amy said. "Don't act like this. Not in front of our son."

David was breathing heavily, clenching his fists at his sides. Amy hadn't been this frightened of him in a long while. It was like one of their old fights before Ryder was able to comprehend what was happening. Staring at David's blazing eyes and reddened skin, Amy recoiled. His face and neck were the color of a tomato and the veins along his throat and arms looked as if they might pop out from beneath his skin. This version of him had been absent for so long, and even still she thought she had never seen him appear quite so angry as he did in that moment.

"You're scaring me," Amy said. She heard her voice come out small and felt pathetic.

Ryder burst into tears then, wailing like he had when he was a toddler, open-mouthed and snotty with a scrunched-up face. Amy rushed to him and pulled him into her arms, feeling his heaving chest against hers as he sobbed. Touching him brought her back to center.

Amy picked Ryder up. He was heavy in her arms, heavier than he had ever been, and Amy wasn't sure if it was because she hadn't carried him recently or if it was a result of the sudden weakness she felt.

"We can't keep this up," Amy said. "We can't keep yo-yoing."

David was still huffing and puffing, but his eyes were large as if he were slowly emerging from a haze, like a swimmer coming up from underwater, breaking the surface, and seeing the sun.

She didn't wait for him to answer. Instead, she hurried up the staircase as fast as she could go with Ryder hanging onto her. She was grateful that she didn't hear any effort from David to follow her.

When she got to Ryder's room, she kicked it open with the toe of her shoe and laid him down on his bed. Already, he had begun to calm himself down to just aggressive sniffles.

"Are you ok, buddy?" Amy asked as she smoothed out his hair.

"He-He-He was so *loud*," Ryder stuttered.

"I know." Amy wanted to cry with him, but she held herself together for Ryder's sake. There was a raw soreness in the back of her throat that threatened to release into sobs at any moment. "I know. I'm going to talk to him about that. He wasn't mad at you, though. He was mad at Mommy. You know that, right? He's not mad at you."

Amy continued to stroke his hair as she spoke. She wasn't sure if the gesture was soothing him or if it was the other way around.

"I-I know," Ryder said.

"Good. Are you ok if I leave you to talk to Daddy?" Amy asked.

Ryder looked down at his feet, wiping his cheeks. "Y-Yes."

Amy kissed his forehead. "Alright, I'll be back soon."

She found David sitting at the bottom of the stairs, rubbing his palms absently as he stared at the front door. He didn't turn to look at her as she approached, and she was strangely grateful for it.

"Jason won't answer my texts either," David said softly. "My calls go straight to voicemail."

Amy gripped the railing as if clutching it tightly might keep her grounded.

"Tiffany never responded. And like I said earlier, Ryder told me he heard them arguing last night. There were lots of car doors slamming, apparently. We have no idea where Braxton is either. I don't know. I'm just concerned."

"It's a Friday. They might be off on a long weekend." He paused for a moment, then added, "They have to be."

There was a break in his voice at the end. Despite herself, Amy drifted down the stairs and sat beside him.

"I shouldn't have raised my voice at you in front of Ryder," David admitted. "I'm really... thrown off by this whole thing. I know it's not an excuse but... I'm sorry."

Amy looked at his hands as he continued to nervously rub his palms. A long moment passed as she watched him, sifting through her thoughts like sand. "I don't think I forgive you," she finally said.

He turned to look at her, and his hands stopped moving.

"Not right now," Amy continued. "I can't even imagine how this might feel for you. I can only speak to how it looks, so I understand the stress you're under." Amy stood back up on her high heels, suddenly feeling very tall. "But don't you dare pull another stunt like that in front of Ryder. He's old enough to remember this stuff now. You tried to humiliate me. Again. I need time to process that. Everyone has told me over and over since we moved here that I need to learn my place. But maybe you need to learn yours."

She had never spoken to him like that, not in all of their years of marriage. But he had never given her a reason to until now.

Chapter 21

Amy was the first one in the house to wake up early that Saturday. She went downstairs and into the kitchen, feeling on edge during the descent. She checked the front door to make sure that it was still locked. It was, but even this gave her little comfort with the knowledge of the four spare keys spread throughout the cul-de-sac.

There could be someone else in her home at any time, hiding out, and waiting to pounce. With her hand still on the unyielding door-knob, she shivered violently at the thought. Amy had stayed up most of the night before, listening for footfalls with strained ears. Though she hadn't heard anything while she was awake, this did not mean that within the handful of hours she had been unconscious, someone had taken the opportunity to sneak in.

Not just someone, though. A Montgomery. She was sure of it now. The average robber wouldn't have sought out something as useless as a marriage certificate. The ring, maybe, but there was no doubt that the theft had been targeted. Only someone in the family would want to steal her evidence. But why?

As Amy brewed herself a mug of coffee, she ran through a mental list of suspects. All of the Montgomery women besides Jenn were up for speculation. Even Tiffany, with her whereabouts being unknown, was not exempt from Amy's consideration. Lily, Richard, and Jason seemed like the most plausible suspects. They were the only ones that

Amy could positively say were on Wisteria Drive in 2004 to see Daisy. Their vigilance would also make the most sense if there had been any foul play involved.

A wave of nausea overcame her. Foul play? Was she really considering that? It didn't seem like Jason and Daisy had an amicable split, at least. Something had gone so wrong that the Montgomerys had worked to bury it by stuffing any known links to her in an attic and pretending not to know that she existed. Jenn at least seemed to think that something was very much amiss.

But those were not the only three who were likely suspects. Any of the men could've been involved too. This included her own husband. She wouldn't give him a pass. Not after Jenn had advised her that it would be wise to keep things close to her chest. Besides, he was the only person who had known for sure where the certificate and ring had been hidden unless he had told someone else, which in itself felt like a betrayal. Any of the men could've snuck out of work with the information David had given them and stolen the slip of paper.

Amy sipped her coffee and felt the steam rush up and flood her face with a warmth that almost tickled. It was a second of pleasantness in a myriad of horror.

Suddenly, her phone buzzed loudly on the table to her right, making her jump and slosh coffee from her mug. She leaned forward to see the caller and snatched the phone.

"Mom?" she asked when she picked up.

Emily breathed out a loud sigh of relief. "Jesus Christ, Amy! You haven't called in two days! I've been so worried about you."

"Oh, Mom." Amy hadn't even realized that she had forgotten to call her mom in all of the hecticness. She had seen the texts from Emily reminding her, asking her if she was alright, but among all that had happened, replying had slipped her mind entirely.

"I'm sorry," Amy said. "Things have just been... busy."

"I assumed," Emily said. "But you're ok, right?"

Amy looked around the kitchen as if someone might be standing in one of the corners listening in.

"I think so," Amy said. Her voice had dropped just to be safe.

"You think?" Emily asked. Her distress was clear.

Amy hunched in her seat, bending over her phone as she dropped her voice as much as she could and recounted everything. She told Emily about Daisy and the certificate, about Tiffany and her supposed fight with Jason, about Jenn's speculation, and about how Jason and Tiffany were nowhere to be seen.

Amy knew that she was telling her mother strange things, establishing a pattern and timeline that could strike suspicion and fear into anyone. At the last minute, she decided to leave out the part about David's explosion the night before and how he had made Ryder cry. She had never told her mother about even her most vicious fights with David.

When Amy was finished, Emily cleared her throat. Amy imagined her sitting up straighter on the other end, processing the information.

"Why are you whispering?" Emily finally asked.

Amy hadn't even realized that she had been hissing the story into the receiver. "I just want to be safe. You know, in case someone is listening."

"It sounds like they already know what you know if they really did steal your things," Emily said. She cleared her throat again and Amy knew that she was preparing to say something she thought was difficult to swallow. "Amy, I don't want to worry you, but something stuck out. You said that David texted you and planned to subtly ask his family about what happened. That could imply that he might have told them about the certificate. When was this?"

"Yesterday at work," Amy answered.

"So, it's possible that the brothers knew that you had it and, unless they immediately texted their wives and let them know, they were the only ones who knew," Emily observed.

She was right. Amy had somehow overlooked this minute detail to focus on the bigger picture.

"I don't feel comfortable with you living there until this is all figured out," Emily continued. "I'm still scheduled to come down this upcoming Friday but... Amy, if I'm being honest, I think I should come over now."

She hated worrying her mother, even if it was for a valid reason. "We don't know where Tiffany and Jason are," Amy insisted. "David says that they're probably on vacation for the weekend."

"I'm sure he thinks that," Emily said sarcastically. "Who doesn't answer their phone on vacation? There's usually more time to be sitting on it!"

"I can't consider the alternative," Amy said. "I can't think about... I can't think about something going wrong."

"You should though," Emily insisted. "It doesn't sound good. I'm going to call off work and come see you."

"Mom..." Amy protested. She knew how much her mom needed her jobs. Leaving so abruptly would only put her in poor standing with the restaurants she worked at. Amy would never forgive herself if Emily had done that for nothing but aimless speculation.

"Don't 'mom' me," Emily said. "This is serious."

"You can't just show up," Amy insisted. "Imagine how that would look. Especially if nothing is wrong."

"Are you seriously telling me that you don't think that *anything* is wrong here?" Emily asked incredulously.

Amy put her thumbnail between her teeth. There was hardly anything to chew on after everything that had unfolded.

"You're right, but maybe plan to come down on Monday. That way you can stay the week and scope things out. And you'll be giving your bosses more of a heads-up. It'll give you time to find someone to cover your shift, too."

Amy didn't know how she was supposed to explain to David why her mom had shown up abruptly at 4 Wisteria Drive so soon after their argument. It seemed more trouble than it was worth, but she couldn't deny the awful anxiety she knew would be quelled by her mother's presence.

"Amy, how am I supposed to expect you to go to that God-forsaken dinner tomorrow with all of them?"

"I'm a big girl," Amy said. "And I have Jenn."

"You're delusional if you think—"

But Amy cut her off. "It's just a few more hours. You'll be over in a little more than two days anyway."

Emily was silent for a moment, chewing on the thought. "That's what you want, then? Me to come on Monday?"

Amy considered the question for a beat before she answered, "Yes."

"Alright," Emily said. "But I'll be leaving at four in the morning on Monday so I'm there early. Be ready for me."

"Ok, Mom," Amy said. Emily's concern was only worsening her own, validating the most distressful thoughts that she had been trying so desperately to push to the back of her mind. "I have to go. Breakfast needs to be made."

"Call me at the end of the night," Emily demanded. "That's my half of the deal. If I'm supposed to wait until Monday you have to call me every day until then, ok?"

"Fine," Amy agreed.

"Alright," Emily said. "Good. Keep me updated."

"Will do, Mom. Bye."

"Goodbye," Emily said before Amy hung up.

Amy had thought that talking to her mother would've made her feel better, but it seemed that Emily's suggestions had only stoked the flames.

Explaining to David why Emily was arriving earlier than expected would be awkward but there was some relief in knowing that her mom, someone who was undoubtedly and unwaveringly in her corner, would be there to witness everything Amy had just described to her.

Amy stood to prepare breakfast. She pulled out a carton of eggs, an onion, a bag of spinach, and some peppers to make omelets. She selected a short knife from the array of options in her knife block, and as she raised it to begin dicing the peppers into tiny cubes, her phone rang again. Amy gave a short huff of annoyance as she went to it, expecting Emily to be calling her back unnecessarily.

Instead, Amy saw that it was Jenn calling and dropped the knife back onto the marble countertop with a light clatter.

"Is everything ok?" Amy asked when she picked up, wasting no time.

"Miranda's over here," Jenn explained. "She's at my place. You're going to want to come over and hear what she has to say."

"Right now?" Amy asked, her eyes falling on the array of food she had taken out of the refrigerator.

"Yeah, that's probably best," Jenn said. "While everyone is still sleeping. The door's unlocked. Just be quiet when you first come in. Tyler is a heavy sleeper, and he usually sleeps in late on the weekends but, you know, just to be safe."

Amy looked at the clock in the kitchen. She had maybe thirty minutes at most before David usually got up.

"Alright," Amy said. "I'll be right over."

Chapter 22

Amy found them in the sitting room, huddled in gray darkness with the shades drawn against the rising sun. Miranda was on the sofa, hugging a thick white blanket to herself as if it were her shield. Jenn was in the armchair next to her, leaning forward with her hands wrapped around a cup of iced coffee. Amy had worn a pair of furry slides that morning, so they both looked at her when she came in, their bodies visibly tensing at the sound of someone entering who wasn't wearing heels.

"What's going on?" Amy asked. She was nearly breathless from her sprint across the street.

"Shh," Jenn hushed her. She motioned for Amy to sit beside her by tapping the chair to her left. Amy obeyed. "I unplugged the cameras but we need to be quiet. Tyler's still sleeping," Jenn said, jabbing her finger at the ceiling.

"What's going on?" Amy asked again, this time in a whisper.

"Miranda?" Jenn prompted, before taking a sip of her drink.

"I noticed that Tiffany was gone too," Miranda explained, pulling the blanket tighter around her. "They've worried me for a while. But now... I can't help but wonder..."

"What?" Amy asked when Miranda hesitated, tilting forward to better hear her. She was pressed for time with the window before David woke up slowly inching to a close.

Miranda sighed out a shaky breath. "Tiffany and I have grown pretty close. We've been here the longest, so I guess it was only natural. Just like it was natural for you and Jenn to have a closer connection. So, I think Tiffany trusted me. She's confided in me a few times about things that... well, things that worried me, to say the least."

"Like what?" Amy asked.

"She told me about how Jason was... um, well, very liberal with his words when he felt she had done something wrong. And I caught her with her sleeves rolled up once and saw bruises. Some of them sort of looked like fingers."

Miranda squirmed her arms out from under the blanket and wrapped one hand around her forearm in a demonstration.

"I asked her what they were from," Miranda continued. "And she told me Jason had grabbed her when she tried to walk away during a fight of theirs. It was a heat-of-moment kind of thing, she said. She told me that it only happened once. But her sleeves weren't ever rolled up again, and, well, I'm not stupid. And she once let it slip that he's very paranoid, always worrying about her cheating on him. Apparently, he's always been really suspicious about it because Braxton doesn't look like him. She acts so timidly when Jason's around. I always knew there was a bit of fear there. And the way she always plays the doting wife, the perfect daughter-in-law... I think it all is a sort of survival tactic."

"Do you know where he might have taken her?" Amy asked. "David said they might be on a long vacation or something."

Miranda scoffed so loudly at the idea that Jenn had to shush her.

"A vacation? When they live right by the beach? And unannounced? Please." Miranda wrapped herself up again in her blanket chrysalis before she continued. "Tiffany told me a week or so ago about Daisy. She phrased everything as just suspicions, though, right after your ring reveal. She told me that she had known that Jason was hiding the secret from her all along because she found the marriage certificate in her attic. And then she said that when you came to the Sunday dinner and brought that ring, things were starting to feel weird. I think... well, I think she saw an out with you. And she wanted you to know but she didn't feel comfortable approaching you the way she did with me. She didn't know you well, after all, and she seems to walk a fine line with Jason. It was best for you to come to the conclusion on your own and to feign ignorance as if you stumbled upon it all in the attic. I think she knew it was less risky for her to do that than to outright tell you. At least then she could pretend not to know about it and say the Montgomerys were careless and stashed it there by accident. So, she told me she went into your house and put the certificate in the attic in a little red trunk. Jenn already told me that you found it."

Amy nodded. She could feel her limbs draining of feeling, her entire body seeming to go slack, numb, and cold.

"She said she used to escape to your house when things were tense with Jason before you moved in. And she told me that she went in and left the certificate up there for you to find before she left you a note."

"Yes," Amy said. Her voice sounded incredibly hoarse. "I found the certificate and put it in my sock drawer. Someone stole it, though."

"Jenn told me that, too," Miranda said. "Tiffany also said that Jason was beginning to get even more paranoid since the ring was found. Apparently, he even outright accused her of having Braxton with someone else. I always thought Braxton looked a bit different than Jason but really, I couldn't see her cheating. She would do anything for that man. Even keep his dirty secrets."

We were all silent for a moment. The idea was absurd. Tiffany, who was always so eager to bend herself into whatever shape the Montgomerys wanted her to be in, would not have dared to cheat on Jason; Amy was certain of it.

"Why did Tiffany tell you all of this?" Amy asked.

"I didn't know at the time. It was all very dark and sounded, well, it sounded kind of unhinged if I'm being honest. Unbelievable, at least. She came over one night all disheveled and without wearing any makeup—you know how odd that is for her—and told me all of this. I now see that it was all true. Hindsight is an awful thing. But I think now it's because she needed someone to know in case... well, in case this happened."

Jenn raised her eyebrows while looking at Amy. "Scary stuff, huh?"

Amy gave a slow nod in agreement. "Do you think they'll be back?"

"I know as much as you do about that."

"Do you want to hear something else that's really weird?" Jenn said. "Braxton isn't with them, wherever they went. I saw him in the backyard of 1 Wisteria."

Amy felt like the air had been knocked out of her. She fell back into her seat, unable to hold her taut posture any longer.

"All roads lead back to Lily and Richard," Miranda mumbled.

"He has to know," Amy realized out loud. "Braxton knows something. I would say we should ask him but the chances of us being able to get him alone are so slim."

"Maybe not today, but we could try tomorrow," Miranda suggested.

"Before dinner," Jenn agreed.

"How are we supposed to sneak away?" Miranda asked. "The last time someone broke rank..." She looked at Amy as both of them recalled the time she had sat out on the patio with the Montgomery brothers.

"I can do it," Amy offered. "It makes more sense if it's me. I've already been known to break rank, and I can tell them I'm going to check on Ryder in the playroom."

"Good plan," Jenn said. She took another small sip of her coffee, then added, "Any updates from you?"

"David and I are in a weird place," Amy said. "He's siding with his family."

"Of course," Jenn said with a roll of her eyes.

"And my mom is coming down on Monday. I told her about everything, and she just wants to scope things out. See for herself."

"You two sound close," Miranda said. "I have no one like that to turn to. It's good she'll be coming. Just make sure it all seems subtle when it happens. Wisteria Drive rarely has visitors. Best not to draw too much attention to it."

Amy nodded in agreement and then checked the ornate clock on the wall just above Miranda's head. She had less than ten minutes left in the tight window she had given herself.

"I should get going," Amy said, rising to her feet. "David usually gets up early. I want to get back before he's awake."

"Makes sense," Miranda said. "Matt won't be up for another hour if he wakes up normally."

"Go on, then," Jenn encouraged. "It's better if we don't give them any more suspicions than they already have."

"Call me with any other updates," Amy said. "And thank you, Miranda, for telling us. I know it was probably hard."

Miranda hugged the blanket around her tightly. "Of course," she said with her eyes downcast.

Amy gave them a parting wave and hurried out of Jenn's house, careful to make sure her slides didn't create any excessive noise against the floor.

She rushed back to 4 Wisteria Drive and held her breath. Inside, the lights were still off and only the crisp morning sunlight was beginning to illuminate the furniture. Amy slowed as she walked into the kitchen, her feet tiptoeing so that she moved almost silently across the floor. When she leaned in, she found the kitchen empty. No one was waiting for her to cook breakfast. The ingredients for the omelets that she had left out on the island appeared undisturbed.

Amy let herself breathe out the breath she had been holding in. Her body relaxed only slightly, accepting the small win.

Without hesitance, she got to work chopping the onion and peppers, though she paused frequently, convinced that she had heard someone stirring near the stairs or above her. But no one descended to confront her. So she spent those precious minutes alone straining to hear above the sound of her racing heart and the rhythmic noise of her knife furiously chopping, hoping to hide her brief absence through work.

Chapter 23

If David suspected that Amy was up to something, he didn't show it. In fact, he didn't display much emotion at all that Saturday or Sunday morning. He was like a shell of a person, lost in his own world of thought and recollection.

Amy couldn't say that she minded his sudden distance. It allowed her to navigate the days without tripping over his anger or confronting him about what he had done.

That Saturday was spent doting on Ryder and making sure that he was content after the horrors of the day before. He seemed to bounce back easily enough, and Amy watched him swim in the pool joyfully, jumping into the water in various poses that made the two of them giggle. It could have been a normal day. They could have been a normal family, laughing easily at silly things. But the new information nibbled at Amy all day, remaining present and loud in her mind.

That Sunday evening came in a hurry. She believed she had covered for herself skillfully with laughter, smiles, and food beforehand, yet she could not feign comfort later that Sunday afternoon as dinnertime neared. Every part of her was resisting the impending confrontation that evening. It felt like she was being pushed forward by some invisible hand and shoved in the direction of her worst fears.

She donned a flowy sundress at around three. It was bright yellow and cheery in contrast with how she felt. Amy paired it with white beige shoes that had five-inch heels. It was a pretty outfit, meant to give no sense of distress. But when she looked at her reflection in the mirror as she smoothed on the last strokes of pink lipstick, even she could see the apprehension in her face. The deepened circles under her eyes did nothing to help her look of unease either. Her reflection made it clear that she wouldn't be able to hide her nerves with makeup or nice clothes.

Every step toward 1 Wisteria Drive took all the strength in her. She had to fight the urge to flee with everything that she could muster.

When they stood at the door of Lily and Richard's house, Amy's heart was pounding so hard she feared the family could hear it. She worried that her limbs were visibly shaking and that her face was a shade of ghostly white.

David turned to her as their feet landed on the black welcome mat. "You look nice today," he observed coolly.

It was the first time he had spoken to her all day. All other instances of him speaking had been passive, usually directed at Ryder but meant for her ears.

Amy gave him the best smile she could manage but she could still tell that her grin likely looked tight and ingenuine.

"Thank you," she said.

Ryder, who was standing between the two of them, gave them both a curious look, wondering what had broken his parents' icy demeanor. Amy was questioning it, too.

David pushed open the door, and Amy felt her body stiffen instinctively. The familiar cold of the air conditioning rushed out to meet them, and Amy took a hesitant, wobbly step inside.

As they walked down the long, darkened hallway, the natural split occurred. With practiced knowledge, Ryder fell behind and went into the playroom, where he joined Kayleigh and Braxton, who were already bent over a pile of toys. Amy took careful note of Braxton as she passed, noticing that he seemed to be unscathed and in good spirits.

Amy walked into the kitchen, and David unceremoniously continued without her, heading toward the back porch. Neither of them exchanged any parting words.

As usual, the women were hard at work in the kitchen. Amy entered and was overcome by the scent of seasoned potatoes lingering in the air, pleasant and heavy.

Miranda and Jenn turned to Amy as she entered and gave her similar wide-eyed looks. They were rigid as they tried to communicate something wordlessly with their forceful stares. Amy froze in place, knowing instantly that something was amiss, but she was unable to identify it.

Lily, who was putting a cookie sheet in the oven, turned and said, "Oh, good. You're finally here. Why don't you get to work chopping some of the vegetables? I left them out on the table there."

Amy felt that it was very difficult to move. She was unsure of what to do or how to act as Jenn and Miranda continued to gape at her, waiting impatiently for her to understand something that she had yet to notice. It took her a long moment to process Lily's request and will her legs to walk.

That's when she heard why Miranda and Jenn had looked so startled. From just around the corner, by where the pantry was, a fourth pair of heels clicked closer and closer. Amy felt as if her limbs were made of ice as she waited for the inevitable.

Tiffany turned the corner with her arms full of boxes of pasta. Her face was painted heavily in makeup that was clearly covering some kind of gray discoloration below her left eye. Despite this and the other wives' shock, Tiffany gave Amy a brilliant, broad smile.

"Oh, hi, Amy," she said as if nothing at all was wrong.

Chapter 24

Amy's mouth hung open as she and Tiffany continued to stare at each other. Throughout that seemingly long stretch of time, Tiffany's smile never flinched. Her face seemed tautly pulled into the grin beneath many layers of makeup.

Lily patted Amy on the cheek. "Close your mouth, honey," she said. "You'll collect flies that way."

Lily's brief touch seemed to release her from her paralysis. Amy blinked hard.

"You never answered my texts. Or my calls," Amy said.

"Oh, yeah." Tiffany put down the boxes of pasta, letting them rattle noisily as they fell from her arms. "Sorry about that. Jason and I were on a little getaway."

"Where did you go?" Amy asked.

"Vacation," Lily chimed in. "Off to Texas for the weekend. I'm so jealous. You all know how much I love it there."

"Oh, it was just a quick visit," Tiffany added.

Jenn, who stood just behind Tiffany, gave Amy a bug-eyed look that seemed to underscore her disbelief.

"Yeah," Amy said. Her skepticism was on full display, but she couldn't summon the energy to care. "That was a *very* quick visit."

Tiffany's smile twitched then with the intent to say something. But it was momentary and if Amy had blinked, she would have missed it. But she didn't.

"Amy, honey, can you chop up those vegetables for me?" Lily asked again.

All eyes were on her then. There was no choice but to take up the task.

The worry she had felt during the long hours leading up to visiting 1 Wisteria Drive had been flushed out of her. In its wake, she felt only anger. Tiffany's tight, practiced smile had washed away any doubt in her mind. It was almost worse than if she had still been gone. Fury boiled in Amy's core, dangerous and growing with every moment that no one acknowledged the strangeness of it all.

This anger did not subside when they sat down for dinner. She had forgone confronting Braxton, deciding that there was no point in putting herself under scrutiny to ask a child questions about his mom when Tiffany was already standing before her. Miranda and Jenn did not seem to mind this decision. In fact, they hadn't seemed to notice at all. They were too focused on Tiffany, watching her every move with analytical precision.

As the Montgomerys filed into the dining room, Amy's eyes fell on Jason. His demanding, broad figure loomed large in the room. Amy saw then, for the first time, just how bitter he appeared. There seemed to be a permanent scowl on his face as if he were eternally disillusioned. His every feature made Amy's stomach churn with a mixture of disgust and fear.

The Montgomerys sat down to eat, falling into their seats in a uniform cascade.

When everyone was seated, Tiffany announced in a candy-sweet voice, "I'd like to say grace tonight."

Amy almost scoffed. The act was perfect. Jason gave an approving smile that sent a rush of revulsion through Amy.

She joined hands with David, feeling his cool palm. His face was stony and emotionless beside her. Jenn's hands, by comparison, were warm and sweaty. Jenn was visibly alarmed, showing great effort to hold herself together.

As Tiffany began to speak that familiar prayer, Amy watched as everyone along the table bowed in unison. Five red and eight brunette heads dipped as Amy kept her own up to watch Tiffany with critical eyes. There was not a stutter or moment of hesitance. Again, she was perfect.

Amy sat tense in her chair, too outraged to eat. It was all so classically Montgomery. Something was seriously wrong and while they all knew it, no one would openly acknowledge it. They were complicit in their own turmoil.

Jenn kept shooting glances at her that were far from subtle, urging her to at least feign normalcy. But Amy couldn't. The idea of putting up the act again was so nonsensical it infuriated her.

Richard noticed Amy's untouched plate and pointed his fork at her. "Don't you like my wife's cooking?" he asked.

"I just haven't been eating much. Or sleeping," Amy said. She could feel herself snapping, liberating herself from wanting to please them like a bird squirming between the bars of its cage.

There was a smile on Richard's face that seemed to suggest that he already knew. "Why's that?"

Amy felt David squeeze her leg under the table. A warning. She moved her leg away from him and said, "Oh, you know. We had a break-in. Things were stolen from us. From me. Out of my sock drawer."

"Is that so?" Richard did not look surprised. Instead, he only seemed mildly annoyed as though he was displeased that she would bring up the topic so brazenly.

"Yes." Amy straightened. There was no going back. Jenn had put down her fork and angled her body toward her. Miranda's eyes flickered between her and Richard rapidly. "Someone stole the ring from the beach. And a marriage certificate."

Tiffany's eyes were trained forward. Her face had fallen, and that taut smile was finally gone. Jason put down his fork and squared his shoulders, his face a strange mixture of raw anger and shock.

"I took them," a voice piped up from the other end of the table. Amy whipped around to see Lily as she took a casual sip from her glass of water.

"Why?" She couldn't believe how nonchalantly it had been admitted. There had been no pushing or probing. Lily had folded without hesitance.

"Anything in the homes *we* purchased is fair game, I should think. And Richard told me that he heard from David that you still had the ring. You know, the one that you promised Kayleigh you would sell. I took the liberty of pawning it myself. And I was going to surprise Kayleigh with the money after dinner."

Amy could barely process what she was hearing. "And the certificate?" she asked.

Lily shrugged. "There's no need to worry about the past, dear."

Amy felt her mouth fall open once more. She looked to David, expecting him to reflect how she felt, to express the shock of the moment, yet his eyes were trained ahead of him, not looking at anyone or anything in particular, but his face had drained of any color. Something about his expression, lacking any surprise or awe, solidified a feeling. Jenn was right. He knew more than he had let on.

Amy felt her eyes narrow into accusatory slits. "What did you *do* to her?"

Lily tittered, a small bout of laughter that sounded very polite in comparison to the situation. "Why must you worry so much about what is already done? You'll get wrinkles from all of that stress. It's not worth it, believe me."

The way she danced around the subject so unabashedly, refusing to even hint at what truly happened to Daisy, made Amy clench her fists.

She looked at Jason, who had not moved in the slightest since the beginning of the conversation. Beside him, Tiffany had begun to silently cry, soundless tears spilling down her cheeks in faint rivers.

"Jason," Amy said. "Where is Daisy?"

He turned to her slowly. His eyes were fiery, alight with an anger Amy had never seen in anyone before, not even in David when he was at his most volatile. The look was primal and unrefined as if beneath his skin he was boiling over with rage that he couldn't hide. It made Amy sit back in her seat slightly, taking away some of her confidence momentarily.

"Why do you care?" he said through gritted teeth.

Tiffany choked on a sob loudly behind him. The sound of her crying was so sharp against the tense, relative quiet that it was startling. Jason, still looking at Amy, seemed passingly annoyed by it.

"You people did something," Amy said. Her voice was loud, louder than she had wanted it to be, but she couldn't help it. "You did something awful, and you won't admit to it."

It was dangerous to hurl such an accusation out there. Somehow, though, Amy wasn't too concerned about the consequences. She knew what she said had truth to it, though to what degree, she was unsure.

This was it. Amy could feel it in the air. This was final.

"You're being hysterical," Richard said, still pointing at her with his fork for emphasis. "There is no need for you to be so emotional right now."

"There isn't?" Amy laughed madly, throwing her head back and letting the hysterics rise from her throat, uncaring. "Ryder, come here."

Amy stood, sending her chair backward noisily, and held out her hand for Ryder to grab. He looked at her for a long moment, visibly weighing up whether to stand or not. For a brief second, Amy thought that he might not come to her side. But then he rose and walked slowly over to his mother, taking her hand in his.

"We're leaving," Amy announced. She bent forward and picked Ryder up. Despite his weight, she turned and walked quickly, a sense of adrenaline guiding her feet, encouraging her to move faster and not look behind her.

She heard another chair move and a bolt of fear shot through her as she imagined Jason rising to grab her in his unyielding grip. But the footsteps clicked against the floor in the familiar sound of high heels, and she felt her shoulders relax slightly.

"David," she heard Richard say from back at the table. "Go get your wife. Talk some sense into her, damn it!"

The sound of his order only made Amy walk faster. She was almost jogging away, flying as quickly as her heeled feet were able to carry her. When she came to the front door, she struggled to open it with Ryder in her arms. Jenn caught up to her then and opened it for her. Seeing her rush to her side made Amy want to cry. Jenn was a true ally after all.

As the three of them quickly left, she heard another person following not far behind them whose footfalls were heavy and solid. She knew it was David stalking behind her and felt nothing but nearly crippling fear at the realization. He was a Montgomery, after all, and he would always do what his father told him to. The alarming sense of terror that zipped throughout her body kept her eyes forward and her feet moving fast enough to keep a good distance between the three of them and David until they were back inside their house.

Inside 4 Wisteria Drive, she put Ryder down on the marble floor.

"Mommy, what's going on?" he asked.

Amy looked at him and saw his panic and confusion. Her heart broke all over again as she kneeled in front of him. "We're leaving. We're moving away," Amy told him. "I'm getting some belongings, and we're leaving."

She wasn't sure how. If she had to call for an Uber, she would wait with her son behind a locked door. It felt like her mind was working too slowly for how quickly things were developing.

"I'll drive," Jenn said, saving her from the possibility of a wait. "I can't be here."

Jenn shook her head rapidly as if trying to physically shake the thought from her mind. Amy saw then that she had tears in her eyes.

"It sounds like they got rid of her," Amy whispered.

Jenn bit her lip. "David's coming. What are we going to do?"

Amy reached up to lock the door and eliminate any possibility of a confrontation, but right at the moment she did, David threw the door open, hitting Amy unintentionally in its wake.

Chapter 25

David's breathing was labored. Amy could hear it before she even saw him, and whether it was from exertion or anger, she was not sure. All she was aware of was that he was panting like a fabled beast, and when she allowed her eyes to rise and meet his, she noticed that his posture was tight and domineering.

Amy rubbed her right hip, which had been hit by the door as he burst in. When David's eyes fell on her, she felt fear rip through her in a torrent. But she stood, despite herself, hoping to appear stronger than she felt.

"Amy," David began.

She held up a hand to stop him and then turned to Jenn. "Take Ryder upstairs and help him pack what he needs." She didn't want Ryder to witness another fight.

Jenn gave her a wide-eyed nod and grabbed Ryder by the hand. Ryder began to cry.

"Pack? Why are you packing?" David asked.

"What do you *mean* 'why am I packing?'" It was taking great effort for her to control her voice. She wanted Ryder out of earshot before she let David have it.

"Amy, where are you supposed to go?"

"Wouldn't you like to know?" Amy found herself walking deeper into the house. She wasn't sure why she was walking further from the door, from her escape, but she found her feet thinking for her again. David followed her.

"Yes, I would actually," he said. "I'd like to know where you're taking our son."

Amy snapped her head around to look at him in the eyes. "Far from here."

"Amy, you can't just take our son somewhere without telling his father," he said. His voice was almost pleading.

"What did they do to her, David?" she asked.

David stopped walking. He looked stunned as though he was surprised she would even ask him.

They were in the kitchen, the dying shreds of daylight streaming into the room and lighting the house in a gray hue. Everything felt eerie, unnatural, and utterly definitive.

"Amy... You're being hysterical," David said.

"That's not an answer."

"Amy... come here..."

He lunged forward, meaning to grab her and take her... where?

Her body worked in reflex. She pulled a knife from the knife block and held it out in front of her.

David's eyes popped wide. Amy imagined that so did her own.

"What the fuck?" David was holding his hands up defensively.

"Don't come near me," Amy said, and her voice sounded shaky, even in her own ears. "Where is Daisy?"

David looked to her, then to the knife, then to her again. The moment felt long between them, seeming to stretch into months and years.

"She's at the bottom of the ocean."

Amy felt the strength in her momentarily fail. The knife dipped in her hand before she corrected it upright again.

"Why?"

"She was a cheat," David said. "Jason found out. It was an accident. He got carried away. You were never supposed to know. The ring must've washed up or it might've slipped off when we were moving her. I don't know, but Amy, it was never supposed to happen."

All of her fears were coming true, being realized in front of her. It was a surreal moment. Amy felt tears spring unbidden to her eyes. Her voice was laden with emotion, wavering with terror.

"You lied," she stated.

"I didn't want to," David said. He put his hand on his chest, just above his heart. "I swear. It was never my intention. You weren't ever supposed to know."

"That you were covering for your brother? Your murdering brother?" Amy took a step forward, brandishing the knife. David took a step back to even out the distance between them, returning both his hands to the air.

"How long did you know?" she asked.

"Amy..."

"The truth!" she yelled. "I want the truth for once!"

"I knew when it happened. My dad called me and Tyler back. Dad took us to get rid of her, and Mom stayed back to clear out her things. We all... except for my mom..."

Amy felt her chest rack with a sob at the realization. "You're just as bad as him," she choked out.

Her husband, the creative, his eyes trained on a bright future. David, who loved clothes and color coordination and playing catch with their son on sunny afternoons. The man who had met her at a crowded, sticky bar and wooed her with discussions about feminism and culture and talks of love and children.

Yet David was none of those things. Those attributes had been an act just like Tiffany with her trained smiles. Practiced. Calculated.

He had plucked her from a crowd, a replica of every other Montgomery woman. Dyed red hair, thin, short, and white. A reflection of his mother.

Amy couldn't drive. She hadn't seen the world beyond the concrete confines of Charlotte.

She had been perfect. Just like Jenn, and just like Miranda and Tiffany – blank canvases ready to be lifted out of their backgrounds and painted in the image of Lily Montgomery.

Amy sobbed, the knife shaking in her hand, uncertain about what to do next. These thoughts and realizations rushed toward her at a blinding and painful speed.

"I didn't want to do it, Amy," David pleaded, staring at the blade instead of her face. "You know I didn't. You know me. They're family. We love each other. We protect each other. Please, you have to understand."

"But you did do it," Amy said, trying to steel herself. "And the five of you were clumsy. You fucked up. You were complacent. You might as well have killed her, too."

"Don't say that." David choked on the words. Was this an act as well?

"And you lied," Amy continued. Tears were running into her mouth, hot and salty. "You were too much of a coward to suffer the consequences. The five of you were too worried about how it would look to let Jason take the fall."

Amy took another step forward. The hallway was at a running distance away now. But where were Jenn and Ryder? It dawned on her then that she didn't have a phone. It was sitting in her purse at 1 Wisteria Drive.

She watched David carefully and saw tears roll down his cheeks. It didn't make her feel any pity, though. She only felt disgust.

"My son can't grow up here," Amy said. "I'd kill myself before I let you raise him."

She broke out into a run with the knife still clutched in a grip that turned her knuckles white.

Amy heard David's feet fall heavy and sure not far behind her.

"JENN!" she screamed. "GET TO THE CAR!"

She wasn't sure if she would make it in time. There were no thoughts in her head, only fear and adrenaline driving her to keep going.

Amy ran out the front door, tearing across the lawn. She was vaguely aware of the way her dress was billowing behind her, carried by the wind like a cape. Every moment between heartbeats felt like an eternity.

And then she was falling.

She felt her body being pushed forward, and she was vaguely aware that she had been met with a great force from behind. Amy fought the instinct to splay out both of her hands as she went down so that she could maintain her grip on the knife.

Amy hit the ground with her arms spread out overhead. The impact nearly knocked all the air from her, and Amy gasped in a painful breath. She felt David fall onto her lower back, and she managed a small groan under his weight.

He was reaching for the knife, clawing up her arm to get at it. She squirmed beneath his weight, finding it difficult to breathe but she continued to fight with what little energy and strength she could muster. Only one thing was certain to her in that moment: If he got the knife, there was nothing stopping him from killing her.

Those seconds where they wrestled on the ground felt like they could have been hours, but it was all happening as quickly as eye blinks. In a quick decision, she pulled herself forward by clawing her fingers into the grass, crying out as she did so at the exertion it took to crawl out from beneath him. As she moved, she attempted to keep her right arm as straight as possible, making the effort seem even clumsier. Only part of her torso had been freed, and Amy felt David begin to fill the gap.

She hoisted herself forward once more, putting more distance between David and the knife, even if it was only momentary.

And then she saw Jenn and Ryder from the corner of her eye. They were running down the street, toward Jenn's house, both of their arms filled with stuffed bags. Amy watched for a mere second as they ran toward Jenn's car. She had bought them enough time. Even if she died there, in the middle of the front lawn of 4 Wisteria Drive with a knife buried in her back, her son would be free. Jenn would make sure that Ryder got away.

But Amy wanted to be with him.

Amy writhed beneath David desperately. She felt him grab at her dress, trying to seize enough fabric to pin her in place. She kicked wildly.

"You stupid bitch!" David yelled. "Give it!"

She heard the car start just yards from her. It purred to life in the distance, the sound barely audible over their struggle. But she was certain she had heard it.

David had heard it, too.

She felt his body stiffen and knew that he was looking at 5 Wisteria Drive.

Amy took the moment's hesitation as an opportunity. She kicked three times as hard as she could, hoping that her heeled shoe would deliver more damage. The last kick connected with something hard that made David groan in pain. She liked to imagine that it was his face, though she couldn't be certain.

As he recovered, she crawled out from beneath him entirely and got to her feet. She had lost both shoes in the struggle and ran across the lawn with bare feet pounding the earth.

She ran toward the car, which loitered in the driveway, waiting for her. Amy didn't dare look back. She couldn't waste time looking anywhere but ahead of her, and she feared that if she turned around, she would see David inches away, closing the distance.

It was there.

Right in front of her.

The car was a metal salvation, waiting for her and gleaming with promise in the dying light.

Amy ran around to the passenger's seat which she found flung open for her. She dove inward and ripped the door shut behind her with a slam. Amy heard Jenn lock the car as soon as the door connected.

David had only been seconds behind her. He threw his body against the closed car door, making Ryder scream. Amy looked at his face in horror as Jenn put the car in reverse.

David's skin was beet red, and his eyes were wild, enraged like an angered animal. The look in them was so alien to her that David seemed like a completely different man at that moment. He was a stranger to her. But maybe he always had been.

As the car sent the three of them backward, he screamed at them, his voice tearing with frustration.

"How dare you? How dare you take my son, Amy? Fuck you! FUCK YOU!"

Amy wanted to look away but couldn't. This rage was unlike anything she had ever seen in him before, even in the midst of those heated fights that had made her shrink beneath his fury. This was who he really was. He was so fascinatingly unfamiliar to her that it was almost hypnotic.

Jenn sped down Wisteria Drive, hitting the brakes so hard at the gate that the three of them were sent painfully forward against their suddenly taut seatbelts. Jenn whimpered as she rolled down the window to punch in the code, seeing David running down the street behind them in the rearview mirror.

For a moment Amy feared that the gate wouldn't open for them. She considered the possibility that one of the Montgomerys might have denied access to anyone leaving, trapping them inside. But when Jenn finished punching in the number, the gate opened dutifully. Jenn rolled up her window immediately and waited for the gate to peel open as David continued his pursuit.

When the gate was open just enough to slip through, Jenn sped out so quickly that it sent Amy against the back of her seat. Jenn clipped the gate in her haste, scraping the side of the car in a grating, metallic crunch. She drove wildly out of Wisteria Drive, speeding down the winding strip of road with her eyes frantically focused on the stretch of asphalt before her.

Amy looked in the side mirror, seeing David for a moment standing within the gateway, breathless and stunned. Wisteria Drive grew more and more distant with each second, fading from view until Jenn turned the corner and it disappeared entirely.

Only when that wretched iron gate was out of view did Amy finally let the knife clatter to the ground.

Chapter 26

They drove for almost half an hour in silence. Amy and Jenn continuously glanced at the mirrors as if they both shared the same nervous habit, and Amy's heart jumped each time there was a car behind them, regardless of the make and model, hoping that it wasn't one of the Montgomerys following them. They never did appear in the rearview mirror, and Amy wasn't sure if that observation should make her feel relieved or even more worried.

After they were both certain they were free, Amy admitted that she didn't have her cell phone in a weary voice.

"I have mine," Jenn announced. "But I don't have my wallet. We're shit out of luck there."

"Can I see your phone? My mom was coming down tomorrow morning, remember? She can meet up with us."

Jenn reached over to hand Amy her phone. It shook unsteadily as she held it out.

"We can pull over if you want," Amy suggested. "I think we should be fine now."

Jenn shook her head violently. "No. I need to get as far away from that place as possible."

Amy didn't argue. She understood.

Amy punched in her mom's number, a string of ten digits that was so familiar to her that it was engraved in her memory. She caught herself holding her breath as it rang, hoping her mom would answer the unknown number.

Emily picked up on the fourth ring.

"Hello?" her mom asked.

Emily's voice sent a wave of relief through her. "Mom, it's me." Amy's voice cracked as fresh tears began to brim in her eyes.

"Amy?" Emily sounded suspicious. "Why are you calling me from this number?"

Amy sighed out a shaky breath. "It's a long story, Mom. We can't be there anymore. We left. We escaped."

The words tasted strange on her tongue. She still was in awe that it had even happened, and the realization that it indeed had been a real experience and not a dream had yet to completely set in.

"Who's we?"

"Jenn, Ryder, and me. I—" Amy's words were cut off as she was overcome by the memory, fresh in her head. She could still feel David's weight holding her down and the fear in her chest that she might die on the grass for her son and all of the Montgomerys to see. "I almost didn't make it."

"Amy... I'm getting in my car now. Where are you at?"

"I don't know," Amy admitted. She was openly crying by then, unable to contain it any longer. She heard Jenn sniff beside her and knew that she felt the same. "We don't have a wallet so we can't drive all the way to you. We don't have gas money, and we can't afford a hotel."

"Jesus, Amy," Emily said. "I'll drive down toward you, and we'll meet somewhere. Try stopping at some point in Georgia or close even South Carolina if you can. And text me every hour where you are so that I know you're ok."

"Ok, Mom," Amy said quietly. "I love you so much. I really thought—"

"I know. Don't even say it. Just get to me." Amy was horrified to hear her mom's voice sounding strained too. "I love you."

"I love you, too." Amy hung up and shivered.

"I can't believe that happened," Jenn mumbled mostly to herself.

"Ryder, are you ok?" Amy asked, turning back in her seat for the first time. She couldn't bring herself to do it earlier and see his face swollen with fear.

Ryder sat stunned in his seat. His eyes were puffy and red from crying, too. "Why did Daddy act that way?" he asked softly.

"Daddy... Daddy isn't who I thought he was. He's not a good person." Amy wiped away a tear from her cheek as she spoke those realizations into the world. Perhaps it was hard for her young son to hear but he needed to know the truth. They both had had enough lies for a lifetime.

"He's a bad guy?"

Amy nodded, unable to say the words herself.

"Like Lex Luthor?"

Amy gave him a small smile. "Yeah, sort of."

She wondered how much he had seen. Had Ryder watched the lengthy, violent struggle on the lawn, or had he just glimpsed it?

Amy turned back around. She found that she couldn't focus on and sort through what he had or hadn't seen. Not now. Not when everything was so fresh.

They drove without speaking for another ten minutes. Jenn's phone had never connected to Bluetooth, so nothing but the wind rushing past the car filled the quiet. Around them, the sky was fading into navy as the night settled in. Jenn flicked on the headlights to guide them before she spoke again.

"What happened?" she asked. Her voice was so low it was almost a whisper.

"He told me everything," Amy said. "They knew. They all did. This whole time. And all the boys they…" Amy looked back at Ryder, who was staring out the window. Still, she whispered the rest. "They threw her in the ocean."

Jenn gasped and her face twisted into a painful contortion as she began to cry again. It was an ugly sadness and one that Amy had been feeling the entire car ride. Jenn took in a staggering gulp of air and then slammed her palm into the steering wheel repeatedly. "I knew it! I fucking knew it!"

She swerved, almost cutting into the opposing lane of traffic, and was met with a chorus of honks.

"Fuck." Jenn sniffled.

"We can pull over if you want," Amy suggested again, hoping Jenn would oblige this time.

Instead, Jenn asked, "Why?"

"Why what?" The question applied to any number of instances.

"Why did he do it? Jason? And then the boys?"

"David said… Jason lost his temper after he learned she had cheated on him."

"Bullshit."

"And he said everyone covered it up to… to protect the family."

"Assholes," she hissed.

"We're good now," Amy said. "We're free now." She wasn't sure if she was trying to comfort Jenn or herself.

"Miranda and Tiffany aren't," Jenn said. "Tiffany… I don't even want to imagine what tonight is going to be like for her. With Jason being as paranoid as he was… and now…" She shook her head. "And those kids. Kayleigh and Braxton. Those poor kids."

"I know." Amy hadn't let herself think about the people they had left behind until then. But now that she had allowed herself to imagine it, it was like a faucet that couldn't be turned off.

She had no idea how Miranda would navigate the situation with Matt. Would they argue? Shout? Fight? Would Matt fold and tell her too? And if so, how would she react to the full truth?

Tiffany didn't stand a chance if Jason turned his shock into violence again. Amy thought of Braxton, who had undoubtedly seen horrors in that home, witnessing whatever was occurring back at Wisteria Drive with his young, impressionable eyes.

"We should go back to them," Jenn said. "Eventually. Not now, obviously. But... I can't bear the thought of them with those *people.*"

"Once we get our bearings," Amy agreed.

"Where are we meeting your mom?" Jenn finally asked. Amy saw that her knuckles were pale as she gripped the steering wheel.

"Georgia," Amy answered. "Or as close as we can get to South Carolina. Basically, as far north as we can get before we run out of gas."

Jenn nodded her understanding. "Get ready for a long night."

Amy gave Ryder a glance and saw that he was slumped in his seat, his head lulling to the side. His eyes were half-open, with one foot in sleep and the other trying to hold him awake. She was pleased to see that he had relaxed enough to succumb to his fatigue. It had been an eventful day for him, to say the least. She only hoped that he hadn't heard and understood their discussion about David just minutes before.

Amy returned her gaze ahead and looked at the highway in front of her. It seemed to stretch on forever in one long, endless snake of grayed asphalt. She knew that she would be staring at a similar scene for hours, and with the little sleep she had gotten the night before, a part of her feared that she would grow weary as the world continued to darken. At that moment, though, she was wide awake.

Chapter 27

I t took over four hours for them to finally pull over. They had made it to just outside of Atlanta, Georgia, where Emily was waiting patiently for them to arrive. The gas light on the dashboard had turned on. Both of them kept repeating how grateful and lucky they were that they had escaped in a car with a nearly full tank.

Amy felt tiredness gnawing at her, but the fright she still felt kept her up, like there was a battle between her sleepiness and the anxiety raging within her.

Somewhere near their third hour of driving, Jenn's phone lit up with an incoming call from Tyler. The two of them had sucked in a sharp breath and held it as they waited for the call to ring out. When her phone finally went dark again, they wordlessly awaited his voicemail, but it never came. He never called her again. It was then that Amy finally thought to stop sharing Jenn's phone location with everyone in the family. She hoped even this rather late decision would save them in the long term. The rest of the ride was filled with little conversation, and Amy was itching to get out of the car.

Amy called Emily as they neared Atlanta to let her know that they were almost there. Emily said that she had sped the entire drive and was waiting for them in a parking lot, and with equally tired voices, they promised to see each other soon. When she hung up, Amy felt a brief flush of solace. With her mother just minutes from her, she finally felt as if she was truly out of the Montgomerys' reach.

Jenn steered the car into a McDonald's parking lot at around one in the morning. The golden arches lit the area around them with an artificial glow. Despite being in a nearly vacant parking lot so late at night, Amy felt more comfortable beneath the aggressive yellow lighting than she had felt in the weeks on Wisteria Drive beneath the warm sun.

Emily's car was parked at the far end of the lot. She had kept the headlights on to signal where she was, but Amy would've recognized that beat-up Honda anywhere.

Jenn pulled into the spot next to the Honda, putting the car in park for the first time in hours. Behind her, Ryder moaned in protest as the abrupt halting of the car seemed to shake him from sleep.

"It's time to get up, buddy," Amy told him in a soft voice. "Grandma is here. We're safe now."

Ryder blinked his heavily lidded eyes and, to no one in particular, asked, "Grandma?"

Amy got out of the car, feeling a strange sensation in her legs as she used them for the first time since they had left Wisteria Drive. She still was barefoot, and the pavement beneath her exposed feet was almost cold at that hour. The pebbles scattered about made her wince when she stepped on them.

Emily got out of her car too. She came around to the other side, her long red hair fluttering in the gentle breeze. Her blue eyes were gaping and fearful, taking in the image of her disheveled daughter.

She didn't say anything. Emily only strode over to Amy and pulled her into her arms, letting Amy feel small again. They stood like that for a moment, utterly speechless, as Amy felt tears prick her eyes once more. She had done so much crying that evening that she felt hollow and drained of all energy.

There was a cacophony of emotions swirling through her, but most of all she felt shame. It felt as though she had reached for the stars with David and had fallen flat on her face. In the process, she had left her mother behind as well as a life that she had admittedly loved. In the end, she had needed to run away from that false image of perfection straight back into her mother's arms. There was a sense of failure there that she couldn't shake.

When Emily finally pulled away, she gave her daughter another look over.

Finally, she said, "What happened to your shoes?"

Amy looked down and wiggled her polished toes against the unkempt pavement. "It's a long story."

Emily nodded curtly, not wanting to push. "Luckily for you, we have a long drive ahead of us."

Jenn got out of the car then. She went around to the other side, unhooked Ryder, and carried him, half-asleep, toward Emily's car.

"It's nice to meet you," Jenn said softly to Emily. "I wish it had been under different circumstances."

Emily looked at Jenn's appearance. She was so well-kept when compared to Amy, and she was still dressed beautifully in a sundress that looked as if it cost two months' worth of Emily's rent. It was clear that Emily had not expected Amy's companion to look so pretty or so well-off in comparison.

Emily kissed Ryder on his cheek and then gave Jenn a gentle, sad smile. "Thank you for saving them."

Jenn's eyes looked glassy as she gave a little nod. "Of course."

Without another word, she went to Emily's car to put Ryder down.

The three of them worked quickly and without speaking. They unpacked the meager belongings from Jenn's Mercedes-Benz and threw them haphazardly into Emily's Honda. It seemed that most of what had been packed were clothes and toys for Ryder. Amy was grateful for that. She knew that Emily still kept a few miscellaneous articles of clothing from Amy's teen years in her apartment. Amy and Jenn could live in old band T-shirts for a bit.

They gave the car one final sweep to make sure that it was entirely cleared. Jenn had taken everything from it, stripping it bare of its aux cord and hand sanitizer as well. The last thing left in there was the knife lying on the passenger's side floor. Amy held it up, watching it glow against the yellow McDonald's light. For the first time, she noticed that it was a serrated bread knife. She emitted a small, breathy laugh.

Emily watched her retrieve the knife without uttering a word but pursed her lips knowing that she would be told the full story soon.

"I think that's everything," Jenn said. The wind had picked up, making the skirt of her dress flutter around her knees.

"Are you planning to just leave the car here?" Emily asked.

"Oh, yeah," Jenn said. "With the keys in it, too. Hopefully, someone will take it. It's Tyler's anyway and—excuse my language—fuck him. I don't want anything to do with it now. I'd rather someone else get some use out of it." She opened the driver's side door and put the keys on the seat. "And, not to darken the mood, but I'm sure the Montgomerys have connections, you know. This car will probably be tracked. We'll talk about all of that stuff later."

Amy was glad they postponed the discussion. As she allowed herself to relax in the presence of her mom, she was beginning to feel the full force of her exhaustion.

The three of them boarded the Honda. Emily had owned the car since Amy was in college, and within its doors, there was a sense of home. Even the faint smell of fast food and dusty floors had a quaint appeal to them.

They pulled out of the McDonald's parking lot sometime after three in the morning, and they were back on the highway again shortly afterward.

Amy stared out at the neon signs and the bright billboards plastered along the highway that whipped past them as they plunged forward toward Charlotte. Toward home. She had had every intention to tell Emily what had happened, but by the time they were on the road for fifteen minutes, her eyelids began to droop and feel heavy. Finally, they closed, and Amy fell asleep.

Chapter 28

Jenn had been unable to sleep and told Emily everything while Amy was out. When Amy came to, they were pulling into the apartment parking garage. She knew that they were there by the way the car shook when they passed over the familiar speed bump her mom had driven over a million times before. As soon as Emily drove over it, Amy knew that they were finally home.

"Did I miss anything?" Amy asked, her voice still groggy with sleep.

"Jenn just filled me in," Emily said. "I'm glad you're back, Amy."

"Me too."

Throughout the elevator up to the fifth floor, the cold sensation of the tiles under her bare feet shocked Amy's senses. Ryder ran down the hall when the elevator doors slid open, tearing toward Emily's apartment as fast as his little legs would take him. He ran that boyish run he always did when he was excited, and the sight made Jenn smile in Amy's direction.

The apartment was almost exactly how she had left it, though it was missing a few pieces that Amy had taken with her to Wisteria Drive. The blender on the counter that David had always said made the best, smoothest smoothies and the coffee maker that Emily had gifted to her as a hand-me-down going-away present were hundreds of miles away now. But other than those few items, the apartment looked the same, as if it had been frozen in time and they were walking through a photograph. The sight of the same furniture and décor she had grown up with made Amy grin softly to herself.

They spilled Ryder's toys out onto the floor in the tiny guest bedroom that Amy had grown up in and cracked the door open to hear him as the three women gathered in the living room. The sofa was a well-worn old thing colored in a sun-stained beige. Against her bare thighs, the material was rather scratchy from age and use. Amy noticed Jenn pulling down the skirt of her dress to create a fabric barrier between her and the couch.

"I won't lie to you girls," Emily began. "You're both in a mess."

It reminded Amy of the way her mom used to chastise her as a child in her calm, measured voice.

"At least we're out," Jenn offered. "I keep thinking about Tiffany and Miranda and Braxton and Kayleigh."

"Me too," Amy said.

"I can't imagine what they're going through. Truly, it must be horrible. But right now, you need to focus on you two. Your game plan. It might seem selfish, but we have to think about ourselves right now. David knows where my apartment is. He also knows it's likely where you ran to."

Amy knew Emily was right. She began to chew at the nail of her pointer finger nervously. Her thumbnails were all but nibbled into nonexistence over the past few weeks.

"I don't have anywhere else to go," Jenn admitted. "I don't have family who still talk to me. Even my sister cut me off a little after I moved to Wisteria Drive with Tyler. Things were starting to get rough between us before I moved but when I married Tyler and went to Florida, she stopped talking to me entirely. And my parents are out of the question."

Jenn had never seemed as fragile or vulnerable as she did then. She had always given off the impression that she was so sure of herself, radiating confidence with each stride and smile. But she was just a woman, one who had been tricked and used just like the rest of the Montgomery women had been.

"This is about all I have to offer," Emily said gesturing around at the small apartment. "And unless Amy has some property I don't know about, this is it."

"Do you think they'll come for us?" Amy asked. It seemed like such a strange assumption that they would be tracked down like prey. But then again, what had happened to Daisy had seemed like a strange assumption only a handful of days ago.

"Look, I'll be frank with you," Emily said. "I don't see them *not* trying something. You both know about a murder and cover-up. Amy, you ran away with David's son. Jenn, you're carrying Tyler's baby. You also stole Tyler's car in your escape. They have every right to seek you out and many opportunities to legally pursue you. Unless you have some pull with the public or the police that you're hiding, they still have the upper hand."

"And we can't prove anything about Daisy," Amy stated. It was something that had nagged at her the entire ride to the McDonald's parking lot, yet she hadn't wanted to speak it into the world with the tensions in Jenn's car being so high already. There was no evidence they could physically hand over that would prove what they knew. There was only the marriage certificate that was likely burnt or otherwise disposed of; the ring that had been pawned off and was no longer on the beach to link Daisy to that location; confessions that hadn't been taped; and a body that had long since been swallowed by the ocean. Simply speaking, they had nothing.

"What if we got one of them to confess?" Jenn said quietly.

"What are you suggesting?" Amy asked.

"I'm saying, what if one of us calls one of the boys and gets a confession out of them?" Jenn said.

"David would never say it again," Amy said. She remembered the look on his face as he laid the truth bare to her. He had been so momentarily unguarded and distraught, pleading for her to understand his side even when it seemed that he himself didn't fully believe it.

"I mean, I could try. Tyler has never been the brightest out of the four of them if we're being honest," Jenn said. Her skin was colorless as she suggested it.

"I doubt he would be willing to over a call," Emily said. "He would be suspicious, especially when you ignored his call on the way here. Not sure that would hold up in court either. It's a two-party consent state."

The three of them were silent for a long moment, turning over desperate, dead-end thoughts until Jenn breathed, "The cameras."

Emily's brow creased. "What cameras?"

"Jenn put up cameras in her house," Amy answered, straightening.

"The kitchens, the living room, the office. They all have indoor cameras," Jenn said.

"And Tyler knows about them?" Emily asked.

Jenn nodded. Her eyes were wide. "I have a clip saved of him waving at the one in the kitchen from when we first got them. That's how we have to do it. We get them to confess on one of the cameras. He knows they're there so he would have to know he's being recorded. We need him to confess in front of one of them."

"Are you saying we should go back?" Amy asked in disbelief.

"I'm only telling you that if you really want to go about pinning them for this, your best bet is to confront Tyler in person," Emily said.

There was a well of silence among them as they considered this. Emily was right, of course, but the prospect of returning to Wisteria Drive and putting Jenn at risk on the off chance that Tyler decided to come clean felt like a massive stretch.

"I could try it," Jenn finally said. "I don't like the idea of Tiffany being there with Jason. I feel like we need to go back with a plan and finish this."

"And if you saved a clip from one of the cameras, I think it would work," Emily mused.

"Jenn…" Amy began.

"No, I mean think about it. If I go missing after you know I went back there, they will open an investigation into my whereabouts the minute you report it. Nothing kicks up a media frenzy quite like a white pregnant woman."

"It's so risky," Amy said. She found herself grabbing Jenn's thin hands. She felt the cool sensation of her gold jewelry and the quick jab of her engagement ring. "We can't risk the possibility of them getting away with another Daisy. And I can't risk losing you."

"I won't be another Daisy," Jenn said. "And neither will Tiffany. Not with you on the outside waiting to report it all."

"This is so needlessly noble, Jenn," Amy groaned.

"What other choice do we have, though?" Jenn made a clipped, exasperated laugh. "I mean, really. It's like your mom said. They know where we are. If we can't get them locked away or something, we could spend the rest of our lives being hunted."

Amy closed her eyes and sighed. Jenn was right. "How are you even supposed to get out of there once you're in?" Amy asked. Behind those gates, she was as good as caged.

They spent the next few hours planning. It was late in the afternoon before they agreed to take a break for Amy to make Ryder a sandwich and to eat for themselves. The plan they had devised still felt flimsy, rather intricate, and based on the assumption of many hypotheticals, but it was the best one they had.

Around seven in the evening, Amy finally let herself fall asleep again, feeling her body start to shut down under her exhaustion. When she finally tucked herself into her childhood bed, snuggled beneath the floral-patterned linen sheets of her teenage years, she slept for twelve hours.

Chapter 29

Amy dressed in an old T-shirt she had made for her high school's Christmas dodgeball tournament. She donned a pair of worn shorts to match that was tight at the waist and a pair of her mom's tennis shoes that were a size too large. It was an ugly outfit of mismatched, discarded elements, but Amy was happy to be free of that wretched sundress. It held too many memories.

Jenn, however, had to continue wearing her dress, but not for lack of hand-me-downs. She had been relieved to take a shower, at least, and freshen up with Emily's few drugstore makeup options. She stuffed her fully charged phone into the deep pockets of her dress.

"I can't believe we're about to make that drive again," she said to Amy.

"Are you sure you're fine with us taking the Honda? And the phone?" Amy asked her mom for the third time that morning. They were some of the few expensive belongings her mom truly owned.

"I don't suppose you have an alternative," Emily said. "Besides, you'll be returning them to me soon."

Amy's chest ached with fearful uncertainty, but she didn't say anything, Instead, she hugged her mom tightly. Emily still smelled of the familiar scent of lilac Tide fabric softener.

"And thank you for taking care of Ryder," she said quietly into the embrace.

Emily pulled away. "Oh, of course! That's no place for children."

Amy nodded in agreement, thinking of Braxton and Kayleigh still on Wisteria Drive without any choice. What would become of Braxton if Tiffany was not around to put herself between him and Jason? And how could Kayleigh go on carrying the guilt of being born a girl in a family of chauvinists? She turned her attention to Ryder then, who sat on the ground staring up at her curiously.

"I'll be back soon, buddy," she told him as she crouched down to level their faces. "I just need to run a quick errand."

"Are you going to see Daddy?" Ryder asked.

She wouldn't lie to him. He had seen too much of that. "Yeah. But I'll be back soon to get you."

"Ok." Ryder reached up and hugged her first, taking her into his short arms. It took a great effort not to cry. When they untangled, she kissed his forehead and smoothed back the chestnut hair that had always reminded her so much of his father's.

Then, she stood. "We should get going. It's a long drive, you know."

It wasn't even ten in the morning, but the day felt as if it were already waning. She hugged Emily again, whispering another thanks into her hair.

Jenn hugged Emily, too. Amy saw the hint of concern in Jenn's features, and Amy grabbed Jenn's hand when she finished her embrace. Amy entangled her fingers in Jenn's and felt their clammy palms meeting.

The two of them walked to the parking lot together with their hands entwined. They didn't speak at all. Jenn pulled out the keys with her free hand and the Honda blinked to life in its parking space.

They broke apart to duck into their seats. Inside the car, the air was muggy from the heat, promising a sweltering day.

Jenn turned the key and breathed out loudly as the car began to purr.

"So, we're going back, huh?" Jenn asked, staring ahead.

"It seems like it," Amy said. The confirmation sent a shiver through her despite the summer warmth around her.

"Hope you enjoyed your break, then." Jenn put the car into reverse. "Off to Hell we go!"

Chapter 30

Jenn dropped Amy off at the shabby hotel that sat not too far from Wisteria Drive. She pulled up to the entrance and waited for Amy to go inside and make a one-night reservation. The lobby of the hotel was dingey and awash in an incredibly dim light that felt foreboding and slightly claustrophobic. But perhaps Amy was simply projecting her mood onto it.

Amy made her reservation with the dreary clerk. He didn't ask why she wasn't holding any belongings. Instead, he only regarded her with tired, unsuspecting eyes.

When everything was set up, Amy jogged back outside. Jenn leaned across the console and took Emily's wallet from Amy's extended hand. She hesitated, looking between Amy and the card as if trying to kill more time. Already, the sun was well on its way to dipping below the horizon and disappearing.

"I'll do it as soon as I can," Jenn said finally as she nervously fiddled with the card. "Just... don't go anywhere just in case. If we miss it, we're screwed."

"I know," Amy said. "I have nowhere to go."

Jenn shifted the car into drive, but Amy put her hand on the opened window to stop her. "This is really brave, Jenn," she said. "Good luck."

Jenn flashed her a haggard smile. "Thanks. I'll see you soon."

"See you soon," Amy echoed. She took her hand off the car and let Jenn drive the Honda out of the parking lot. She watched Jenn get back onto the road before disappearing into the sparse line of cars.

Only when Emily's car was out of sight did Amy return to the lobby. She pulled the room key out of her pocket and got into the vacant elevator. The room key was now only one of two belongings that Amy had on her besides the clothes on her back.

Her room number was 215, and when the doors slid open, it turned out to be the room right in front of her.

Inside, the room reeked of old smoke and must. Even at a glance, the furniture appeared to be well-used.

Amy took a moment to reflect on the scene compared to the house she had lived in on Wisteria Drive, decorated to appear wealthy, smart, and sophisticated. That house had been built to intimidate its guests and flatter its owners. It had always been so bright with its clean white furniture and ample natural light. By comparison, the hotel room before her was so muted it was almost dark. The two places were like different worlds, despite being just down the road from each other.

But something about the room around her was alive with a life that Wisteria Drive had always lacked. Its imperfections were on display, not hidden away in trunks and sand. She could appreciate that, at least.

Amy walked over to the desk, which had been scratched over and over until it was almost entirely a web of thin lines.

Jenn would be at the gate at the end of Wisteria Drive any minute now. Their little neighborhood was a quick drive from the dingy hotel. She couldn't imagine Jenn's fear as those heavy iron doors slowly opened for her and she drove a strange car onto the street instead of the Mercedes-Benz. She would have a lot to explain. Amy only hoped that she could sell it.

She pulled out Emily's phone, opened Jenn's home security app to the kitchen's view, and flipped on the sound.

Then, she waited.

Chapter 31

Amy jumped when Jenn and Tyler finally moved into view. After what felt like hours of looking at a stagnant image of Jenn's kitchen, she almost couldn't believe it when they finally stepped into frame like actors moving onto a stage. Her breathing quickened as the moisture in her mouth disappeared.

With a shaky finger, Amy pressed the button to ensure that a clip was saved from the live stream. She then hunched over the phone and held her breath.

"... Tyler," Jenn was saying as Amy turned up the volume.

"What do you want from me, huh?" Tyler asked. His voice was still rather unclear, and it took Amy a moment to understand what he had said. It was especially hard to concentrate with her chest feeling so painfully tight.

"I want you to tell me," Jenn said. "In your own words."

"Tell you what?"

"About Daisy," Jenn said. Amy could hear her voice getting smaller, begging Tyler to trust her with her tone. Her back was to the camera, but Amy could see Tyler's annoyed expression clearly.

"What about her?"

"Where is she?"

"I'm sure your friend Amy told you," Tyler said. "Why do you need to hear it from me?"

"Because Amy could've lied. I ran away from them for you. I stole her mom's wallet and car for you. I want to hear it from your own lips. I want to know your truth."

There was a chasm of silence.

"She's in the ocean," Tyler stated evenly.

"And you put her there, yes?"

There was no audible response, and Amy watched Tyler nod almost imperceptibly. That wouldn't do.

"After... after Jason beat Daisy to death, you decided to dump her in the ocean," Jenn prompted.

"I didn't want to. You can't imagine the pressure they put on us."

"Pressure?"

"To look perfect," Tyler said.

"You look far from it right now," Jenn said. The air hitched in Amy's throat. Jenn was walking a fine line now.

"I didn't have a choice." Tyler's voice was rising. He spoke rapidly in defensiveness as his shoulders became visibly tense. "It was either that or lose my trust fund and throw my brother under the bus. I couldn't do that."

"And that's how they got you to move back here, isn't it? They hung this secret and your trust fund over your head, huh?"

"What do you want me to say to you, Jenn?"

"So, you admit that Jason killed her, and you five boys covered it up then?"

Another moment of nothingness stretched out, electrifying Amy with panic.

"Why are you asking so many questions?" Tyler finally asked.

"Did you?"

"I already told you."

"I want to hear you say it or... or I swear to God Tyler I will run away again and this time you'll never find me. And... and I will abort this baby. It might be a baby boy, too. In fact, I feel it in my bones that it is. A little son. But I'll get rid of him. I will. I won't have a baby with you if you can't be honest."

Jenn's voice cracked convincingly with the statement. Even while Amy knew it was a bluff, Jenn had sold it even to her. Jenn had been the perfect bait. She held the best leverage they could ever use against a Montgomery. As Jenn had once said, there were few things that the Montgomerys loved more than tanned, red-headed women and the prospect of sons.

Amy watched Tyler's face twist with outrage. Jenn had used the most effective ultimatum anyone could have. But the suggestion had also put her in a very dangerous position. Would Tyler have the same temper as his brother?

"Don't even suggest that." Tyler's voice continued to rise like a wave coming to a crest. "Why the fuck would you ever say that?"

"I mean it," Jenn said. "Tell me!"

"Alright! Jason lost control! Is that what you want me to say? He lost control and took things too far. He's only human, for fuck's sake."

Amy did not like the edge to his words, the way his tone was swelling. His face was becoming visibly red on the camera's feed. She had heard the same sharp rise in David's voice before as well. Amy straightened up in her seat. Even through the phone, she could feel everything moving south as Tyler's rage built. Jenn had played her most impressive card, but it had been too much.

"So, yeah, we helped him out. That's what family does, Jenn. You obviously wouldn't know that with that shithole you called home. I took you from that, Jenn! Me! You should be thanking me."

Amy could hear the muffled sound of Jenn crying, whimpering softly as her shoulders shook. Without seeing her face, Amy couldn't tell if she was exaggerating it or if her tears were truly the result of Tyler's mounting anger.

"Don't give me that," Tyler said. "Don't get all emotional on me. Every family has its secrets. All of them. I don't know what you expected. Really, Jenn. Calm down."

Amy grabbed the phone in her slick hand. They had the confession. There was no need to watch any more of their conversation. But Amy sat there, frozen in worry as she watched intently. She should have been calling the cops, but something was wrong. It was as though the three of them were teetering on the edge of something awful, and Amy needed to make sure that they weren't going to fall over before she so much as moved.

"You won't hurt another woman again," Jenn said in an undulating voice between sniffles.

Amy knew that it was the wrong thing to say to him instantly.

"Are you not fucking listening to me? I didn't kill her, Jenn!" He leaned closer as though to grab her.

"Don't touch me," Jenn murmured.

Amy felt her stomach drop.

"Tyler, I said don't—"

His hand pulled back. Amy didn't need to see more. She was on her feet in an instant, moving toward the door.

Her body acted without guidance from her mind and typed in the three-digit number.

One low ring. A click.

Chapter 32

"Nine-one-one, what's your emergency?"

"I think there's been an assault," Amy said. Her throat felt cracked and dry. "On 5 Wisteria Drive. The man who lives there, he's dangerous. I just– We have evidence that he disposed of a dead body. A woman who was murdered. Please hurry. The men on that street helped make a woman disappear."

She was in the process of hanging up as she fled the room. Within moments, her feet were pounding the road.

Each inhale felt like a knife in her throat and chest, leaving a sharp, metallic taste in her mouth. Her speed was wild, almost unmanageable, but she refused to slow down.

She wouldn't let herself think deeply about what had happened to Jenn. Not yet. All Amy willed herself to dwell on during that sprint was the way her lungs were rejecting the exertion.

As she rounded the corner, Wisteria Drive sprawled before her, gated in by those long iron doors, keeping strangers out and secrets in. It was almost completely dark out, and the streetlights dotted the cul-de-sac with golden globes of light. As always, the world beyond the gate was ominously mute.

Between the eerie stillness and her sharp intakes of breath, she could hear sirens behind her as she neared the entrance. She knew that the police had rounded the corner when she saw the rhythmic flicker of red, blue, red, blue wash over the gate.

The police car pulled up beside her, slowing as it approached the gate.

"Ma'am…" an officer began from his vehicle.

"I made the call," Amy said wildly. "Jenn… is in… 5… we have proof now."

"Ma'am, we'll need you to calm down," the officer said.

"I… live here. Code," Amy said breathlessly, ignoring his advice. She jabbed a finger at the gate. "08 25 80." The day Lily and Richard had gotten married.

The officer communicated this to the other officer in the passenger seat. The passenger, a balding, plump man, stepped out and punched the code in as instructed.

The driving officer turned back to her, "You should sit down."

"No," Amy refused as she struggled to catch her breath. "I have to make… sure she's… ok."

She heard the gate whine open, leisurely and with a moan as if inviting them in was incredibly exhausting work. Amy entered with the police, despite the instructions from the officers telling her to do just the opposite.

Amy did, however, stand outside as the officers entered the house after Tyler had opened the door to them and stepped aside for their admittance. She waited on the front lawn with her hands clasped over her mouth to stifle a sob that was threatening to emerge from the back of her throat.

But there was no shouting or an audible struggle. Amy was not sure what to make of this. Each passing moment was another opportunity for the scene to escalate.

Her muscles were taut as she shook aside any of the potential risks forming in her head. Would the police even believe her? A woman in a worn high school T-shirt against the Montgomerys?

The officer who had pulled over beside her outside the gate exited the home and approached her in a saunter.

"You said on the call that this man was dangerous," he stated.

Amy nodded vigorously, her eyes never leaving the front door. She didn't notice at first that all around her, Wisteria Drive was coming alive with even more lights, and curious eyes were beginning to peek out from between blinds.

"You said he was involved in a murder," the officer continued.

"They all were," Amy said. "All of the men. And Lily, the mother. She knew, too."

"We're going to need a statement."

"Please," Amy said. "I need to see that she's ok first." She couldn't think of anything or any time beyond the moment they were in.

The officer nodded tersely, looking displeased.

Amy knew then that her fear was well-placed. They didn't believe her. They assumed that it was another domestic battery report from rich people who could pay their way out of it. They put no stock into what Amy had to say. Who would believe the prestigious Montgomerys would do such a horrible thing? How could people with such immaculate homes and lawns do something so dirty? Amy knew the feeling of that doubt. She had stewed in it for months. It wasn't new to her, but the skepticism from a stranger stung worse than it ever had from David.

The wait continued to feel as though it was lasting the whole night and sucking Amy into its vacuum of time. It had only been minutes, in reality, when the first people emerged.

When Jenn surfaced, her eyes were downcast and big, recounting horrors Amy had only just begun to imagine. Amy rushed to her and saw on the short jog that Jenn's lip had been split. Otherwise, within a glance, she seemed fine, if not completely alarmed.

"Jenn!" Amy exclaimed. "Are you ok?"

Jenn looked at her, visibly confused and pleased at once. "Why are you here? I was supposed to pick you up after."

"I saw him start to hit you and ran," Amy explained. "What happened?"

"He slapped me," Jenn said. She pressed the pad of her thumb to the bloody cut of her lip as if realizing for the first time that it was there. "I fell down, he hit me so hard. And then he started apologizing over and over. He was pleading. Amy..." Jenn gave a radiant grin despite her lip and the circumstances. "He looked so pathetic."

Something inflated in Amy's chest then. They had done it. In her pocket, Emily's phone held the damning confession that could free them. Around them, the street was being painted in a consistent pattern of red and blue. Even if the officers didn't believe her and Jenn now, they had the proof to prove them wrong.

At that moment, it felt like it was just the two of them, and Amy let herself return Jenn's smile, beginning to accept their victory.

That was until they realized that there were more people than expected on 5 Wisteria Drive's lawn.

"Can I help you officers with something?" came a deep voice from the edge of the front yard, close to the street behind them.

Amy and Jenn both turned in a synchronized motion to see Richard approaching, hugging his arms to his chest and appearing perplexed.

"There was a domestic abuse report," the officer who had been standing by them said.

Richard's eyes fell on the two women, and for a moment, Amy saw a flicker of anger flash across his features. He had not expected them there, and as usual, they were posing a massive inconvenience.

"Domestic abuse? From my son? That's impossible," Richard said. All of his features were trained perfectly, and he appeared utterly flabbergasted by the suggestion even as Jenn continued to bleed. He was a good actor; Amy would give him that.

"It wouldn't be the first time, would it?" Amy said. She felt emboldened by the scene at her back and the officer flanked behind her.

"What could that possibly mean?" He narrowed his eyes into slits. The motion seemed like a dare. He wanted her to say it, thinking that she had nothing to back her claim.

"I don't need to explain it to you," Amy said. "In fact, Tyler will. He confessed and we have it recorded."

Richard didn't let on that he was affected by this news. Instead, he took a step forward and dropped his voice.

"We can figure a way out of this, can't we?"

"You might try," Amy said. "And you might succeed with them." Amy jabbed her thumb at the officer behind her. "But I'll put the recording everywhere. It will be on every social site. I won't balk, no matter the price."

Richard's apathetic face stared down at her for a long moment, and Amy briefly feared that he would take a swing at her despite the police around them.

Finally, he spoke in a cold monotone. "I see."

Tyler was taken out of the house then. He wasn't handcuffed, but the other officer walked beside him, watching him closely.

"I could get used to that image," Amy said to Jenn.

"Seems we'll be seeing a lot of it. Five more versions of it, hopefully," Jenn said.

It was cocky, but Amy didn't mind. She hoped so, too.

As Tyler lowered himself into the police car, he flashed a desperate look to his father, who only stared back at him with an expression that suggested that he was calculating the situation but couldn't help at the moment. Perhaps it was the first time in any of the Montgomery brothers' lives that their father and money couldn't save them immediately.

Part 4

Chapter 33

S omehow, they were listened to.

Amy and Jenn had known that the odds were stacked against them from the moment they started discussing their plan in Emily's kitchen. The Montgomerys were too affluent and proud. As Emily had always said, the Montgomerys had more money than God.

But the police watched the confession, saw Jenn's assault at the end of the recording, and dug. It was not, of course, without pressure. The Mongomery wives uploaded the video onto every social media platform they had in their arsenal as promised. The public outrage mounted, and the police reacted under the social scrutiny that followed. Jenn and Amy often said afterward that without the option to make the confession public, they might have never held the police's attention.

It helped, too, that as the investigation continued, it brought a closer look at Treasensure. In truth, that was where it seemed most of the investigation's efforts were at times. Soon it became clear that the vague description of the company's purpose had always been intentional. The business sold malware protection that acted as a Trojan horse. Once installed, the software gave Treasensure the freedom to pillage as they pleased. This was among other counts of fraud that Treasensure had stacked up over the years to create a collection of white-collar scams. Federal investigators were quick to swoop in on the case when they smelled blood in the water, and their attention promised a separate, thorough, and lengthy investigation on top of it all. The dual investigations repositioned them in the public eye, and the Montgomerys quickly went from victors to villains.

And because of the Montgomerys' wealth, the murder and financial investigations were turned into a spectacle that others devoured. Their faces graced the covers of the gossip magazines Amy had read all summer. The Montgomerys were deemed fascinatingly out of touch. With the public spotlight on the case, everything seemed to move at an accelerated rate. And with all of the bad press and years of isolation, no one came forward to help provide money for their steep bail; the Montgomery wives certainly didn't feel inclined to.

They were scarred and traumatized, but they were free. None of them was quite so eager to step back into that cage again.

Even Tiffany, who had gone to such lengths to protect and please Jason, held her tongue. During the night Amy and Jenn had fled Wisteria Drive, she had screamed herself hoarse, begging to be freed from the room Jason had locked her in. Now, it seemed she had no words left for him.

Investigators found records of Jason Montgomery and Daisy Stevens' 2004 marriage. According to their investigation, Daisy and Jason had gotten married in New York shortly after Jason had graduated from NYU. Daisy's sister had reported her missing over eleven years ago when she had first run off with Jason and eloped, neglecting to finish her college studies in the process. No one listened, though. Her sister had no proof to present, and she had been waved away, called hysterical, and deemed dramatic. Daisy's elopement was consensual, so by the time she was really missing, nobody took the case seriously. She had died in silence because of it.

The rest tumbled into place when the police found this lead. It didn't take them long before they found Daisy's ring in a pawn shop not far from Wisteria Drive. It had been unsold and unharmed. Lily had never given the money she got for it to Kayleigh.

When they finally had enough to arrest him, Jason confessed to it all and threw his brothers under the bus as well. It seemed that their familial loyalty only ran so deep and in so many directions.

The other Montgomerys fell neatly with Jason.

Amy went to the trials and watched all of the convictions as they were handed out. Not only was she frequently called upon to be a witness for the prosecution—a role she had filled gladly—but she remained in the courtroom for every moment she was not needed as well. She had had to testify in all cases besides Jason's, who was the only Mongomery to plead guilty and take a deal. The others had too much pride for it and intended to draw out the process for as long as they could.

Attending the court sessions was a great pastime of Amy's, one that was certainly better than reading gossip magazines and lounging all day. Being there to watch the trials unfold filled her with a mixture of dread and pleasure. Despite this uncomfortable and occasionally painful concoction of feelings, she found herself carving time out for it without hesitance, ensuring that it was her second priority just below her resumed college studies.

Amy took special satisfaction when she sat in the courtroom to watch David receive his sentence. Amy had dressed prettily for the trial in a gray pantsuit that she knew David would have liked. She combined it with a neutral top and a pair of blue flats.

Before she had arrived that day, she assumed that it would be hard to look at him under the circumstances, yet when she was there, she couldn't tear her eyes away.

In those moments, Amy was not certain of what she felt. She had been married to him for seven years. That was a long time to love someone you didn't know. She had slept with a stranger and carried his child. She had trusted in someone who, in the end, would've rather killed her than harm his reputation. After seven long years, she hadn't learned a thing about him. Anything he had told her to sweeten her up could've been a lie. Everything she had told him in confidence was used to his advantage.

So, she watched him carefully in the courtroom, examining his features for some hint she could've overlooked yet was always there. But all she ever saw was his face, the one she had fallen in love with, the one she had uprooted everything for. All the while, he avoided her stare as if it might blister him if he acknowledged it. She wished it could have.

As he was given five years in prison, Amy wasn't sure what she felt. There was a surge of relief that was met with a rise of sadness in her. Sorrow and comfort mixed in her chest, swirling into an unpleasant mixture as the echoes of him screaming "FUCK YOU" in Jenn's driveway still rang in her ears.

But the sadness she felt was not misplaced and directed toward David. It was a selfish feeling, one born from the knowledge that she would be alone and that this strange moment they shared in the courtroom hanging on the words of his conviction was the last moment of "them" and not "her."

Ryder would not grow up with a father figure. David had made sure of that.

When he walked out of the courtroom, he gave her a disappointed shake of his head, holding her gaze finally, but said nothing. Amy thought later that it was perhaps for the best.

All of the other Montgomery men received a range of prison time for what they did to Daisy. Tyler was given additional time for assaulting Jenn. Lily faced her sentencing stoically, though already, her well-kept appearance was fading, with her roots growing in gray as they led her out in handcuffs. Amy wondered how long it would take prison to erode her pride as well.

Amy had removed her focus from the Montgomerys after the sentencing around Daisy; she did not feel as obligated to keep up with their financial legal blunders but was happy for the added blows they would deliver as these trials geared up.

It was a relief to have them put away, especially when the Montgomerys' legal powers had loomed so large throughout the process. The women were pleased that the Montgomerys had received anything, but they all quietly wished it had been an infinite sentence, one that would have eliminated the threat of them entirely. They knew that with some good behavior and a few well-placed bribes, they would be out soon. This refuge was only temporary and already dripping away.

It wasn't enough.

There would always be a feeling of danger, one that they couldn't shake even with their abusers and manipulators behind bars. It would linger like a bitter taste in their mouths, dwelling over years and miles. That damage was deep but not entirely insurmountable.

The Montgomerys had left four women to fend for themselves. They had stripped their wives of everything and left only trauma in their wake. It was how they were raised, in their blood, and as essential to the Montgomerys' makeup as brown hair and testosterone.

Chapter 34

They gave themselves one year after the trials.

Twelve months seemed like enough time to get back onto their feet and find a safe place to start anew.

With Lily set to come out in just a few years in the most optimistic estimate, the Montgomery wives assumed that one year would be enough time to find their bearings. Wisteria Drive was only a temporary place to settle. Perhaps it always had been.

Their discussions around moving had begun as early as that August following the night Tyler was arrested. In the weeks afterward, all of the wives had moved into 2 Wisteria Drive with Tiffany, feeling more comfortable as a pack than as individuals. Those large, vacant homes that had been left to them had always had too much space, too much room for error, and too many places to hide. Besides, Tiffany had made it clear that she didn't like to sleep in such a spacious house alone. So, when she had offered to let them fill in the many rooms, all of the women had accepted without hesitance. With ten bedrooms to speak of, it wasn't a tight squeeze.

Emily was even able to move into the house with them. After Tyler's arrest and Jenn and Amy's report, Emily had driven the long journey down to Wisteria Drive. Her intentions had purely been to return Ryder now that the coast was clear, but Amy had extended the offer. Emily had gladly agreed to the opportunity to watch her daughter more closely and moved into the second guest room on the first floor not too long afterward.

As September neared, none of them were particularly eager to send the kids back to school. It would mean that the house would be emptier, devoid of children's laughter and play during the daytime. The women all knew without directly addressing it that they would miss their juvenile innocence.

When September finally appeared and school resumed for Kayleigh, work began for Miranda after several years of inactivity. She went to work as a waitress with Emily, which had been Miranda's job in her life before Matt. In fact, they had met at one of her waitressing jobs and he had teased her relentlessly about the profession ever since. His jokes had silenced her from speaking about it, but she had always liked the work and had been happy to take it back up.

As time passed, Jenn began to moan about her pregnancy. She had learned the hard way that it wasn't all that the movies and magazines had promised. As her belly swelled, she started to complain about the aches and pains endlessly, wishing for a glass of wine or an extra cup of iced coffee. But sometimes Amy caught her staring down at the hand on her belly with a warm smile and Amy could see her understand what every mother knew: It would all be worth it when she welcomed her baby girl in just a few months.

Tiffany, however, was easily the most affected by the July events. It took her many weeks before she could even speak about what had happened to her and it was mid-September when she revealed everything to the women, who listened with hungry curiosity.

Jason had been abusive toward her from the moment they had married. They had tried desperately for months to conceive but to no avail. All the while, Jason had punished her for this infertility. Brutally. Despite all of her tests saying that she was viable, she could not get pregnant, and when it became clear to her that the fault was not her own, she turned to other means.

Braxton was the result of an anonymous donation from a sperm bank. Tiffany would have done anything to please Jason despite his faults and cruelty, even keeping such a secret. Even going behind his back and conceiving with a stranger's help.

The abuse only stopped when she was pregnant with Braxton, who seemed to have unintentionally allowed her to live nine months of pleasure. Yet when Braxton was born looking different than Jason and it became clear that more children would be an uphill climb, the abuse returned, perhaps even more violent than before. As she got closer to the Daisy secret, it only worsened, and when Jason discovered she was leaving breadcrumbs for Amy, he hit her in the face, something he had never done before because even he had been smart enough to know that a bruised eye gave up the game. That's why he had driven her away, to the hotel down the street, the same one that Amy had been in the night Tyler was arrested. They had waited there overnight to see how she healed. It had ended up being a minor bruise—as small as a nickel—that Tiffany had deftly covered with layers of foundation.

The night Jenn and Amy had escaped Wisteria Drive was perhaps the most harrowing time for Tiffany. Jason had locked her in their bedroom, refusing to allow her out for fear that she would run away, too. She was kept there until the police arrived on Wisteria Drive, all the while debating whether or not to hurl herself out of the window for a chance at running and finding help for her and Braxton. Fortunately, she had been found before that desperation had truly taken hold. When she emerged, led out by the police, she was hungry but free.

And yet she still missed Jason after all of his violence and faults. Even after weeks of her claiming to have grown calloused, Amy had walked past Tiffany's bedroom on the way to her own one night and heard her muffled crying. Jason had shamelessly beaten her and left her to feel as though without him something large was missing from her life. Amy couldn't imagine how things were twisted up in Tiffany's head. She could barely fathom what her own husband had done. Tiffany spent many afternoons down at the shore, and Amy suspected that she stared out at the vast ocean trying to sift through these thoughts. Or perhaps she was looking for more evidence of Daisy in the sand, tiny trinkets as a reminder of the life her husband took. Amy hoped that Tiffany one day got the closure that had been robbed from Daisy. But for now, she only found broken shells and tears as salty as the sea.

The women spent the rest of the summer functioning as a sort of community, moving around each other with grace and rarely mentioning the horrors that the cul-de-sac had witnessed. Perhaps David was right all along. It simply took time for Amy to settle in and by the fall, Amy actually began to feel mostly at ease.

It wasn't until October that Miranda finally mustered up the courage to ask about Daisy and break the unspoken silence on the matter.

Daisy Stevens was not hard to find. A quick Google search unveiled her sister's social media profiles and an article from Daisy's hometown paper in Ohio where her sister had implored others to take her disappearance seriously.

Jenn, who had held the phone during the search, tapped on her Daisy's sister's Instagram first. They immediately were able to recognize Daisy in the occasional throwback photos her sister posted. She was a mirror image of them, after all.

There she was, smiling back up at them with a face that looked just like their own. She had been pretty and shorter than most of the friends she was pictured with. Her hair was a bright red, and her skin was tanned. The perfect Montgomery wife.

In her pictures, Daisy seemed to be glowing with a happiness that they now knew Jason had squashed. She was frozen in time, etched in pixels, forever smiling.

Daisy, without any intention of doing so, had saved them all. Her memory had exposed the Montgomerys for what they were. They had been privileged and arrogant and, most of all, carelessly sloppy. They had preyed on vulnerable women and beat them back in line when they strayed from their restrictive expectations. They had taken their wives from their homes and families and given them trauma and burden in return.

Daisy could have been any of them.

She had been all of them.

Acknowledgements

It takes a village to write a book. This was underscored in the long process of pulling together Wisteria Drive. I leaned on many people for support when creating this story, perhaps even more so than with my previous work.

Of all the people I have to thank, of course, my family is first and foremost. I am nothing without them.

I want to thank my sister, Kalli, for encouraging me even when I expressed my doubts to her. She is always my voice of reason. And I want to thank her for playing Polly Pockets with me when we were younger; without that, I wouldn't have had the name inspiration for David.

My mom, Kerri, is also someone who deserves my endless gratitude. I will never forget how she told me to bet on myself by publishing *Sirens*. She started the snowball effect that led me to publish this book as well. Her support means more to me than anything else that comes from publishing my stories. Thank you, Mom. Always.

And my dad, Chuck, read one of the very first drafts of this book and gave feedback on it even when Wisteria Drive strayed from his nonfiction reading diet. His support then meant everything and ultimately led to this final copy. So I wanted to say thank you, Dad.

I would also like to thank my cover designer, Gabby. She has a talent for cutting right to the best and most important parts of everything from conversations to art. This cover was no different, and I'm thankful again for her keen eye.

My editor, Suzy, worked tirelessly with me to thoroughly look through Wisteria Drive and provide the feedback it needed to become the story it was meant to be. I cannot express how much I appreciated her red pen.

And then, there are all of my beta readers. Thank you to Dawn and David from the writing group at my local library, who took the time out of their busy schedules to give this nearly finalized draft a read. They gave me feedback on Wisteria Drive to get it ready for publishing, and I will always be thankful for their unnecessary kindness and dedication to the craft of writing.

I am also thankful to my writing club, in general, for always giving me fresh ideas and a sense of community.

There is also Craig to thank, who gives me great perspectives, feedback, and grammatical edits from an ocean away. He is always thorough as he weeds through my stories, so I wanted to say thank you to him once again.

And finally, I need to say thank you to you, the reader. You did not have to pick up or purchase this book. You did not have to read it to these final pages or form your own opinions on the story. But you gave Wisteria Drive a chance, and that is the greatest thing I can ask for as a writer. So thank you for reading. I will always appreciate your time.

About the Author

Chloe Ruffennach is the author of the 2023 novel *Sirens*. She enjoys a quiet life in Pittsburgh, Pennsylvania, where she works in marketing when she is not writing worlds and characters into existence. If she is not found reading or writing, she can be spotted cuddling the love of her life: Karma, her cat.

You can find Chloe everywhere at @crruffennach.

www.ingramcontent.com/pod-product-compliance
Lightning Source LLC
Chambersburg PA
CBHW072101300726

48975CB00003B/652